Chris is a former civil servant who spent the last twenty years of his working life as a union official representing colleagues and members in the crawlspace of privatised UK government service. An elected member of the left-wing Public and Commercial Services (PCS) union's National Executive for a decade, he was awarded the Distinguished Life Membership of PCS in 2019. He is semi-retired and lives in Telford.

This is a work of fiction. Names, characters, businesses, places, events and incidents are either the product of the author's imagination or used in a fictitious manner. Any resemblance to actual persons, living or dead, or actual events is purely coincidental.

SCRAPS FROM THE CAPTAIN'S TABLE

Chris Morrison

SCRAPS FROM THE
CAPTAIN'S TABLE

Vanguard Press

VANGUARD PAPERBACK

© Copyright **2023**
Chris Morrison

The right of Chris Morrison to be identified as author of
this work has been asserted by them in accordance with the
Copyright, Designs and Patents Act 1988.

All Rights Reserved

No reproduction, copy or transmission of this publication
may be made without written permission.
No paragraph of this publication may be reproduced,
copied or transmitted save with the written permission of the
publisher, or in accordance with the provisions
of the Copyright Act 1956 (as amended).

Any person who commits any unauthorised act in relation to
this publication may be liable to criminal
prosecution and civil claims for damages.

A CIP catalogue record for this title is
available from the British Library.

ISBN 978 1 80016 607 3

*Vanguard Press is an imprint of
Pegasus Elliot Mackenzie Publishers Ltd.*
www.pegasuspublishers.com

First Published in **2023**

**Vanguard Press
Sheraton House Castle Park
Cambridge England**
Printed & Bound in Great Britain

To Andy and Dave for the happiest years of what
I laughingly call my career

Acknowledgments

To Alan Morrison and Kevin Greenway for taking the time to read my early drafts. Kim Hendry for the inspiration. Hikma for finding me when I was lost. All my friends and comrades in PCS for support over the years. The management and staff at Eighty Six'd, Truffles, the Coracle, the Tontine, the Golden Ball, and the Horse and Jockey for always providing a warm seat in the corner.

Finally my thanks to the staff at Vanguard Press for pulling the manuscript over the line.

"I stare at her name tag I think to myself
Both you and I, we never asked for any of this."
New Model Army, 225

Prologue

The year 1709 was when this madness started. It says so in the history books. Right here on our doorstep, a few roundabouts away from Telford town centre, down the road in Coalbrookdale village. 'The birthplace of the Industrial Revolution' That's what the signposts say. Those scarred furnace walls are a permanent reminder of hard days gone by.

Nowadays we skirt around the issue: how we got from there to here and all the suffering involved. We're raised to celebrate 'our' English heritage, but which England would that be? Them or us. Look closely, there's barely a space set aside to salute the working class – the foundation stone of Empire. They've denied our ancestors' stories, buried them under rich people's history. The statues are reserved for those upper-class glory hunters – the bosses and the landowners. It is their well-fed faces that line the gallery walls.

'Don't worry, you'll get your rewards in Heaven' the Church would console us from the pulpit. Jam tomorrow – just like the modern politicians promise.

So, pull up a chair and park yourself because it's important you understand how the politics of consensus has deceived us. We teach our children the advance in Industry moved hand in hand with social enlightenment, as though by an unlikely miracle thousands of lives lost to deprivation and disease on the banks of the Severn were dying for a shared cause – all part of a liberal masterplan. Consensus advises people like us to be patient, to await the refreshing torrents from capitalism's trickle-down effect, to accept our forebears died content knowing they could claim consolation that future generations had better chances to read and write and to avoid hunger because they themselves had lived and sacrificed.

But tell me would that advice be correct?

Was it always inevitable our class would advance? That working people like us would gain literacy. Or we would achieve the vote? That we would establish the Welfare State? Between the unruly slabs of Bedlam Furnace is there a Blairite social contract between rich and poor? Of course not. Consensus be damned – our forebears paid in blood for everything we have today. Exhausted, exploited, beaten, imprisoned, transported– no-one ever met them halfway.

We've become complacent. Here in the twenty-first century we've forgotten the unpleasant truth our ancestors understood too well – the rich are our enemy, and the class war will never be over until it's won. While we turn away thinking those days are long gone, behind the jingle-jangle distractions of modern life our class is in retreat, the rich are stealing back our meagre gains and transferring our nation's wealth to their offshore bank vaults.

Captain Pinkbeard, 2009

Part 1
A different horizon

May 2003

All I had was uncertainty and confusion. You need to understand I hadn't been bought or sold but bartered away. I felt powerless. I was owned, and I guess I always had been, but I'd never thought of it that way. It was humiliating, that's what it was. The decision makers didn't even allow me the satisfaction of possessing a price tag so I might know my value but pushing curiosity to one side I reasoned I was only a makeweight and barely worth a mention. A fixture or a fitting, perhaps more or less valuable than a computer or a cupboard, all no doubt recorded as a footnote near the bottom of the Transfer balance sheet. Yes, against my will I had been privatised by the government. Outsourced. Little more than a specimen in a test-tube. An insignificant detail in the free-market's great social experiment casually tossed from one employer to another, from this pile onto that pile, from civil servant to corporate bootlick, and yet my government still had the cheek to tell the world that I'd been empowered and set free.

'Typical' I sighed as I opened my email drafts folder pondering an expletive-infected response to the announcement of my enforced transfer. Something to nurture the chip on my shoulder – to raise me onto the moral high ground. The email I planned to create would be a searing rejection of their decision, proving conclusively the country had been wrong to abandon talents such as mine to the vagaries of the marketplace. Aye, a draft sitting proudly for a month or two next to the open-ended crime sheet that constituted my long-standing, forever in my back pocket, never-to-be-sent resignation letter – 'The Reasons I'm Leaving.' But what was the point? I slumped in my chair. Yes, exactly that – what was the point of diffusing my anger through unsent data? Sometimes winning the argument isn't enough, you must win the battle. And I was the loser, we all were.

Twenty years as an anonymous public servant and New Labour had rewarded me with a letter from the Minister – 'thank you for your hard work, your achievements and your loyalty' – now fuck off. The instruction remained unspoken. Ha! I've only myself to blame, I'll never forgive myself for voting for them. Or at least not until the next time I vote for them. 'My life as Labour voting fodder' – that's another in my drafts folder. I open and update it from time to time when Blair feels the need to reach out to the middle classes.

'No matter.' 'Move on.' 'Get over it.' That's the advice the local managers give.

Alas, the congratulations went to Tex4Tex for they had won the flagship contract and the easy profits that arrived with the gravy train. I'd never heard of them before, but they were now my employer, and while I sat at my desk fuming, I imagined chinless city types were launching champagne breakfasts in the company's honour. Aye, the vultures were circling ready to pick our bones. Bleak though it seemed, while I shuddered at the thought of the sales team's self-congratulatory rugger-bugger joshing and bonhomie I did see the joke. It wasn't all bad news. There was at least something for the financiers to worry about the morning after the night before. Between me and you, I trust Tex4Tex had read the small print well, because they'd won more than profit and a place for their lips on the tit of UK PLC. They had also won the right to manage the blockers, the scruffs, the cynics, the unions, the hippies, the public service idealists, the lefties, the inflexible pedants, the jobsworths, the weirdoes and all the oddballs that only the civil service broad church could ever tolerate. Yes, in the wise words of the singing Swedes, The Winner Takes It All, and the terms of the contract meant that included seething, resentful misfits like us. So I hope Tex4Tex savoured victory well and I looked forward to that moment when the rich widow they had taken for an innocent, seduced, and then proposed to, introduces them to her kids from hell and gleefully passes them the ultimate management cop-out note – "Yours to deal with."

And that I guess will be where I came in – Jack Pinkbeard. Captain Pinkbeard to friends and acquaintances. Not a real pirate of course but pirate lite as it were, more like a team mascot. Just a young punk growing older, larger, and hairier by the year, letting nature take its course. Add a half jacket, pipe, boots and waistcoat and the look just came together. Don't get me wrong, it wasn't deliberate styling, at least not at first, it was others who gave me the title of Captain Pinkbeard. Initially I just indulged them and let them think whatever they thought, but over time I grew into the assumed role of site buccaneer. There was never a reason to change course, it suited me so well. I was both an outsider and part of the team, and by accident a walking advert for civil service tolerance.

Now I suppose you might think a man allowing himself to be presented to the world as a seafaring rover has a cheery outgoing big-hearted personality to match it, but that wasn't me. Far from it, I may have got my signature look by accident, but I stuck with it because it celebrated my otherness. Though I say so myself Captain Pinkbeard had a forbidding look. I liked it that way, I wanted my look to say – 'back off and leave me be'. While colleagues imposed their interpretation upon me, behind my red beard wall my eyes impassively watched the world go by. If folk thought I was a jolly pirate without a care and approached me for a chat and a yo-ho-ho, then who was I to argue, and if others thought my unkempt style was dragging down the tone that was fine too. It appealed to the stubborn punk who still lurked within me. Both interpretations suited my purpose. You see I wasn't gregarious, but I wasn't shy either. I was quiet. Quiet, but opinionated. I wanted to be distant. I didn't impose myself on people, but if they thought that meant I'd be grateful for their attention well they were usually wrong.

I suppose what I'm saying is that I was not a man you'd see behind the windows at a high street bank or flirting with customers on a reception desk. No, I wasn't one of those staff destined for the in-house brochures, or employee of the month awards, and despite privatisation and my new corporate home I intended to keep it that way. I didn't intend to change. Over the years I'd come to appreciate the way Captain Pinkbeard had set me apart from the failing greyness of working life, and as I grew into the role of team misfit, I had learned to enjoy the irony that my identity also suited a career drifting quietly on the waves since its inception. Don't get me wrong, I knew my job of course, and whisper it quietly through sheer longevity I was on occasion surprisingly good at it, but my career was stagnant. My name didn't appear on even the longest-term promotion lists. This injustice didn't matter to me though, I understood and readily accepted the truth, supposed oddballs may be accepted in the easy-come easy-go civil service but they don't advance too high. Without tears I resigned myself to the coastal path to retirement rather than make the sacrifices necessary to advance my career on the fast road.

Nonetheless, putting my becalmed career to one side, I was at ease most of the time. Compared to real workers, the private sector workers I overheard at the bar in the local, I thought the civil service was an acceptable compromise – a life of continued public sector obscurity with a guaranteed index-linked safety net pension at the end. And I'd kept to my side of the bargain for two decades or more. It was only now, as the public sector closed its doors on me and kicked me out into the street that I realised I'd been cheated and my government had reneged on that mythical deal.

Overall, I approached this announcement of privatisation with trepidation. I was afraid this transfer might well scupper my career plans, or rather more precisely, it might scupper my lack of career plans. It sounded like a come-uppance, like the gods were punishing me for years of drift. What's more, privatisation might require me to engage with my career, force me to change. Surely there would be no point to privatisation if it didn't lead to change? Yes, it might force me to adapt, to straighten me out, to fit in, to learn their ways, and I didn't like the sound of that.

Maybe you sympathise, maybe you don't, but answer me this: why should I be the one to change? It seemed so unfair. It's a point of principle from the old school playground, here I really did hold the moral high ground, surely the private sector should bend to me. Those were the rules, after all I was here first.

June 2003

With crossed-fingers and pausing for a deep breath, I pressed send and accepted the email invitation to the 'Getting 2 Know U' session. It was time to confront my fears.

I'd like to consider myself fair-minded, I guess we all do, but I'm sure you'll understand when I explain that as a lifelong public servant I instinctively feared and distrusted my new employer. You could call it the fear of the unknown and I generously applied the term to the whole of private industry. I knew so little about Tex4Tex, but what I'd gleaned from conversations with the office know-it-alls made me uneasy. The prevailing view was that Tex4Tex were very controlling – they had an opinion on how we should look and how we should behave both in and out of work. We were led to believe every staff member was to be regarded as a walking advertisement for the company and our behaviours mustn't let the team down. The gossip said we shouldn't be seen drinking, we shouldn't be seen gambling, and even adultery might bring the company into disrepute and generate bad publicity.

It all sounded very extreme and unlikely. Sacked for infidelity? Seriously? Surely, the gossip was just hot air, and the fears were misplaced. Of course, there was never smoke without fire, but I kept my cool as I listened to the paranoia. After all, for the adulterers there was always defence in numbers, it stood to reason they couldn't sack us all.

Days later with a combination of curiosity and dread, I shuffled onto the cavernous floor space of the Telford International Centre between my colleagues Paula and Tony, anxiously awaiting my first Tex4Tex gathering to begin. Our gang instinctively found our place even though there were no seat reservations. Some things never change – suits at the front, scruffs at the back, and as we parked ourselves as close to the back row as we could get, the contrasts with those old public-sector days from a week or two before struck me immediately. You see in the recent past staff consultation would be handled in the joyless perfunctory manner that a dog might consult with a lamppost. An unshaven manager in a sweatshirt and corduroy kegs pulling up a chair, apologising for wasting our time, passing a few weak comments about the noise outside, jovially offering his Polo mints around and then delivering twenty minutes of taxpayer-funded apathy and defeatism.

"This has to be done, I have been told to say this, I don't like it either and whoops there goes my script," and sure enough we would shrug politely at his clumsiness as the notes slid off his knee to the floor. Today as my eyes scanned the International Centre ceiling and I contemplated an uncertain future it was hard to believe those memories of slapdash management may one day be recycled under the 'good old days'.

Today would be different, our new employer was putting on a show. Tina Turner was belting out *Simply the Best* from somewhere in the tiled ceiling while coloured spotlights picked out movement on the platform. Gloria from HR stood in the wings with a hand-held camera filming the audience for posterity. To her side a huge slideshow on a dropdown screen confronted attendees. It bore images of smart wholesome employees with haircuts you could slice your bread with carrying the message of the future. Tex4Tex was in town to hard sell itself to those of us who had no choice but to buy. The buffet had arrived fresh, and staff tossed jackets on to seats upon arrival and walked purposefully over to grab their free dinner while taking a minute to consume the spectacle. This was to be an Event. All this money spent to impress us. After years of public sector cutbacks, it was an unaccustomed feeling.

Of course, just to drag us all back to reality and dampen the anticipation, our traitorous, turncoat civil service management were also here seated in the front rows. They were the ones who had provided the detail that enabled my smooth transfer. Canny enough to keep their opinions to themselves while the union campaign against the transfer was in play, they quickly adapted to the new mood by dropping their casual sweaters and corduroys. Our supervisors had dressed up in their wedding suits and ties to greet our conqueror, attracting laughter and the occasional catcall from the back.

"Oi, you've left the price tag on."

Yes, privatisation offered a new dawn for middle-managers – a chance to reset the game. At last hard-working restricted public sector leaders were going to be given a sack of cash, a blank sheet of paper and the power to make a difference. Or at least that's what they thought, for that's the privatisation script. But power is elusive, it jumps through your hands like a bar of soap, you think you have it but then it's gone. Surely even they must realise that. It's the laws of nature. There can only ever be one captain on the ship, and I comforted myself all these talentless backsliding double-dealers would surely be for the Plank if there was any justice. Now that would be a consolation. No one likes a Judas.

Aye, only one captain, and ours was about to take the stage. My first ever CEO – 'call me Herb' Nilsson, began his contribution in a West Coast lilt. He was smooth easy listening, Tony Bennett in a business suit. Yes, compared to his scruffy grey civil service predecessors Herb was a picture of clean-cut enlightenment selling the American dream to rural Shropshire. He began by recounting the 'fascinating story of Tex4Tex; forty years and rising'.

Indeed.

I know what you're thinking, I yawned too. For the record, our company history was the fascinating story of outsourcing, repeated all over the world – service, process, and structure but without a mention of invention or creativity. Ha! 'They never made anything but money,' I jeered inwardly as he talked about expansion, acquisition, and mergers. Apparently once 'we' were Dallas Technology Services, Texan Technology Services, transformed to Texas Technical Services, Techxans, Techs for Texas, until finally, or perhaps currently, Tex4Tex.

Yes, Herb seemed excited by this 'evolution, dare I say revolution'. As he talked, he paced across the platform, chatting easily about himself and the company. I supposed he must have done this speech a hundred times to new hires. The odd thing was he didn't seem remotely embarrassed talking about his many personal successes. It seemed natural. He wasn't bragging, or lording it over us, but nonetheless I'd have been mortified to walk in those shoes speaking those words. It felt so immodest, so lacking in self-deprecation, so unBritish. Yes, a combination of God, family, hard work, and relentless ambition had brought him this far, within twenty miles of the bright lights of Wolverhampton, and at no point did he bother to ask himself whether it had been worth it.

I suppose it was all about personal goals and targets. Having said that, however grumpy this old curmudgeon may get, I cannot deny he was a triumph. I looked around and realised my cynicism was in the minority, maybe out of date even. Whilst a few of us cursed this easy surrender to the invaders, others clung to every word and story from this worldly American with his globe-trotting personal history. It was hard not to appreciate the attraction. He had ambition, and it had been rewarded. Whilst we'd plodded away in Shropshire, Herb had worked in cities we'd only seen on the news – Washington, Cairo, Moscow, Tel Aviv. He'd rubbed shoulders with corrupt dictators and tax-avoiding billionaires. It was a life well led. The way Herb spoke, rootless living in permanent transit seemed easy, exciting, and most of all, dutiful.

"You see my story is the company story, and I hope that Our Story will soon be Your Story. Because the Tex4Tex story is best told by its folks, and that's whether I'm in the boardroom meeting and greeting senators, or like you at your local soccer team chatting to your neighbour."

The spotlight followed him as he strolled confidently across the platform prompting his audience to adapt and fit in, to forget the past and embrace the future. His words promised that if we adjusted successfully then there could be hotel minibars in exotic cities within our grasp.

He stopped pacing, momentarily transfixed. Pausing in the centre of the stage he placed his hand on his chest for added sincerity.

"Like you I was transferred to Tex4Tex from another company. I hadn't applied to join, but impressed with the mission, the vision, and the drive, I seized the chance to change and create a new story for myself and the family I love. It can be done, I'm the proof."

It was surely meant as a moment for the tears of a TV evangelist, but my dry eyes were drawn to a pony-tailed young man a few rows in front laughing uncontrollably while others tried desperately to quieten him.

"But they just don't get it" he snorted in ridicule. "This is Telford, not Texas. It'll never happen!"

Alongside me, Tony sat shaking his head, his plate of free food dangerously overloaded and each wobble required countermeasures to keep the construction in place. I listened to my friend while keeping a watchful eye out for debris.

"But I don't want to change, that young fella's right, I'd get a kicking if I walked into the pub in Wolvo bragging about the company I work for."

Pointing to our department head who was sat with the spotlights bouncing off his bald head in the attention-seeking first row, Tony added, "Look at that useless twat Cliff Wiley." He paused and stopped for a bite of his roll, "Jeez, privatisation is bad enough without our limp dick civil service managers suddenly developing hard-ons for their careers." He stopped again, belched, and then restarted. "I mean I bet the hypocrite has probably been up all night practising the company song." Again, he stopped, patted his chest, and sighed. I thought indigestion might have beaten Tony and he'd finished for good this time, but then he realised he had more insight I would benefit from hearing and burst into life again.

"I mean if he really wanted to work in the private sector why didn't he fuck off years ago?"

That was indeed a good question and one asked of their conniving bosses by thousands of public servants over the last twenty years. As my peeved friend sank lower in his seat delicately lifting the white plate of food onto his belly, Herb milked the last of what applause he had, and we came to the serious part.

The HR director stepped to the lectern at the right side of the stage. She asked us to call her Rose. History will recall that over time she'd acquire many names from her rivals, but Texas Rose was the usual one – the one we lower grades used. Her first task was to assure us that just because they were Texans then we shouldn't dismiss them as a bunch of red-neck racists looking to lynch communists, suspected communists, potential communists, or potential suspected communists.

I breathed easier, at least that was one fear ticked off my list.

In her words Tex4Tex were more complicated and modern than I'd expected. They loved the world and all its diversity, employing people in a thousand countries from one end of the globe to the other – Brazilians, Chinese, Koreans, Austrians and Australians and

Indians. Not I guess the rebellious American Indians who hilariously kicked Custer's ass, but real Indians, tens of thousands of them in India apparently. So that was good I suppose, although a little disconcerting. And Tex4Tex were going to keep our terms unchanged, or more precisely they 'currently had no plans to change contractual legally binding terms'.

However, they did want to see some cultural changes.

Now, I didn't get this culture thing entirely, but the way Rose made the case it didn't sound like a day trip to the museum. She was warning us our old colleagues who'd stayed in-house must now be treated as 'our customers' as we were now their supplier. She emphasised it was important we maintained 'a professional distance' between ourselves and those we'd worked alongside, and in many cases slept alongside for twenty years. To guide us in our labours we had our Tex4Tex Values and our 'Codes of Ethics and Behaviours', and she lifted and waved a snazzy blue folder at Gloria's camera for effect as she passed on the message. Above all, we should bear in mind we all had a shared interest in the success of the contract "otherwise," Rose gravely stated, "the situation might become complicated."

Was that a threat? Judging by the nodding heads at the front, apparently not. These were the economic facts of life she promised an audience of public servants that barely understood such things. Only weeks before we'd have walked out on mass if a manager suggested we should share the bosses' pain, but in our changed circumstances it sounded fair enough; we would share the harvest and the famine.

Assuming of course there would be a harvest.

Not before time, the gathering reached 'Your Questions'.

I was tense even though I reasoned the call for questions meant we must be close to the end, and I'd survived this far. From my seat near the back row, I could see wiser heads going down to check on shoes and examine mobile phones hoping we would get through the rest of the meeting unscathed and avoid the imposition of HR's wandering microphone. I locked my hands in my lap and offered a silent prayer to whichever gods may be listening.

"Please make it volunteers only".

I didn't need to worry though, fortunately for myself and the rest of the semi-detached there were plenty of ambitious sycophants anxious to draw attention to themselves in front of the new masters. Their arms reached skywards straining for attention.

'Can I refresh my skills?'

'Can I work overseas?'

'Can I move to company terms?'

"Can I have an improved mobile phone?"

'I must drive to work, can I have a company car?'

Good grief, I thought, and picked at my nails. What was wrong with these people?

I'm no expert, but Rose's answer should of course have been a sarcastic 'welcome to you all, enthusiastic non-descript fellows, your subservience to your new corporate oppressors has been noted'. But there was no such luck. Blow me, she said she was taken aback by such straightforward and honest questioning, and thought it boded well for the future of the contract that such engaged people had come on board. And yes, of course she could take a few more questions.

By my side Tony couldn't contain himself.

"Okay, let's see who the wannabe twats are," he said. Simultaneously, Paula shifted on my left.

As Paula's hand rose, I noticed some in local management had moved uneasily in their seats as the roving microphone innocently descended upon 5ft 2ins of trouble, one of the few union officials with the decency to follow their members through the gates to the private sector. I'm ashamed to say I instinctively leaned away, I wanted to be invisible as my long-standing colleague reached out to grab the microphone.

"You say how much your values are family values, so can you now confirm the site nursery will remain open?"

"Good question," said Tony, backtracking his earlier opinion.

Indeed, it was another good question – was the all-conquering multi-national goon squad planning to bulldoze the nursery? That's what the union leaflets claimed, although the accusation had of course been denied by a furious management.

There was a moment of silence. Even the bored momentarily placed their sandwiches back on the plates waiting for a response.

Consider this: if my life was a film then surely this was the perfect dramatic moment for Tex4Tex to bare their fangs, and for gun-toting guards to crash in with a pack of hissing rottweilers to escort the unbelievers to the salt mines. It would be a moment of truth, like that scene in *V* when sexy Commander Diane reticulates her jaw and swallows the rat whole, and although you still fancy her and you would if you could, you know for sure the liaison won't end well. I must be honest brothers and sisters, I had half hoped something like that would happen, if only to prove my suspicions about Tex4Tex right. But Rose was made of sterner stuff, she merely shrugged the question aside saying they 'currently have no plans to close the nursery'. However, she added 'the company were talking to the customer about future needs, and users would be notified if there was any change in the arrangement'. Crisis averted; managers nodded to each other in approval as the microphone quickly raced as far away from Paula as possible. Her failure to get a follow-up became apparent. Frustrated she returned to her seat muttering sarcastically, "Great. So now I'm no longer a working parent I'm only a nursery user and consumer of corporate resources. Thank God for Tex4Tex values, I don't know how I coped without any personal values before they turned up five minutes ago." Muttering complete, she pulled out a mobile phone, and angrily jabbed a picture of her husband before she began texting.

Only moments later we came to my personal highlight of the matinee.

"I have a beard," said a man with a beard, "do I have to shave it off?" I felt self-conscious and gave my scruffy luxuriance a little tug just to make sure it was still there. This was the breaking point for me as I was literally as attached to my beard as it was to me.

Rose smiled down benevolently. She'd probably heard this question a thousand times before.

"Of course not, the Clean Shave policy came from the old Tex4Tex in our Dallas days, we've all moved on together since then. So long as your beards are trim and tidy, we have no problem." She said it seriously, despite her smile, as though tolerating people with beards was challenging some great social taboo. "No, we employ many men with beards, and who knows maybe even a few women with beards too." She relaxed again and laughed at her own joke, for she was in great humour now – absolute comedy gold judging by the thigh-slapping hilarity amongst the sycophants, "and we even have managers who have beards. Look!" and as she said it all the managers on the platform turned and pointed towards a man in a turban at the far end of the row, and they were laughing and pointing at him because he too had a beard and was a manager!

Ha! I guess you had to be there.

"Stand up Rohit, so they can all see you," she instructed as the light picked him out from the shadows. He did as he was told and he bowed to her before smiling sheepishly out to the audience while pale managers clapped him to show they weren't the least offended by his beard. They enjoyed it because they thought it was hilarious.

There was a strangled gasp from the audience, and a moment of toe-curling clarity for many of us as they pointed and laughed at the only non-white face on the platform. Cruel though it seemed, and with apologies to Rohit, I felt comforted. Since the days of Thatcher we in the public sector had been led to believe we were inferior to the modern efficient private sector. We represented the past; we had been told repeatedly we had nothing to offer modern Britain except an invoice. Yet in that single moment we civil servants realised a historic truth, one not covered in the privatisation script; their bosses were dickheads too. Maybe there was a hope in the darkness.

October 2003

Occasionally I try to recall the precise date or moment in time when Tex4Tex stopped being 'they' and became 'we'. This was our first loyalty test and it mattered to our leaders. Within weeks of the transfer, most managers had effortlessly learnt and embraced the 'we' word. It was an article of faith, a religious conversion if you like, it made it easy to self-identify as an insider: Were you us or them? Were you the past or the future?

These questions were all part of the process of assimilation. There was to be no opting out – assimilation was compulsory. Speaking the truth that I only worked here and wasn't paid enough to care wasn't considered a good enough excuse to avoid re-education. I didn't like this obligation to sign-up to corporate standards, muddling by had always been good enough before, but did my opinion matter? Who knows? They never asked my opinion. Tex4Tex rolled on regardless. The loyalty tests kept coming and the new broom kept on sweeping. And by the autumn when our new masters had gained their sea-legs as it were, they decided it was time for the next step, bring out the big guns and roll out their Values Training. Never one to half-sell themselves

Tex4Tex called the induction course Excellence Through Endeavour – Risk and Opportunity.

Now here's the rub. The way I saw it I didn't need Values Training or re-energising. I didn't want to take part or contribute, and I didn't need to find a space for corporate ethics in my heart. No, I knew my job, so all I asked was for the company to leave me alone from Monday to Friday, and then praise be I'd go to the pub, get wankered, Wolves would win on Saturday and there'd be fish and chips on the way home. That was as close to perfection as my week ever got. My failure to belong hadn't bothered me so far in what we laughably term my career path. No, it wasn't a problem for me, like millions of others in darkest disenfranchised England I get by from one pay day to another and that's all I need. I was born working class, and that's how I intend to die. Others may hunt a treasure map shortcut to greater pressure and responsibility, but I just aspire to be content in my own skin.

I guess my team leader, Roger, must have agreed with me deep down.

"All the bad eggs in one basket" was how he described our scheduled Values session. "I told him I'd rather teach Tex4Tex values to the Children of the Damned than you, Paula, and Tony" was his abrupt statement on the issue. He was ignored by the powers above. Despite Roger's well-intentioned advice unit leader Cliff Wiley had insisted our presence at the Values Workshop was compulsory otherwise the unit wouldn't be able to tick a box indicating all staff had attended a Values Workshop, and that might prevent the whole account ticking the box stating everyone had attended a Values Workshop. Most importantly we staff would lose our opportunity to earn certificates proving we had attended a Values Workshop and had passed our Values Training.

Not of course that anyone failed Values Training.

A week later and accepting my fate, I mused on the futility of corporate morality as I shifted my weight and rocked my chair back until it rested against one of the whiteboards in the training wing. This had been revamped for the occasion by the newly created 'Inspiration Team' to remove blocking formalising barriers such as tables to create a relaxing chilled-out atmosphere conducive to learning. Whilst I could admire the effort it did simply resemble an infants school classroom inhabited by giants with marker pens and beanbags scattered between the whiteboards.

Our tutor arrived with a clatter against the swing doors as his bags and laptop pushed through. It was Martin Monk, one of the new guys from the first wave of 'real' Tex-4-Texans to storm our barricades. There were already a few like him on site parading about like pious crusaders amongst the backward folk of Shropshire. I knew little about Martin, except that he was Roger's equivalent as a team leader in the unit and that in private his team referred to him as Martin Sidepartin, a tribute to his clean-cut loyalty to the cause of Tex4Tex. We all assumed he slept in a suit and tie just in case the phone rang.

As you can imagine it therefore came as a surprise when Martin began the session by removing his tie with a flourish for the occasion, pulling apart his top button, and rolling up his sleeves. It was a statement of intent – we were obviously going to see Martin Monk Unchained. Or at least I presumed that was the theory, but to see him 'dressed-down' in front of me, well I felt uncomfortable and embarrassed like when I saw that picture of William Hague in a baseball hat. It seemed strange and unnatural and I fought an urge to run, I was worried we might be enticed to let our guard down and this may be one of those revolting occasions when we might be pressured to have a group hug or prayer or be invited to share something secret about ourselves with the rest of the attendees. As if prompted, I rehearsed my official secret I keep for these occasions.

"My wife didn't leave me. I keep her chained in the cellar."

And why not tell a lie? I mean frankly I like my colleagues, but they can fuck off if they want to pry and judge. I don't see why I should be open about myself just because my trainer tells me to, and I don't know why others do either. Surely comrades the right not to contribute to poxy team bonding exercises is the forgotten human right?

Anyways, that debate will have to wait for another day because Martin was speaking,

"I'd like to begin by telling you about a remarkable Estonian peasant called Igor. He didn't like communism and after years of suffering he bravely escaped his homeland by jumping ship at Tallinn. A year later, he started cleaning toilets in Tex4Tex Atlanta office, worked all the hours of the day, never took a break or a holiday, caught the bosses' eye, and you know what?" He nodded with approval. "He is now Head of Tex4Tex Estonia." He clapped his hands together. "So what does this story tell you about our great company?"

There was an embarrassed pause before we realised this could be fun, and decided to pitch in. Maybe this wouldn't be such a wasted afternoon after all?

"Is it that we employ illegal immigrants?"

"No, but nice try."

"Did he swim the Atlantic?"

"No, it's about him and us."

Tony arched an eyebrow. "You say that he worked in the toilets and caught the bosses' eye?"

"Don't even go there."

But the instruction was ignored. Tony carried on.

"So, let's get this right, this bloke hated the Commies so he swam the Baltic to escape them. He'd rather spend his life cleaning the toilets for some Atlantan fat arse, but we sent him back anyway."

"No. I think you're missing the point." Martin was already just starting to get a little flustered, whereas Tony was just starting to warm to his task.

"Is it that cleaning toilets is suitable training for management?" We all laughed at Paula's preposterous idea. Everyone knows you wouldn't trust a manager to do a vital job like clean the toilets.

"No, I think you're getting distracted by the toilet."

"Is it that people with stupid names get on fast?" Paula was speaking again, "I mean I looked in the Tex4Tex corporate address book, and there are some of the stupidest names I've ever seen. It's like the Americans want their kids to hate them. There's a load of them – Igors, Wolfgangs, Hortense, Herberts, Willies, Juniper Berrysmith that was one, Herman Grizzlie, Canapé Woodsmith..."

Tony butted in excitedly.

"Yes, I know I found one the other day, Rhoda Dendron. I kid you not. You know one day I'm going to send them all a blanket email asking how they cope."

"That's a great idea," I laughed.

"Well, Mr Captain Pinkbeard, you can look forward to receiving an email then."

Martin's stern intervention drew us back to our quest for a certificate in Values.

"No, the point I am trying to make is that Igor wanted to be the head of Estonia. It was his dream to return to his homeland as a successful businessman. The point I'm making is that through Tex4Tex you can achieve your dreams if you are prepared to work hard enough." Martin took a step forward. He stood above and in front of me.

"What is your ambition, Pinkbeard?"

Now that was a tough one. Not to be head of Corporate Estonia that's for sure. I guessed that I hoped for an admin mix-up and immediate retirement on a greatly enhanced pension, but it was hardly a goal I could work towards. I'd like to be renationalised to go back into the warm cocoon of civil service oblivion, but I doubted Tex4Tex would help me there either.

"I want Wolves to win the League," I piped up.

Martin stepped in, "No, what ambition do you want for yourself Pinkbeard?"

Now that was another hard one and I stroked my beard for effect.

"I want to be in the crowd when Wolves win the League."

"Jeez, how long do you want to live Pinky?" Paula's tribe didn't like yam-yams.

"No," Tony corrected her, "supporting Wolves is a great thing. My dream is your dream." He clicked his fingers for effect. "Make it happen Martin."

"No, I really don't think that even Tex4Tex can make Wolves a good team."

"But that's not true. The company makes billions and trillions and probably gazillions. It could easily invest in Wolves and bring back the Glory Days to the Old Gold."

"No, I really don't think so, we'd want to do something for the staff."

"Okay then, how about committing to keeping the nursery open?" Paula was never going to let a chance to keep piling on the pressure slip by.

"No, but we want to do something for all staff, not just Wolves fans, not just mothers, but everyone."

"Right, so the nursery is for mothers, but not for fathers then?" Under her breath Paula added the words 'sexist twat' but she made sure it was loud enough for all of us to hear.

Martin sighed and rolled his eyes. I feared his values workshop was already collapsing like a tiring Springbok with the yapping hunting dogs closing in.

"Tell me this then, Martin," I leaned forward. "Are company cars for everyone or just for managers? Is the executive bonus for everyone or just for managers?"

"Yes, the captain is right again. Where's my company car?" demanded Tony. There was a brief stand-off as Martin glared at us, and we returned the compliment. We were adopting the values of our environment. It really was just like an infants' school. I half expected Martin to push Tony to the floor and draw cat's whiskers on his face, but after gathering himself, our teacher changed tack.

"You see out there, in the car park, what can you tell me about it?"

"It's concrete."

"It's raining."

Now I don't want to seem dumb, but it just looked like a car park. Built for purpose. It was hard to work out what on earth our lunatic trainer was after.

And how did he do it? How can a man be simultaneously dull and deranged? Answer me that, shipmates.

There was a pause. Extended pause, and then a bit more pause.

"It's got a lot of cars in it."

"Yes, brilliant Paula," Martin Sidepartin clapped his hands together enthusiastically as though he was encouraged by the lively progress we were making. "The car park is full. It's full because Tex4Tex employs us all. We are world beaters in our field. That is why the company can employ so many."

Tony put his hand up. "Mm, I know you won't remember because you weren't here, but I think you'll find the car park was full when we were civil servants as well." We nodded in support. "It isn't as though Tex4Tex invented computers and sold them to the UK government and created the jobs. The jobs were here anyway, it's only the employer that changed." Tony pointed his finger at our trainer again, making it clear he was blaming Martin personally for the transfer in ownership.

Martin brushed Tony's statement away as though it were a mere technicality.

"Nonetheless, this contract will be a huge success, and who knows what might have happened if it wasn't for Tex4Tex stepping in." He said it passionately as though the British government would have to go back to using the abacus without Tex4Tex. He looked up. "And do you know the secret of our success?"

'The secret of our success?' Well, the questions weren't getting any easier. We could be here all day. I glanced at my watch. To break the silence, and hurry things along, I ventured out.

"Look. I'm just throwing this up for discussion, and please stop me if you think I'm guessing, but is it our secret sauce?"

While Tony and Paula convulsed, Martin, his face reddening by the second, stared in utter disbelief at this ludicrous imposter into his corporation.

"IT'S OUR VALUES AND VALUES SYSTEM!" he shrieked. He turned away, clenching, and unclenching his fists, as though he was quite deliberately taking a break to calm himself. And then, after a few seconds, he walked over to the easel with an A1 pad of white paper on it. He lifted his pen briefly before thinking again and lowering it back to his side. After a few seconds he turned quickly, blew out his cheeks and faced the class. Martin was wagging his pen at me, like he was contemplating whether to shoot me with it, but at the same time he had this deranged smile on his face.

I noticed the pen had Project Telford inscribed in gold along the shaft. Neat. While I was wondering where he got the pen, Martin continued.

"You know Pinkbeard, you're right, our values are a bit like our secret sauce. The secret sauce to our success." But before I could modestly inform the room it was a lucky guess inspired by a visit to a takeaway, he had moved on.

He stood over Paula.

"Paula, how would you increase your value to the company?"

"I dunno," she answered carelessly, "by resigning?"

"Oh, come on Paula, I know you can do better than this, show a bit of interest." He glared his disappointment at her briefly, before taking out a marker pan and drawing the child-like black outline of a bucket on a nearby whiteboard. He then changed pens and completed a blue line across the centre of the transparent bucket. When he had finished, he stood back for a moment to admire his handy work. He spun around to face us.

"Colleagues," he said magnanimously, "your career is like a bucket, a bucket with a hole in it." Well, my friends this was a turn-up. I glanced at the others to see if this was the knowledge he needed to impart, and the course had ended. But no such luck. "Your value to Tex4Tex is the level of water in the bucket. But because of the hole, and the level of water your value is constantly diminishing as your knowledge becomes outdated. Paula, bearing in mind you can't stop the leak, how would you make the level of water rise?"

She shrugged. "Maybe get a smaller bucket?"

"No! No! No!. By training, by constantly learning and refreshing your knowledge. By pouring more water into the top! Tex4Tex will help you in your constant desire to improve yourself." He stared down at us. "You see you can't ever stand still and think you've learned enough. Technology is always advancing and forcing us to grow."

He did seem to be making a point to us.

"So Tex4Tex is a bit like a bloodstream then and a working man's constant battle with dehydration and rehydration."

"Well, yes Pinkbeard, good. Healthy blood flowing all around the body is important as it flows from your feet to your brain."

"Aye, and the level of alcohol in your bloodstream represents your value to the company. The level of alcohol is falling as you nip to the toilet hoping to meet the next head of Estonia, and it can only be topped up by frequent visits to the pub."

"Well, I don't like your imagery, but in principle you're getting there."

"So what?" Tony leapt in. "I get it. Well done, Pinky. Thank you for finally explaining Values to me." He tugged at my arm, so he could address me directly and ignore Martin.

"So, what you're saying is the more alcohol you drink the greater your value to Tex4Tex?"

Whilst I nodded my approval with a smile and a wink, Martin turned away again, and quietly stared out of the window at the car park for a half a minute or so. He then quite deliberately walked to the table in the corner and took out Project Telford one final time and signed three forms one after the other. As he moved away to gaze out of the opposite window his right hand gestured for us to collect our certificates of completion. He kept his back to us the whole time. As we collected our certificates of Achievement in Values Training and left the room Paula turned briefly to glance over her shoulder.

"Do you think he'll be okay? I think we might have broken his brain."

"Don't worry Paula, a couple of cold showers and he'll have washed our public sector filth off," Tony replied cheerfully. "Nice pen though. Project Telford. Bostin."

I looked down at my certificate. It said, "Pinkbeard has passed his Values Training." Bless him, Martin didn't even know my Christian name."

2004-2005

I read that some of our best and brightest from the metropolitan elite have impromptu career plans mapped out on scraps of paper in coffee houses. Not me.

"Join the civil service," they said, "it's a job for life" they said, "great pension for free" they said. And from back-office admin I had drifted further back, so far back I fell into the private sector. You see I work in information Technology, so unlike those of you who sit in front of a computer and drive it, I'm under the bonnet helping it tick over smoothly. Or at least that's the theory my friends, because as we all know history teaches us government computers have a mind of their own.

For those not steeped in IT gobbledegook computers speak in English on screen, but they talk to each other in their own language. Only people with translation skills can instruct computers to do what we want, and we call these interpreters Developers and their instructions Code. Computers are modern beasts, when they fail to do what we want, we can't fiddle with the aerial or bash them on the lid yelling 'bugger, bugger' like Dad fixing the old black and white. No, we must take out the old code and replace it with new code providing the right instruction. To do this we shut the computers down, substitute the old code for the new and then we push it all back in the computer's guts in an act of minor surgery we call a 'Release.' After that it is fingers crossed and hey presto we trust it all lights up again when we press the Start button. I'm sure it's apparent to you by now, we don't give computers legs, or they quite understandably would run amok like Yul Brynner in *Westworld* seeking to avoid this weekly disembowelment.

But whilst most computer programmes follow simple tasks and routines the challenge is to get them to harmonise so they can perform all their duties concurrently. Through mission creep the individual programmes merge to become a computer system running multiple simple duties, and when that goal is achieved it allows the bosses to sack workers to offset the initial expenditure. From there on employers follow the economics of scale adding more simple tasks to maximise the savings, but as a downside the more complicated the system becomes the greater the chance of failure. And when the inevitable happens then well blow me, shiver me timbers, what are the odds? 'Do you know we've just sacked the workers who could do the job manually?' What a calamity! Yes, even in information technology the laws of nature apply – the bigger they come, the harder they fall comrades. Never mind at least we can console ourselves in the certainty that at the heart of the collapse of capitalism there will be a computer screen with an error message.

To minimise failures and ensure the new code will succeed a developer will rehearse it in a mock-up test environment. When satisfied with a mock-up the code is 'released onto the box' and 'placed in a live environment'. In other words, the rehearsal is over but tomorrow it's for real in front of an audience when the users get to drive the computer again. It sounds straightforward doesn't it, except developers are low grades. We are not trusted to unilaterally take down a computer system, perform an upgrade and put it on the box because it undermines an entire management hierarchy and is of course the road to anarchy. No, management need to ensure one upgrade to one single programme doesn't bring all the others down through incompatibility and it can be identified if it does. Therefore, forms need to be filled, releases need to be scheduled, decisions need to be owned, an audit trail created, and most importantly, backs need to be covered.

I guess the point I'm making is that the Hollywood idea of computers being under the sole protection of a bearded geeky genius shouting 'eureka!' and saving the day is not true, and maybe never has been. Computing isn't about inspiration at all, it is about following process and not making a mistake, it is about communications and teamwork. It's a military activity where everyone has their role and each link in the chain is as important as the next. The developer can't see the end-user, and because of shift-work and remote working neither can oversee the Release. The managers plan the workload, but they can't perform any of the roles they are responsible for, and the department head commissioning the work is usually only interested in the draft Press Office wording. And at the end of the day if Jo the cleaner pulls the wrong plug out when she turns on the Hoover then the screen goes dark, or dead, or quiet – a multi-million contract dependent on a minimum wage employee. Each part is as important as the next, comrades.

The basic rule is this, all areas require the others to provide accurate honest information at the right time to identify weaknesses and improve performance, and most important of all the organisation should work as a coherent unit. And of course, when we were civil servants, we were a single unit, maybe not coherent but we had potential. Although we techies didn't work in the offices as end-users many of us had started our careers there, and while we only had some inkling of the purpose of our code and the business of the department, we still felt a kinship with the end-user because we shared the same employer.

For better or more probably worse, privatisation had placed a barrier between the computer folk and the end-users who we were instructed to regard as our customers and not our colleagues. Where once information had been shared freely now there was a contract and a price, and it created agendas which never existed before. Previously our loyalty to the department had been unquestioned, but these days we had the loyalty to 'our computer system' and the multinational sitting tenant to balance. Over time rumours surfaced of developers in Tex4Tex identifying faults in the system but being instructed by local management not to correct them until the department paid for the fix to the problem it hadn't yet realised existed. It was computing Munchhausen's by proxy, the patient needed to know how clever we were and how much we cared before we fixed them. Or else we wouldn't fix them.

You didn't need Old Mother Shipton to tell you where this path was leading, but we were told running costs had to be lowered, and of course risk-taking was the route to both profit and cost-saving. I guess our managers must have passed their meetings with the department with crossed fingers behind their backs. It was best all round if we never openly stated the level of risk of running computers with known errors, but we privately pursued a working theory the government accepted and understood the basis of the game –risk-taking came with an element of risk.

For the time being the department's computer system was riding the waves as smoothly as ever, but if you paid attention below the decks under the flooring you could hear rats nibbling on cables.

February 2004

You must be wondering when I was going to find the time and space to say something kind about my employer – take a walk in their shoes and see things from their point of view. Aye, and I guess you may be feeling sorry for the poor multinational so-and-so with the misfortune of being forced to employ unwilling old soaks like me. Yes, I guess the bad feeling can cut both ways.

Well, to be fair, and for the sake of balance, even I could see there were good things a kind-hearted boss could now provide with a corporate Amex and a snout in the Tex4Tex Kind Hearts Fund. Although it wasn't common practice everywhere, on Roger's team cakes and chocolates appeared on desks on Fridays, and flowers were sent when staff ailed. His behaviour proved to be the right kind of bribery and it encouraged the idea we were a family of friends and colleagues inside the Tex4Tex Big Tent. In some teams these little things mattered because it presented kind leaders with an opportunity to show their appreciation, and who knows, maybe they even made a lasting difference, but in other teams with other bosses, there were mixed signals. In those teams it was like watching terrible pushy parents buying back affection from the teenage children they beat and belittled.

The dye was cast in such a manner management would continue to try to balance carrot and stick with an amateurish display of psychobabble they called management discretion, common-sense and team-spirit.

And then one low winter sun morning I too was swept up. For a moment I too became an advocate of freedom from the chains of government. All too briefly, but I cannot deny it happened. Don't press me for details. I can't recall quite when it happened, but I guess it must have been over a weekend. It was there on a Monday, it must have been a Monday, true love in the tea-point – the Coffematix3000.

She was tall and sleek with buttons in all the right places as far as this old grump was concerned. A temperature modulated passport to happiness. She caught me off guard. I don't deny it, comrades as I realised even in this moral vacuum there was beauty and tenderness. Like a butterfly on a battlefield.

My friends – the Coffeematix3000 – what's not to like? Coffee and tea in all varieties, differing levels of milk substitute and sweetener adjusted to tastes. But that's not all – soup, dayglo soft drinks and delight of delight, choco-milk. Not chocolate, not milk, and possibly for reasons of patent, apparently not cocoa either.

And best of all it was free.

For some former public servants this seemingly endless supply of free coffee was viewed suspiciously. It could be considered an undeclared taxable benefit, and some questioned the propriety of the arrangement. Not for me though – Pinkbeard, the private sector entrepreneur now had a tax-free perk courtesy of Tex4Tex, and I intended to drink my way to a twenty percent boost in my relative net overall income. Feeling I'd been liberated from drudgery I happily threw away my financially uncompetitive teabags and prepared for the new century. Like others I awaited my turn in the queue, but on quiet days I merely took my coffee to the back and started queuing again drink in hand. Okay, I admit it, some days I just threw a hot cup away in the sink as a celebration of decadent wastefulness so I could briefly replicate those grotesque toffs lighting a cigar with a £50 note.

Anyway, it was there in the tea-point my latest tale began.

"Tragic about Old Sheila."

It was the voice of Paula in conversation with Tony. "I tell you they should burn out those old smoke rooms. I think I'd rather work in Chernobyl than in there. I mean the doctor said she had the lungs of the Marlboro' Man."

"Oh, I didn't know she smoked, I never saw her in the smoke room," answered a bored Tony as the queue shuffled forward.

"No, that's the point," replied Paula animated. "She was one of those cleaners given the task of airing the place. They let her take the carpet tiles home before they cleaned it out. She's the first passive smoker in history to catch lung cancer from stain proof polypropylene. Who'd have thought it? She was the one needing the ten-year warranty not the carpet."

Before Paula could develop her story, our leader, Roger appeared in the doorway. A very timely arrival as we'd just reached the front of the queue. A moment of fortune recorded by the sighing further down the line.

"Well, I was going to wonder aloud why the so-called 'most valued' members of my team are stood around chatting, but now I'm here I think I'll join you. And what's more I'm feeling reckless so I'm thinking I'll have one of those salty soup-like monstrosities into the bargain.' He was gesturing vaguely at the Coffeematix.

"But can you guess today's flavour?" smiled Paula sweetly as she covered the label and pressed the combination before presenting the beige plastic cup to her leader.

"Thank you, Paula for issuing the challenge," Roger raised his cup in acknowledgment, "and of course these days a challenge is not to be avoided. A challenge is to be welcomed." He turned and gravely addressed the rest of the tea-point. "Let me remind you, here in Tex4Tex a challenge is another blessed opportunity for us go-getters to shine."

Then he cautiously sniffed the aroma before presenting his findings to the audience.

"All I can say without tasting it is that it smells of boiling underpants and looks like milky vomit. Soo, if you were to press me, I'd have to say chicken-flavoured soup extract." He carried the confident air of an aficionado. Paula nodded her acknowledgment of his expertise. With the affirmation Roger took a swift nip of the boiling chemicals, while I quietly listed this rival for the Coffeematix affection.

Turning to Tony, a triumphant Roger continued.

"I take it this note is from you?"

Removing a folded lined sheet of A4 from his top pocket he read it aloud for the benefit of the tea-point occupants.

"Dear Roger, as you may know post-privatisation there are many rumours of redundancy, and I would like you to know I am prepared to sacrifice myself if the company reluctantly makes the necessary decision to throw expensively pensioned baggage overboard to help to keep this flagship contract afloat. If you feel unable to support my request, will you please provide me with the name of a manager who will? Secondly, if I am to be considered irreplaceable would you please interpret this note as a request for Events in my honour, bonuses, or promotion as a reward for my enforced loyalty. Your loyal colleague, Tony."

"Very, very moving," murmured Paula touching Tony's upper arm. "I love the way Tex4Tex has produced this spirit of self-sacrifice amongst us.'

"Thank you, Paula. I'm so glad you noticed. I just wanted to give something back,' responded Tony pretending to wipe a tear from his eyes. "It's like the corporate posters say. Us big old oaks are in the way, it's time to let the saplings grow. It's the young ones I'm doing it for."

"Well, Tony,' replied Roger, calmly asserting himself, "whilst I've seen more convincing tears from disgraced politicians, I promise you in the event they announce redundancies that I'll give it my best shot 'cos to be honest you've been here for fifteen years and you're still no use to man nor beast."

It was the insult Tony wanted to hear.

"Great. Thanks, Roger. You're the best!"

The conversation about Tony's desire to depart this earthly paradise continued back at our terminals. The topic suited our mood of the month – spending our imagined redundancy payments was our favourite waste of time. We may have been privatised, but to everyone's surprise we'd kept the value of our pensions, allowing us life options and a safety net if it all went kaboom. This happy-go-lucky approach to the prospect of redundancies wasn't universal, it was interpreted by some new hires as a sign of both disloyalty to the company as well as an injustice. It offended them on a personal level because we had better pensions than they did, therefore, given our new account sensitivity, as far as we were concerned it was a small act of defiance talking so openly about our anticipated windfall.

"You're not going to get enough to live off though, are you? You're not exactly in the golden years?" commented Paula referring to the mythical period of civil service entitlements in the early Fifties when minimum age met maximum pension uplift.

"Well, it's funny you should say that," Tony answered enthusiastically, "because you know I'm forty-five, and I know I'm forty-five, but owing to a completely, definitely, totally, unforeseen, out of character, key- in cock-up at the point of transfer when our HR records could be checked and amended, apparently I am now unfortunately fifty-four, and have given thirty years loyal service for Queen and country."

"You know sometimes I just curse these sausage fingers," he smiled and winked, holding the guilty hands up for inspection. "But what can I do? I tell you, I'm nearly ten years closer to death than I thought I was nine months ago, and it feels great! And look at this," he declared proudly. He was pointing to a counter in the top right-hand of the screen. "I linked the union pension and redundancy calculator to the timer on the PC, and now I can watch my pension entitlement rise by the day."

We were in awe at his ability to find a life- relevant use for his IT skills.

"You are indeed a genius and so young looking for your age," said Roger, appearing over Tony's shoulder where he'd been lurking, quietly listening. "In fact, I could say I never knew there were such hidden depths to your talents." Tony began to shrink in his seat in response to Roger's enthusiasm. "In fact, I could say your comatose career prospects are the result of you being sorely underused. Maybe I need to stretch and develop you? More work? Harder, more challenging work? Maybe I need to expand your potential?"

"Please God, no Roger. Don't say these nice things about me," Tony pleaded. Roger was grinning, he was enjoying himself. He pushed the keyboards to one side and rested on the newly available space.

"I have to say you've been hiding your light under a bushel all this time. Who'd have thought it? You are exactly the kind of modest, humble, talented, resourceful, independent-minded, risk-taking employee that makes Tex4Tex the obscenely profitable bully boys of the outsourcing Industry."

Roger patted his hand on Tony's shoulder.

"Believe me, I would have tried, but it appears in all honesty I can't spare you for this non-existent redundancy round or possibly even the real one when it rolls into town, as it surely will one day."

As Tony slumped in his seat, not sure whether to take his boss seriously, and unsure whether to challenge him, Roger pulled out the note constituting Tony's unofficial redundancy request, folded it carefully, dipped it in his chicken soup, placed it in his mouth and slowly began chewing. We watched in amazement as Tony's desire for expensive liberation lay in tatters through his own genius.

"But this isn't fair, you can't eat his redundancy request."

"Can't I, Paula? Can't I?"

"But surely, you've got to reward his moment of genius, a word you used yourself."

"Paula, I will. His request for redundancy has been refused because he has shown hitherto untapped skills. The use of those skills in deliberately falsifying his HR records will need to be rectified, and if Tony can't correct the error, then I will need to make HR aware, and who knows what those pedants may do."

It was a bitter pill.

"You see this, Tony" Roger continued, pulling the paper out of his mouth, and tossing it in the bin.

"That's your career, that is."

He was joking of course.

March 2004

You know those times when you were bored at school and any distraction would be seized upon? Well, the modern office is not so far away from those days. Childish in memory, but perhaps this demonstrates the carefree stability of our working environment before Tex4Tex picked up an axe and began home improvements. I recall one of the little things used to break the monotony of the working day was an announcement over the public address system. It gave us all a chance to stop tapping the keys and lift our eyes from the screen. Of course, the arrival of site wide email would eventually consign these aural distractions to history, but there was a brief period where Neanderthal and Cro-Magnon co-existed and that space is where this story belongs.

The security guards had the responsibility to make loudspeaker announcements to a bewitched audience. Bless me, as everyone knows guards are not trained newsreaders, and there was usually a quiet giggle at their expense. All the staff had their favourite announcers, and everyone's favourite was Dean Hammond, a lumbering walrus of a guard– he was the by-word in hopeless. Over the years Dean had seemingly perfected a technique of confusing the written message to the point it became irrelevant. For all we knew there could have been terrorists storming the guard hut in the car park, but we would still have been cackling merrily with our feet resting on the desk. Through a range of strategies, the gravity of the announcement would be lost; he may get a coughing fit, he may talk off mic while the mike was still on. At times he may even have been simultaneously eating and reading. Once, I swear comrades, he even belched into the ears of one thousand five hundred people. Dean, to everyone's amusement, had an almost one hundred per cent record honed over the years of not quite getting anything right. It is perhaps one of those small personal misfortunes that occupying the security room he never got to hear the rounds of applause and cheering following those occasions when he mispronounced the names of senior managers or visiting dignitaries.

Yes, on reflection it was a miracle our tie-up with that Korean multinational ever proceeded.

It must have been about eleven thirty when the loudspeakers crackled into life.

Peep!

"This a reminder that there will be a union meeting in Meeting Point House today. Everyone is invited."

Peep!

"Sorry the meeting is at noon with the union."

Peep!

"Sorry, only union members can attend the meeting....House Point"

As the loudspeaker peeped out and it was clear there were no more corrections, as some amongst us reached for our jackets, a small group of new Tex4Tex managers appeared from Cliff Wiley's office alongside the man himself. In their company was HR director Texas Rose, a woman whose name already invoked fear on site. It was not always clear to me why she invoked this fear, but workers whispered she had the ear of our increasingly distant CEO Herb and she was the power behind the throne. She was his gatekeeper. To win him over, you first needed to win her approval was the accepted logic. In less than a year Rose had been granted A-list celebrity status by the middle managers. She was the accessible face of senior management, and she never ate alone, the ambitious rising leaders would invade her table seeking her favour – a queen and her courtiers. Part of me felt sorry for her being constantly fawned on by pushy managers and I imagined she showered twice a day to clear away the lickspittle droplets. Lesser folk invoked her name – they claimed they spoke for her and conjured up the fear of She Who Must Be Obeyed while they passed on their interpretation of her thoughts. In doing so they conveniently placed themselves close to power in the minds of their underlings.

"Don't do this." I heard Rose say the deal won't get over the line." Or sometimes they would hide behind her shadow, "No, I can't say why exactly because it's all hush-hush, but you should know Rose would be angry if she heard about it."

And there she was, site royalty, in the centre of the office blocking the main passageway to the exit. Close enough for me to ask for her autograph if I'd wanted it but that wasn't my intention. I was puzzled. What was she doing here with Wiley? It felt safe to assume she hadn't dropped in on her way to the union meeting.

She positioned herself in the narrow corridor between the lines of desks with her back to the exit and smiled at her companions. She rubbed her hands together before unleashing her Texan drawl.

"Over here, everyone. Let's see who the union blockers are!"

Her courtiers all laughed as expected, and a smarmy looking twat of a graduate flourished a notebook and pen for their further amusement. There was a moment when those who'd risen to put their jackets on stood there with one hand in their sleeve apparently caught in the act of belonging to a union, and not quite knowing what their next move should be. It was a temporary stand-off. They were caught between the Old World and the New, and worst luck, the self-appointed Conquistadors were blocking the doorway taking names.

"Oh, for Christ's sake. I wasn't going to bother but this is a disgrace."

It was Paula speaking. She stood and put her coat on while the managers stared in disbelief at her audacity and the graduate scribbled. Tony rose next and beckoned me to stand alongside. I dutifully responded As Paula walked down the office calmly doing up her buttons, a few others had by now taken courage from Paula's defiance and they were preparing to leave for the union meeting. Tony was more vocal in his disobedience, no doubt anxious as ever to be the centre of attention. This development suited me well as I quietly dropped in behind him.

"That's *Spartacus*. S-P-A-R-T-A-C-U-S. Spartacus!" Tony shouted down the room at the graduate. I began wandering after them, but first turned to see a bemused Roger with his arms spread wondering where the hell his team were going. As Tony approached the managers he gestured towards Wiley and began winding up the outsiders by talking Telford.

"Ow bist jockey, you coming to the union meeting? You're still a union member, aren't you Cliff?"

"No used to be. I resigned, didn't see the point any more." Wiley had replied in a deadpan manner, but he was looking awkward and momentarily stared at his shoes. He liked to play both ways and he didn't want to be caught siding against long-standing colleagues, but there again he didn't want to side against our new colleagues and future line managers either.

Paula blocked his retreat, and penned him in.

"Yes, to be fair, Tony he probably resigned over principle. If you remember when Cliff spoke at the big meetings, he said he'd leave the union if we didn't strike over privatisation, and he'd never work a day for those 'red-neck bastards'."

She turned to me and rolled her eyes. "I guess he must have adapted his political position in the light of circumstances."

She made me laugh.

By now we were right in front of them. Wiley's face was already reddening, Tony was about to turn it purple with fury.

"Yes, you're right, Paula. Good point, but I think you're being harsh. Cliff is entitled to change his opinion, after all everybody knows civil service managers have always been socialist firebrands in the pub but grovelling union bashing brown nose toadies in the workplace, so we shouldn't expect too much of him. He's only reverting to type. Keep it to yourself, but he's still a tatty civil servant underneath his suit." Tony pulled Paula's arm to slow her down and jokingly wagged a finger in her face as if to tell her off. "No, we should accept this is the best of all possible worlds. Let's take a lesson from Cliff, I think we should all move on, don't you?"

Tony beamed as he held the door open for Paula to walk through.

"Ta-ra abit!"

As we passed the closing door, we heard Wiley bellow, "Roger, my office now!" and began wondering whether we wanted to return at all. Paula continued to the union meeting to find out about the state of the nursery campaign, but me and Tony split with her on our way to the Tommy Botfield, the recently opened local Wetherspoons.

Drinking at lunchtime? I can hear your eyebrows rising as I write it. Of course, you're right, returning to work with beer on your breath in the early days of Tex4Tex was officially a career breaker and disciplinary offence, yet in practice a tolerant boss could turn a blind eye. Therefore, on days like these it seemed entirely rational that as we'd made our bed we may as well stay out all day. Provided we weren't discovered we convinced ourselves we were doing our boss a favour by not compromising his principles. It was a risk but if no one contacted us, we gambled we could put meetings in our calendar, or perhaps take retrospective leave to be safe. We could always catch-up tomorrow. Ha! Yes, those were the days – if you'd told us Wetherspoons sold soft drinks we'd never have believed you.

It was two hours' drinking later, when a tired looking Roger came in to join us. He was kind enough to buy a round as he sat there with an orange juice explaining developments.

"Well, I've had two meetings with Cliff – one with Texas Rose in attendance, and then I waited for another opportunity an hour later when he had calmed down without her presence. Officially, Tony, you are covering for Brainstorm who has finally been signed off sick. The good news is that before Brainstorm finished, he provided a software release going into Live this afternoon and you're supporting it as punishment for taking the piss out of them." He pressed his palms to the table. "Let me make it clear, in case anyone asks, I am, as we speak, literally dragging you two screaming from the union meeting and forcing you back to work."

Roger then took a moment to survey the table, and what I modestly considered to be an impressive looking collection of stacked used glasses with their tell-tale beer-rings. He continued. "Unofficially, I had a chat with Cliff, and he knows they can't stop people attending union meetings, however much the Texans may want to. He doesn't want to take sides on this. You know you really shouldn't have said what you did. You forced him to make a decision" The Horror!

Roger took a sip of his orange, while we wondered what the punishment might have been in other circumstances, after all there was little chance Wiley would have put it to Texas Rose that she had foolishly provoked the aggressive response from experienced confident staff.

Roger sighed, "I think he feels a bit bad about being caught up with them. He also has correctly guessed you two would never waste two hours at a union meeting if the pubs were open and there was drinking to be done.

So, we've got a problem Tony. You're on the way to getting drunk and can't come back to work, and Texas Rose has made it her business to ruin your afternoon and needs to see your name on sign-off."

Tony responded diagonally.

"Is she really terrifying then? Is she so frightening a manager as senior as Wiley is running scared?"

"Well, as you know Tony, Cliff has always been a career shapeshifter not a manager. He follows whichever way the wind blows and makes sure the direction of travel is in his own best interests. So, basically, in answer to your question, 'yes', he is afraid. Do you remember, when the civil service managers used to say, 'as far as you're concerned, I'm God' and we'd all laugh at the pomposity? Well nowadays when the Texans bang the table the managers directly beneath them start jumping. To be honest I don't think the suits could believe their eyes when you three walked out taking the piss. It was like watching the kid at Tiananmen Square standing in front of the tanks trying to sell the Militant."

Tony shrugged, before continuing sarcastically, "Okay then, bostin. Just bostin. I mean just absolutely fucking bostin. I'm working from home then. I mean Brainstorm maybe mad but generally his code is spot-on, so fingers crossed they won't need me."

Now at some point later Roger must have returned to work. His message had given Tony a problem of logistics. Now he had to support the Live Release but couldn't return to the office with alcohol in his system. Our warped logic was therefore that Tony had no choice but to carry on drinking nearby until the Release was on the box. As a friend I supported him, and to be fair it was always my round anyway on alternate pints. I guess at some point Tony must've decided we needed some food to soak up the alcohol as it was of course only sensible to gorge ourselves after drinking for three hours on an empty stomach.

I remember it was dusk when I woke. My memory of Roger leaving had disappeared into the alcohol void. Our table was cleared except for the plate I had been resting my face upon; curry and chips I guessed. I looked across and saw Tony was stood outside in the concrete beer garden, a pint glass in one hand and a mobile phone in the other. He was pacing up and down as he held the mobile to his ear and a couple of times he crashed into chairs and tables. He looked up as I came out, proffered a hankie for me to wipe my face and made the eternal thumbs-up gesture meaning it was my round and he wanted another drink.

Despite his inability to stand up straight or still, his phone manner was impeccable bar the occasional swear word of frustration. I had always been impressed by his ability to defy the wear and tear instructions of beer. Aye, sometimes you should take your hat off and accept the presence of a superior constitution. It must've been twenty minutes later when he returned to the cavernous interior to begin his next pint.

"Everything okay?" I asked.

"Well sort of, being pissed doesn't help, but probably isn't the issue."

"So, what's the problem?"

"It's Brainstorm. He's the problem. For some reason, he'd caught the bug about learning a new language, and he obviously thought this Release would be a good test to trial his knowledge. So of course, the frigging download instructions were all in French! None of them bastards on his team had even made a cursory check before they approved them, because they were so intent on stitching me up." He started laughing, completing with a hacking smoker's cough before he continued.

"So of course, they phone me as Technical Live Support, and ask if I can translate this for them." He scanned the ceiling briefly for dramatic effect before returning to me. "I mean, of course I fuckin' can't! I'm not Thierry Henry!"

Tony was trying to be angry, but he couldn't stop laughing and coughing. Without the magic work phone in his hand, he had transformed merrily back into a drunk. "While you've been crashed and offline, I've been talking with some sap who's implementing the Release, and he's been sat there with an internet translator open. And let me tell you, we'd have done it in half the time if Brainstorm's French hadn't been so hopeless."

When he'd finished laughing, and coughing, spluttering, and retching, he held up his glass. "To Brainstorm. Crazy non-conformity may have finally got the better of him and he has ruined my afternoon. His hovercraft is truly full of eels, but we'll rue the day when oddball techies are merely cogs on a production line."

He downed the pint in one, and then staggered to the toilet to throw up. It had been his second successful release of the day.

April 2004

When I returned from my second or third trip of the morning to the coffee machine Paula was already reading aloud the email announcement breaking the news our account had adopted Tex4Tex corporate standards of attire. She looked close to pain because she was laughing so hard.

I had been worried this day might come. Here it was.

"Pinky, I love you to pieces but your grunge-pirate style won't cut any mustard with the dress code police," she lectured me. Satisfied at having passed on the lesson she calmed slightly, pointing at the screen while she looked me up and down. "Man at C&A. I can't wait."

I tried to feign a small amount of concern. As it happened Roger had already warned me privately of the announcement twenty-four hours earlier. Paula's news was old news.

"Why surely I'm business casual?" I smiled as I half protested, provocatively preening myself in front of her, momentarily noting the dirty buttons and cat-hairs on my waistcoat.

Gorgeous! Stylish but lived in. Still got it. Tony wolf-whistled his support from across the bank of four, and I bowed stiffly in response before taking my seat.

I hoped my posing might bring an end to a potentially damaging discussion but Roger, my leader, was not having it. He'd informed me the day before he wanted to stamp out any talk of the dress code on his team. He didn't want any fuss because he'd already had to fight off a half-hearted attempt by Martin 'Sidepartin' Monk to force the business to move against me for lowering standards. 'Management point-scoring, nothing to worry about,' was how a composed Roger had described it to me.

Anxious to impart further knowledge, my team leader pulled up his feet and slid into action. Using his hands on the desk to haul himself towards us on a swivel chair, he was ready to deliver the sanctioned official view to his audience.

"Actually Paula, Jack's pirate gear is not far off the required Tex4Tex standards. He doesn't do t-shirts, polo shirts or jeans. He always wears a collar of a kind, always wears a jacket however preposterous, and always wears trousers not jeans."

Then he turned to me, lifting his feet off the ground again while he swung round.

"Perhaps if you promised to wash them occasionally, tone down the earrings and ringlets, hide the tattoos, comb your hair, and trim the beard a bit you might just sneak through. And at the end of the day, in modern Britain they can't sack you for looking like a pirate anyway." He stopped talking for a moment, pausing to clarify his position on the dress code. "And that's important. They can pressure you, they can make you feel unwelcome, they can even ruin your career but," he patted my lower arm in a comforting manner, "frankly you've had a twenty-year head-start on them."

He smiled to show no hard feelings for his little joke as he steered me through my first difficult waters of privatisation. He knew I didn't like the thought of being the focal point of a higher-grade spat, let alone criticised for the way I'd dressed for twenty years, but Roger appeared to have everything in hand.

This was a false alarm. That's where I'd file it. Not the first either. As far as we could tell the company had these tough policies, but they wouldn't apply them if it didn't suit the local business. So long as the workplace was flowing smoothly managers had been granted power and discretion to seemingly ignore Dallas HQ, or at least that's how it appeared. I allowed myself to believe every policy was advisory. If I wanted to get on, I would have to adapt to Tex4Tex standards, if I was happy where I was then it was down to me. That's how I read the tea leaves.

Yes, looking on the bright side, my first winter in the private sector could have been worse. So far, and fingers crossed, drinking and dress code apart, the company hadn't been too bad. Yet in the months since Day One Year Zero while everything still looked familiar the workplace had been pushed ever so slightly out of kilter. It was all a bit Stepford Wives. Imagine living and working inside the before and after shots of a difficult Spot the Difference competition.

This is where we belonged in the first year.

That's not to say all the differences were unwelcome or hard to spot. In the first six months post-transfer the company pulled down the low hanging fruit, and we witnessed an instant improvement in our environment. Stale old tobacco- coated meeting rooms with their drab impersonal numerical titles were freshened, personalised, and renamed after famous catalysts from Shropshire's glorious century of iron, coke, and typhoid.

"I'm entering Abraham Darby by the back door, and I'm going to be bashing around inside him all day," Tony would joke. Okay, I admit it, I'd laughed along the first dozen times he said it.

In my office tired worn carpets had been replaced, faded vanilla corridor walls repainted azure blue, and conveniently those depressing union noticeboards with their tatty prophecies of doom were quietly removed over the course of a single weekend. Those same walls now carried glass-cased motivational posters containing uplifting pictures of dolphins or whales breaching in sparkling oceans. There was one of multi-coloured children playing together under giant redwood, and there was another I recall of American eagles soaring over snow-capped mountains. The posters had cryptic messages in the footnote for all of us to consume: 'A snowflake is a fragile thing but looks what happens when they work together; Fun is being part of a team, all working together in good company'.

I laughed when I saw them although the posters neither raised my morale nor motivated me. I wondered what the Shropshire Ironmasters the company had honoured would make of the cloying sentimentality. The posters left the impression British bosses had finally lost the will to impose the hellfire and brimstone aspect of their Protestant exhortations to work harder as though they'd undergone a fashionable Blairite makeover, blurting over dead Diana, and hoping we'd work ourselves into the ground for the sake of the whales, the planet, and the profits.

It didn't seem important at the time, it seemed churlish to make a fuss, but with hindsight this seems relevant, so I'll pass it on. You see Tex4Tex were cross charging the department for the office refurbishment, and despite the department's role in letting our environment deteriorate through cost-cutting, they paid the invoice willingly. They'd privatised us to save money, but thanks to Tex4Tex the department was already on a spending spree. Privatisation had loosened the purse strings. It was a most unexpected outcome. Yet while I sniggered at the political machinations, thinking this won't last, on the top floor in a sinister development, the boardroom had been unofficially renamed the war room. Behind the locked door, the room was occupied by dark-suited managers placing yellow post-it notes on the whiteboard while the enthusiastic attendees roared their approval. You see we in Tex4Tex were no longer to be timid civil servants, we were training to become company warriors. In the Outsourcing business it was the survival of the fittest; it was dog-eat-dog, it was a jungle out-there, and in here too, and we intended to be the kings. It was war. Or at least it was war if you could convince yourself our soldiers and the Taliban only traded flame-mail across the canyons at Tora-Bora.

Yes, corporation business was a matter of life and death for our testosterone-fuelled leaders, but with the death part replaced by your inexplicable disappearance from the list of invitees to tomorrow's power breakfast. A strangely Orwellian outcome. Managers disappeared as though they had never existed, only to be reinvented months later toeing the company line on a project far, far, away.

Everything seemed to matter much more now in the private sector, every slight was emphasised, every mistake had a price tag attached. They said that if a manager wasn't in a meeting by eight thirty then they may as well go home because they'd been usurped. Of course, whilst there was a comic element to this hyper-competitive gung-ho militarist approach, our Tex4Tex managers were truly planning their own assault on the enemy. No, not the heavily armed Taliban shooting back but our former soft-bellied colleagues in 'the customer'. As the company pushed its feet under the desk Tex4Tex began planning to identify and exploit the weaknesses in the contract to increase profit margins at the taxpayer's expense. A task made much simpler when you consider they were identifying weaknesses in the contract our managers themselves had edited and approved prior to their own transfer.

It was a time for our managers to settle scores with former colleagues. You see Tex4Tex, aided and abetted by our local management, weren't just conspiring to bite the government hand that feeds. If the game played out properly, we were going to rip the whole frigging arm off.

No matter who was exploiting who, and we assumed the department must have anticipated confrontation, on balance it was so far so good inside Tex4Tex. It was only when you read the frustrated suspicious memos from our sidelined trade union you appreciated how far we'd drifted in such a short time. To attend a union meeting and listen to Paula and the remaining union reps was to hear an echo from a disappearing world of agreements and certainty. It was to be reminded of what those linguistic practitioners say, everything in the sentence before the word 'but' can be discarded. They had no plans to close the nursery but...they guaranteed job security but... they had no plans to change our terms but... They wanted continuity and as little change as possible but...

But there'd be no point privatising us if they weren't going to change anything! It wasn't complicated, and that was the unspoken truth.

But what would change look like? What form would it take? That's what none of us, even the union, could answer. Perhaps the quiet morning when Paula read aloud the latest missive from HR about the dress code would prove to be a stalking horse, an outlier of more aggressive change to come.

All around me the evidence of the underfunded dog-eared civil service was being quietly removed as if it had never existed, and the comforting familiar questioning cynicism of the public-sector was in retreat alongside it. While I stood still in time, other staff were voluntarily smartening themselves up, aligning to newly imported standards.

Every month team heroes were acclaimed and garlanded with trips to Alton Towers alongside never to be discussed cash rewards in brown envelopes. Promotion lists were steadily cleared as staff advanced, the pipeline of work was flowing, and glory be, overtime was granted upon request. But on the dark side, the dress code had been adopted without any kickback, terms like blockers and change resisters readily entered our vocabulary, and lads' lunchtime 'knitting circles' in public houses quietly disintegrated.

The company was winning the Culture War, the battle for hearts and minds.

It was like the first scenes in a horror movie where the aliens seemed pleasant enough and used all the right words, but on quiet days I could easily convince myself somewhere in Wolverhampton along the banks of the Shropshire Union there was a warehouse, and like the *Invasion of the Body Snatchers*, pods were being created wearing our faces but without our distinctive identities.

May 2004

When I first transferred, I'd expected rotting skulls hanging from the gates of the car park, or necklaces made from the teeth of 'disappeared' malcontents, but it hadn't worked out that way. Far from it, you see there had been weeks when I could kid myself not much had changed and I would easily muddle through anonymously. Maybe I was just a civil servant on extended secondment and the enemy tanks would roll harmlessly over our trenches, but then increasingly there were days when I faced reality, when I witnessed change first-hand, and had to accept our public sector past had gone forever.

This may only be a short tale for even these years later my old eyes still tear up at the acknowledgment of the lessons I learned, and the lessons I should have learned. Bear with me friends for it is important to my story.

This was the first big lie, the first unmistakeable sign we couldn't take Tex4Tex at their word.

And yet the day had begun as usual, I strolled towards my desk coffee in hand (button number 71 – extra milk and sugar) at 9.30 and prepared to take my battered derby hat and green army jacket off. I was fresh and fired up for a 'hard day at the coalface', which was how my bosses referred to computer working. However, Paula was not here, and Jolly Roger was also nowhere to be seen. It was odd, I felt like the cat entering the room only to find the furniture rearranged. I wanted to sniff the air to make sure it was safe.

The mystery was soon resolved when Tony beckoned me over conspiratorially, and then before I had reached him, in his customary manner he shouted across the bank of four desks.

"She must have fucked something up. She's been in there with Roger for an hour.' He was pointing to the Reynolds room. "He must be giving her a right bollocking."

And then he grinned at the crude suggestion. As much as I liked him and his uncomplicated easy-to-read nature, at times he made me want to despair. However, on this matter he appeared to be right. Computers were radiating heat and light, bags were under tables, but the desks were vacant. I was confused; it seemed so unlikely she could be in trouble.

Now normally, Paula, well, she kind of took care of me and by the time I arrived at my desk first thing, she had agendas and timetables printed out, and sometimes even a biscuit or two. I never asked her, she just did it out of affection for this lovable old rogue. I often told her she was like my little workhorse, so it was a little off-putting I don't deny it when I had to turn my own computer on, and clear yesterday's to-do post-its off the monitor. It threatened to sour my normally mellow mood.

It may have been two coffees and a toilet stop later when they returned. Paula's eyes were red where she must have been crying. Alongside her Roger looked pale and tense, his arms hung self-consciously at his side as though he desperately wanted to reach out and comfort her, but of course he couldn't. Those were the rules, otherwise we'd all be hugging her. As Paula looked up and saw the pair of us gawking, she barely acknowledged us, just put her head down, picked up her bags, reached for her coat, folded it across her bags, and began to leave without even putting it on.

I guess she wanted to place distance and dignity between herself and the prying eyes.

"Paula, it'll be all right, I'll sort something,' Roger called hopelessly to the back of her head as she sauntered away searching for the mobile phone in her pocket. The other teams temporarily turned their faces away from the screens to watch as this office fixture, one of our stabilisers, left in a state of distress. Within ten minutes Roger had called us into the Reynolds Room to share the news.

"Well, the powers-that-be have decided, surprise, surprise, to break their promise to staff and close the nursery." His fists tapped the table. "Although they are prepared to compensate her for a year, she is thinking of resigning as she's insulted by the insinuation this is about money. To her mind it's about disruption to her children and her family, as well as a breach of trust by the employer, and one made by local bosses who can easily afford stay at home wives and private education for their kids let alone nursery fees. Basically, she's getting angrier by the minute, saying this proves they're all liars and they always have been. So, I've sent her home if only to stop her sending flame-mail to all and sundry and getting herself into trouble."

"But surely she's not really going to resign. Is she? I'd miss her if she left and no mistaking."

"Well, I hope not, Jack because she's a treasure to have on the team, and to be honest you two lads don't have so many fans on site that you can afford to lose any." I nodded back to Roger acknowledging this probable truth. Tony, however, was not at all pleased by the insinuation our ill-disciplined maverick ways were not the absolute toast of the contract.

"Hang on! hang on! This has got nothing to do with us. She had kids. They've closed the nursery. What's this got to do with me? I mean I support her, and it'd be nice for her if her kids are close, but really this is not my problem. Blame the bosses, not us. I mean I like her, but wake up everyone, here in the private sector her nursery is my pay rise."

Roger rocked back in his seat. He looked furious at Tony's selfishness.

"Tony, are you so blind you can't see what's in front of you?" He came forward again, his arms grasping the edges of the table. "Don't you see Paula is the glue that holds this team together? She writes up the minutes, she prints off agendas and keeps you two facing forwards when you get distracted. She even answers the phone without a second thought when you two are in the pub or out for a smoke. She's hard-working and dependable, like a little workhorse, she does all the jobs no one cares about, covers for you two, and then she still delivers on the technical stuff."

"So why don't you promote her then?" Tony continued to challenge Roger, trying to play the bluff.

"Why Tony I'd like to, but I've let her down, or rather," he looked up, "we've all let her down. The extra work she does is not individual, it doesn't scream 'look at me'. She could easily do high quality work, but her better nature gets in the way. She gets no credit for the union stuff, and she props up you two chancers day in and day out. To get her promoted I'd have to balance it out by putting you two into the Under Supervision process, and even that might not work."

There was a pause.

Tony was breathing heavily as though his ego was audibly deflating. He hadn't expected to hear the message. I knew for a fact he thought he was the blue-eyed boy on the team, the next cab off the rank for promotion. When he wasn't in the pub drinking, or in the office requesting redundancy, he was complaining about the injustice of his non-promotion. He was our star striker, and women couldn't even play football, he hadn't even considered Paula as a potential rival, or that he might have to buck up his ideas. Dead man's shoes – that was the way these things had always worked. Like replaced like. In Tony's mind it would be positive discrimination if women benefitted through dead man's shoes.

It was Roger who spoke next.

"Do you know the expression your colleague is your competitor? That's what they say. It means you work together as a team, but you also need to be seen to be better than the others to be promoted. Even the others must know you're the best. "

"So, what's that got to do with anything?"

"Well, Paula is too much of a team player, she wants the team to succeed, and she doesn't stick the knife in when she should for her own benefit. To be honest, instead of covering for you, she should let you two fail every now and then just to reflect how good and reliable she is. That way maybe others would notice her."

Tony shrugged at listening to the truth while Roger continued his monologue.

"You see the Tex4Tex leadership team are like a viper's' pit fizzing and boiling with personal ambition and vanity. To address the problem of what truly awful people they all are, they need to make selfishness a virtue, so they portray it as toughness and resolution. Knifing your best mate in the back is a kind of rite of passage. They've all done it, and they expect others to stoop to their level. To advance, she needs to prove she's a bastard. Rest assured in Blair's competition-friendly Britain Paula's hard work and selfless team spirit is not what leadership is about."

"So how can we help?" I asked, "My bosses may want me to take advantage of her misfortune, but I don't like all this change and I do not want to see my friends and colleagues cry."

"Well, thank you, captain, at least you understand this." Roger said this to me whilst avoiding Tony's withering gaze. "To help persuade her to stay I need to make a case for her promotion and cover the added expense if she must find extra costs. And to help her cause I need you two to try and be a bit more self-sufficient, so she gets the time to pick up training and better-quality work."

I nodded my reply while Tony grunted his agreement.

Paula remained off work for a week or two while she considered her resignation and searched for affordable childcare. We were told, typical of Paula, she had phoned Roger while she was away to keep reminding him of little things that needed doing – budgets that required preparation, expense claims that had to be submitted. It surprised me at the time but in her absence, I started to learn critical admin roles I'd overlooked before and had previously needed Paula to manage for me. I worked out which processes required which forms, which forms belonged in which folders, and which passwords opened them. Whilst I was pleased with myself and the progress I was making, I became aware of all the responsibility I'd thoughtlessly outsourced to Paula without offering any reward or respect. I felt as guilty as the others.

The good news was that within the fortnight it was agreed Paula was to return to us part-time as she couldn't find the support she needed, and to be honest she preferred to be with her kids rather than spending all her time in a workplace she perceived as having stabbed her in the back. However, Roger assured us her part-time status shouldn't affect her promotion case, after all there were rules and policies about these things.

Paula breezed into the office on her new hours, and for once I was there to see her arrive instead of the other way around. She beamed as she put a new picture of her children on the desk beside her to keep her motivated by life's important things during the dull working day. Comrades, the blonde boy did indeed look a 'little rascal' as she said. For the first time I began to understand how her family had kept her balanced and rounded and not those of us in the workplace. I was a little put out to realise I was not as important to her as I'd thought, but I was comforted she was still my friend and still my colleague, and I was sure she would never be my competitor.

It was a good ten minutes catching up on gossip before she realised there was a meeting to go to. She laughed with embarrassment as I handed her the agenda, the previous minutes I'd printed off, a spare pen and blank paper, and instructed her 'get back to work Part-time Paula.'

"Aye, aye, captain' she saluted and laughed.

When she'd gone Roger came over to me.

"You know, Jack, that's a nice thing you did there. Keep it up."

"Thanks, Roger. Good people deserve to be happy, don't they? None of us asked for this."

Although Roger gave Paula the training she needed and much higher quality work, and as he promised he would he wrote and submitted promotion cases that year, and for years after it was never to happen. When push came to shove, the powers that be the ones who closed the nursery, the ones who inhabited the viper's pit, they said she didn't have the 'right stuff' to be leadership material. Good for her.

June 2004

A cultural highlight of the new regime occurred every quarter when our leaders would be whisked away to all-nighter management summits to enable them to privately, yet collectively, judge and assess their staff. Although this was presented to staff as voluntary team-bonding, the Leadership Team Ranking sessions were compulsory, and God help any leaders with priorities placed above the company.

"Don't worry, your child will still be sick when you get back." That was the message.

The outcome of the offsite deliberations was the Universal Ranking List which purported to map the pay and performance of all our workmates in the global family of Tex4Tex. However, it was more than just a pretty wall chart to cheer up the boardroom, apparently the Ranking List would help decide our future careers and reward strategies. Ridiculous! A preposterous idea, I know. But whilst you or I might laugh out loud at the crass stupidity of comparing Pinkbeard with his Mumbai counterpart, it did not do well to point this out or draw attention to oneself, not least because I was paid five times more than my comparator.

Yes, the Ranking List was an important 'Performance Tool', so important we were told it was top secret. Leaders spent a long night publicly appraising their staff, although they weren't allowed to share the information with the same staff. When we quizzed Roger about confidentiality, he would repeat he was only authorised to tell us was that out of two hundred thousand Tex4Tex employees none of us were in the bottom dozen, because if we were there'd be trouble. Like other leaders across the globe Roger would often return from what appeared to be pointless ranking sessions fuming he hadn't got his way, and other leaders were in favour and therefore their pieces were advancing around the board far quicker than his own.

It was shortly after one of these summits Roger approached me with an offer of new work. Normally 'opportunities' were something I was happy to leave to my occasional promotion-seeking colleague Tony, so this development came as a surprise to me.

"I admit I had originally thought of giving this important task to another more ambitious worker but bearing in mind your lowly position on the Ranking List and knowing how it is my sacred duty as a leader to start you moving in the right direction, I thought a little responsibility may do you some good and give you a chance to shine." Roger anticipated my question and continued. "Of course, I'd love to tell you where you are on our segment of the global design, but rules are rules, and of course performance management is highly confidential." He kept his head down, but I knew he was loving teasing me. "And that's why they take the managers away for an overnighter piss-up to minimise any chance of gossip spreading." He put a finger to his lips to emphasise the secrecy. "Yes, the Ranking List is a hush-hush top secret corporate activity whose findings are only shared with me on a need-to-know basis, and only to others such as division leaders, unit leaders, human resources, all the personal secretaries, their mates, the barmaid in the social club, and anyone else who happens to be in on the joke or knows the password to the share drive is Passw0rd123. "But not me?"

"Absolutely not. But, and maybe I'm overstretching myself here, but between you and me, what I can say is that you're running neck and neck with Whiskey Robson." Well, the news was a blow, whilst I had no delusions regarding my talents; Daddy Redeyes had been dead for three months. I was caught amidships. I had no desire to become a company man, but equally I had no great desire to be forced to walk the plank either. However, Roger was quite upbeat, dismissal for my many perceived failings was not on the cards and his view was I only needed to show improvement. The way he put it the problem wasn't what I did it was how I looked while I did it – the shaggy beard, those clothes, the detached air. He said it needed to be progressed upon. Apparently, it was an accepted Tex4Tex sociological fact, people who looked or dressed outside social norms must have psychological weaknesses, or a history of bad blood in the family.

So, I guess you could say I wasn't walking the plank, but I was walking a tightrope. It wasn't as though I wasn't good enough to do the job, Roger assured me everything was within my control. I didn't need to be any better I just needed to be seen to slightly more engaged than I was before. Roger advised I needed to create a moment where he could say to other managers 'Pinkbeard's turned the corner'. He just needed me to show willing to win people over. 'Like a bone-headed footballer kissing his badge and clenching his fist to the Kop before aimlessly hoofing the ball into them' was how he put it. Now I'd seen Wolves play in the bad years, I thought this was something I might be able to replicate without difficulty. A crass over-the-top display of enthusiasm with no thought to an end-goal seemed a potential win-win, and besides it seemed I had no choice but to accept this mysterious opportunity.

Within minutes it was apparent Roger was planning to provide me with an opportunity in mentoring. Of course, you realise by now we had been forcibly transferred into Tex4Tex and the company had inherited a disgruntled workforce made up of legacy staff who never chose to work for them. To change the demographics, behind the scenes Tex4Tex had begun quietly diluting the influence of the ageing ex-civil servants by recruiting young impressionable apprentices from Telford, and awful pompous university graduates who acted as though they were the beneficiaries of Manifest Destiny. The theory was that the fresh starts would give the account a new look. Bless their naivety. The reality was different of course, all the new workers were to be disappointed whatever their backgrounds. Tex4Tex recruited them as cheap labour, filled their pockets full of promises before quietly abandoning them to life on the hamster wheel.

Roger outlined his proposal.

"Calum is going to be our first apprentice in the unit. He'll be joining Martin Monk's team, the poor sod. In fact, Martin has been bragging how he practically pulled Calum from the tank himself based on mindset, attitudes, values, blah, blah, blah etc, etc, etc. The way Martin bigged it up they didn't so much interview him as give him a full psychometric test and internal body search. Unfortunately, as Martin Sidepartin has had the foresight to send his entire team on Values Training Stage Two today, his protégée is going to need someone from my team of blockers to mind him for a day."

As you can guess, after a year into the contract Martin Monk had developed from minor player into Roger's direct rival. Martin seemed to relish his role as an evangelical true blood Tex4Texan (except from Hampshire). At the time I had little contact with him but looking back I should have noticed how he had a way of getting under easy-going Roger's skin, and I should have worried about this ability to infuriate. As it was, I just put the rivalry and Roger's bickering down to management politics and let it pass.

"Do not fear Roger," I assured him "I shall be Baloo the Bear and he shall be my Mowgli."

"Great, I'm counting on you, but for Christ's sake don't teach him the secret of man's red fire. Show him the toilets, the canteen, the emergency exits, get him a pass, and then, most important of all for the ambitious new recruits, show him the recruitment pages in *Computer Weekly*. At least that way, he can move on quickly to correct his mistakes."

As it worked out the newest addition to our unit spent most of the morning shaking hands and jawing with various management nobodies, and it was lunchtime before he got to meet a real person. But I wasn't going to let him waste his lunch hour sat alone in the canteen. I wanted him to feel like he was part of the team from day one.

"Tell me Calum, do you like networking? Making contacts in an informal environment? Being a team player, a real team player, and not a brown-nose?" I could see he did. "Tell me Calum, do you believe in risk-taking? Taking make or break decisions every day?" I could see he did.

"Well, Wetherspoons it is then" and just to get us started I pulled my hip flask out and offered it over.

I guess the rest is history. Calum broke the ice with so many people that same afternoon, he was better known and more popular in a single day than many of his colleagues had been after years of toil. My fondest memory was Tony teaching him the Sir Edmund Hillary game. This game for those who do not know is where you try to climb from one end of the office to the other without touching the floor. You think it sounds easy? Let me tell you it is a game of skill, strategy, and no little agility. Perhaps we should have stopped Calum when he fell off the radiator for the first time and dragged down two productivity posters as well as a light stand before hitting the floor, but he gamely insisted on trying again. To the sound of cheers, he clambered on the desk by the door and stepped onto the photocopier to gather the applause before launching his next attempt.

In retrospect I should have intervened to protect my charge, such a commotion outside Wiley's office was not a wise move. Whilst we welcomed this robust new member to our unit Wiley was less impressed. Yes, he was a bit angry in fact. There he was a manager with thirty years' experience having a 'difficult conversation' in the middle of the office at the top of his voice with our new hire. It was like watching seal-clubbing hoping the pup might somehow escape, but also understanding the overwhelming odds against it. I stood close by Calum; I knew it was easier for Wiley if the weakest separated from the crowd. Besides, he seemed a nice lad to me, and after all it was his first day, and getting drunk with your team was an old-fashioned rite of passage to my mind. Surely if a young man can't make a few mistakes, then what's the world coming to?

"Well, captain, that's yet another deep hole I've had to dig you out of," Roger confided in me a couple of days later. "Martin Monk is furious. He wants to sack Calum because the boy is on probation, and therefore he can. He thinks sacking soft teenagers will make him look like a hard man. Cliff Wiley, however, is for the time-being at least, mildly amused by you leading the lad astray and tainting him with your ancient public sector ethos of team-bonding down a pint glass. All told, we've had to calm Martin down, and so to pacify him and prevent him from raising a formal complaint I'm giving you an informal verbal warning about your lunchtime drinking."

I smiled. Genuinely, what was the point of an informal warning? An invisible slap on the wrist.

Roger caught my eye. He turned serious.

"And to be honest, you need to listen to me here, this isn't a joke. Thanks to you Calum might easily have had his probation ended on his first day, maybe a record of sorts. Seriously, young new hires can't get away with the kind of things you did at their age and still get away with now. The rules are applied to them in a far tougher way than they have ever been applied to you or me. You should be grateful for that fact, and not push your luck. And I can't emphasise this enough, you're not a civil servant any more, you must stop parading your difference in their face. I've already spoken to Tony as well. His daily lunchtime refuelling also needs to end if he wants a promotion."

I looked at my boots ready to apologise. I wanted to make it clear I didn't want to let Roger, or Calum, down, but my leader carried on regardless.

"I've had to step in and share the blame in return for ownership of the resource called Calum. Hardly anyone's come out of this clean. At the end of it, you've made Martin look foolish in recommending the lad so highly." As he spoke, I noticed a grin moving across his lips, he was struggling to keep a straight face.

"Believe it or not, the way Martin put it to Wiley, you'd have thought I'd planned it like this." And now he was smiling. His rival in the doghouse, a new resource on the team, lunchtime drinking outlawed. He'd played a blinder.

August 2004

Gather round my friends, put the kettle on, sit down and pay attention. There's some vital information I must pass on.

Where once our workforce had been homogenous and unionised within eighteen months it was divided between ex-civil servants and several hundred new recruits. The new recruits, Tex4Tex direct hires like Calum, were on 'flexible' company contracts known as Standard. In contrast my terms were widely referred to as Image because they were an image of the terms I had with my previous employer, the civil service. From a legal standpoint the central difference was that the Image terms were contractual, and still subject to negotiation with my trade union however weak it may be, whereas the Standard terms for new recruits were imposed upon the individual, and their supposed flexibility rested in the hands of the employer who could alter or withdraw them at will.

Society term it a two-tier workforce – shipmates doing the same job and sat next to each other, but with different terms and conditions which in turn led inevitably to different rates of pay and treatment. Aye, it's a brain-buster I know but commonplace. It's unfathomable how Britain got here, and doubly unfathomable we chose to stay.

Understandably, a cultural divide arrived with the two-tier workforce, because unsurprisingly we staff didn't embrace our enforced diversity. Those on Standard resented our Image term security and our pensions. They called us Untouchables because we were partly defended by our union collective bargaining and were consequently much harder to pressure or discipline. In kind we resented their bonuses, healthcare, and their supposed fast-tracking careers. We saw them as management favourites.

Yes, in my office we had a two-tier workforce with all the trimmings. Two sets of workers on different terms, both feeling cheated, and rather than soothe the wound management seemed to encourage the resentment and bad feeling. It was as though petty uninformed jealousies were considered a form of healthy competition. Every week or two Tony would ask us to listen to his latest gripe proving once and for all we Image folk were second-class citizens– "the blacks of Tex4Tex – he called us. After a while I learned to tune him out. To my mind who was on top was irrelevant, it was divide and conquer in its purest form, and Tony was dancing to their tune. As far as I could interpret we disunited workers were only fighting over scraps from the captain's table to begin with.

Let's be clear, I wasn't unsympathetic to Tony's grumbles however crudely he expressed them. What we were witnessing was a benign form of ethnic cleansing – a sort of term and condition genocide. We Image unionised ex-civil servants resembled a perennially dwindling number of free Sioux roaming the American plains, our lifestyle and identity being methodically erased from history. Our story would surely end at the first generation. I surmised Tex4Tex wanted us to believe the only safe future was inside the Reservation, or to be more precise to surrender our union terms and transfer to the company package. But deciding to transfer terms voluntarily wasn't so easy for everyone. There were mixed messages. In a further confusion, the Real Tex Standard community was also split between the have and the have-nots. Flexible discretionary terms were a mixed blessing, but it was surely far, far better if you were in the position to exercise discretion upon yourself and your friends without union interference. Yes, it was the strangest thing for an ex-civil servant to witness, that staff's development in the superior, efficient private sector was not based on productivity and 'achievements in the fields of excellence' as it said in the brochures, but largely on a leader's judgment of your 'Behaviours.'

'He plays cricket at the weekend for the Jolly Shrewbees so he must be a good egg' was the rationale, 'and besides my team needs a happy left arm bowler, they're worth their weight in gold.'

The supposed freedom accompanying the individual contracts was little more than industrialised toadying. Many of my long-standing colleagues who had been lagging in the civil service, (and with good reason), learnt the company song, lost their Midland's twang, exercised their brown tongue, and surrendered union terms. Having shed their skins, they expected to advance rapidly through nothing but unquestioning loyalty to Tex4Tex. As news spread of the success of these brave pioneers more Image staff were motivated to become company insiders so they too could get a chance to wolf down a bigger share of the cake. Yes, if you paid attention to the office grapevine then you heard unchallenged tales of how ex-civil servants were taking advantage of opportunities falling into the laps of the brave; Tosser A had surrendered union terms and now had health care, Idiot B had wangled himself a company car, Jammy Git C finally had her teeth fixed. All over the site off the record conversations were taking place with managers grinning like idiots as though they couldn't believe their good fortune – 'Of course, I'd love to give you a massive individual pay rise, but your union won't let me. Please sign here.'

It was therefore no surprise when owing to 'unprecedented demand' all ex-civil servants were to be formally offered the chance to move to company terms. We were to be allowed thirty days to decide on this once-in-a career offer to change employment packages or stay trapped on union terms forever.

It was a moment of truth but when staff pored over the minutiae of terms and conditions it was clear there was no comparison. We ex-civil servants had more leave, guaranteed overtime, better redundancy provisions and pension, and of course whilst you could surrender union terms if you had them, those outside collective bargaining wouldn't be allowed to opt in for the security of union protection. For Christ's sake, it wasn't rocket science, comrades! You only had to ask yourself why the company wouldn't want people represented by a trade union. However the rumour mill was spinning on full cycle, and at the bar of the social club tiresome know-it-alls would offer their views on the distraction and say they'd had it on good authority this leader or that leader had said staff who didn't switch from union terms would be frozen out, would be supporting old unvalued Legacy systems, and never be given the chance to advance themselves by working with the latest software on the newest projects.

Although this analysis was intended to be frightening, as you can imagine, comrades, the picture of career stagnation rocked my boat big style. The idea I would somehow be left undisturbed by the company if I remained on Image terms was precisely what I wanted to hear. I hoped it meant I could come in at nine, read my emails, and go home at midday like one of those workers in Russia before they got Gorbachev, Glasnost, and a work ethic. On the one hand the prospect of transferring contracts of employment provided me with an unlikely shot at career progression and advancement; on the other, the safer prospect of an afternoon of beetroot vodka and *Countdown* curled up on the sofa with Carol Vorderman.

For me, there was no choice to make, I would remain on union terms, but for those who had career goals or ex-wives to pay for, this was a difficult time. It was a decision on a precipice. Aye, imagine you've spent fifteen years grumbling about the outcome of union negotiations, and then someone points a gun at your head and asks, 'do you feel lucky, punk?"

As Roger finished reading from the management script at the team meeting, Tony was as ever full of questions. He had already forgotten that only days before he'd been bemoaning the good fortune of those on company contracts.

"So, what you're saying is if I move over then I lose my pension and redundancy, but I may get a larger pay rise at some point in the future? Surely that's blackmail? Oh, sure it's okay for you with your management hat on, but blackmail, just blackmail for the rest of us."

Roger was probably half-expecting the comment.

"Well, thank you Tony for your contribution. I shall feed it back," he said with a sigh. "However, I do wish you wouldn't assume because I'm a manager I'm going gung-ho over this, or I'm planning to transfer terms myself." Roger had his serious head on again. "I'll tell you something, not everyone on company terms is rising fast, and if you switch then you will not be solely compared to the trailblazers you'll also be compared to the low paid new recruits as well as the slowest in the herd. Just because they don't publish it, or negotiate on it, don't think they don't have a pay system. The seniors want us all to think we are indebted to them for every penny of every pay rise, but it's a management process just like everything else. It just happens to be invisible to staff."

"So, you're saying we shouldn't transfer then?"

"No, I need to get my words right here. It's an individual decision. What I'm saying is you should ask yourself why? Why would any company make this offer?"

Within weeks we had our answer.

We were assured later it was of course purely a coincidence the announcement had so quickly followed the entreaties to surrender our redundancy and pensions terms, but one day the grave news arrived the bean-counters in Texas had realised the corporation wasn't as profitable as they had promised the New York stockholders. Initially it seemed a remote problem, but the gravity of the bad news was that rather than sack the handful of bean-counters who'd made the false promises we had to accept the blame for their incompetence. Redundancy, at least that's what I think they announced, for it was hard to know what else an outplacement strategy could be.

Looking back, it seemed there was always an outplacement exercise running somewhere in Tex4Tex

Global, and I'm surprised we never saw the big picture, or thought it might ever apply to us. Yes, it all balanced itself out – there were contracts won and contracts lost. For example, the contract with Baghdad council had been struggling since the USAF bombed Iraq, however as if to compensate, our contract with the USAF had never been performing so strongly. It was like a kind of corporate karma unless you were caught in the storm.

Now it would be our turn.

October 2004

Of course, my analysis was simplistic. I openly admit I didn't understand the levers of power, and I guess that's why they never let me anywhere near them, but as far as I could tell there had been no need for a redundancy round in the first place. After all, we had plenty of work in Telford. We were still bidding for shiny, brand new, expensive IT projects from the department, and if I were a betting man, I'd say the odds were that HR were hiring permanent staff whilst simultaneously working on the drafts for the public announcement that we were overstaffed and needed to downsize.

Furthermore, my argument ran, and surely most important of all, our account profits were jaw-droppingly real. We could ignore whatever was happening elsewhere on planet Tex4Tex. Everyone knew a government contract was a non-stop gravy train; it was a present which just kept on giving. Job losses made no sense. The only conclusion left to draw was that decent people would lose their jobs for no other reason than to allow our supine local bosses to take a soft option and tick a box saying Telford managers had bought in to the bad news and would impose the pain on their staff.

For those of us sat at our desks consuming the process, we would have preferred to think management must have wrestled with their collective conscience for weeks, examining every alternative to the grief a global redundancy exercise would cause, but that proved to be a fanciful notion. We quickly realised the truth; the account had only ever been a day or two away from announcing job losses. The evidence had been staring us in the face all along. Those months of judging, assessing, and ranking had produced a workable scoring mechanism, one stating numerically whether shipmates were fit for Tex4Tex future purpose or not. Yes, management had been ready prepared for months, it just needed someone to fire the starter's pistol.

Now if those rankings alone were all that mattered then I knew I was hovering somewhere close to the relegation zone, but within days it was made clear to me our team was not in the firing line. A triumphant Roger returned from Wiley's room informing us he had made the case sparing our team from the scythe. He channelled Gracie Fields and told us we were the crew "that drills the hole that holds the spring, that drives the rod that turns the knob, that works the thingummy bob" and therefore irreplaceable.

Bizarre though it may sound, the news was bittersweet. My feelings were mixed at best towards future employment with Tex4Tex, and I wasn't the only one with misgivings over my non-selection for redundancy. Many ex-civil servants felt the Gold Rush had briefly visited Shropshire, and a once-in-a- lifetime possibility was pulling away. Over a jar in the pub Tony would complain he wanted to leave but now he felt trapped. It was as though resigning from a detested employer without a massive contractual redundancy payment was selling out some almighty principle and had never occurred to him. He fumed throughout the entire consultation process, and he wasn't alone. Over the weeks I witnessed what seemed to be an endless stream of ex-civil servants like Tony filling the hours bemoaning their luck at having been so highly skilled the company couldn't possibly consider selecting them. Some would protest the misfortune in the middle of the corridor or tea-point knowingly overheard by fellow Tex4Tex staff at genuine risk of redundancy on statutory terms without a thought to their feelings. And one Tuesday morning Roger sat there with a smile and an arched eyebrow as Tony wasted a whole team meeting on the injustice of Roger protecting our jobs. He demanded Roger reconsider and personally intervene to ensure Tony lost his job on the most expensive terms available.

But Tony was to remain out of luck, Roger was not going to intervene to help his team surrender jobs. He said permanent jobs belonged to the community not the individual. It was a principled stand. However, Roger's views weren't shared across the office. Where he had tried to shield us from the process Martin Monk had enthusiastically signed up his own team. If sacking a few underlings could earn Martin some career brownie points, then where was the harm? Every cloud has a silver lining, or so he thought.

A month or so later, at ten on Judgment Day, Ralph Ebbrell's phone rang opposite Monk's desk. As Ralph stood to leave for the short walk to Wiley's office where HR's hatchet man James Brunt had taken residency for the day, he signalled a request to Paula, our union official, to accompany him. All the teams in the room stopped working and stared, we all knew what this meant. We'd never seen a public dismissal before. Ralph returned ten minutes later, slumped at his desk, and gazed at his PC before briefly opening his top desk drawer and then deliberately, violently, slamming it shut. We all watched helpless but passive, unsure what to do as Ralph pushed his head down into his hands. From my angle I could see a screensaver of his smiling family appear over his shoulder.

I was quickly distracted from worrying about Ralph. Moments after he sat down Kristy's phone rang. Initially she didn't respond, perhaps hoping another might fall into the trap. As she picked it up, she started crying without even hearing the words. She struggled to her feet but broke down and colleagues gathered round to physically assist her on the path to dismissal as Paula followed in tow, a fresh notepad in her hands. It was a routine Paula would complete several times in the next two hours and be repeated hundreds of times across the site.

In the melee surrounding Kristy, Ralph must have slipped out unnoticed without saying goodbye. After twenty years steady service he simply abandoned his desk leaving papers and messages across the horizontal. I thought it was the last I'd see of him.

The tide bringing back the shipwreck's debris arrived a few weeks after Judgment Day. It was a typical Telford raining in-fits-and-starts Tuesday and we were working on some project or other when Tony nudged me.

"Are you watching this? It's unbelievable." And then as he dropped his head behind his PC Tony sniggered and pointed towards the sight of Martin Monk resting his backside on the edge of graduate Toby Mullett's desk.

A red-faced Toby dialled the numbers while Martin read them out carefully as though he was teaching Toby to use the phone. Contact made, Martin snatched the phone from Toby's hand and took a deep breath.

"Is that Ralph? Ralph Ebbrell? Hi there."

"Good, good. How are you?" Without waiting for a reply from the man he'd selected for redundancy, he moved on. "Listen, Ralph we've got a problem with your code, and if you're free I'd like to ask you to help Toby with it as he's taken over your workload. Will you do that? Thanks."

And task completed he handed Ralph's old desk phone to Toby to enable Ralph to help Toby with Ralph's old work.

"Toe curling," Tony said, and sniggered once more, "where will it end?"

A week later, Toby tried to contact Ralph again, only to be embarrassed, as he sat there with a phone in his hand while the line went dead. It was the Silence of the Just, just exacting revenge. Over the next month it became apparent that relying on the goodwill of ex-employees who might possess an understandable grudge to bear was not just an embarrassing problem, but a vulnerability. Who knows what trick Ralph might have told Toby to try?

A rumour gained currency that management had severed the employment of the wrong people, and our service agreements with the department were imperilled by the loss of experienced staff. The gossip's stark conclusion stated that loyally signing up to global job cuts was proving to be an act of ritual disembowelment by our local managers. Our jobs had been safe before, but now the redundancy round had loosened the stones.

The account had to move to paper over the cracks. And so it was Night Owls Consultancy slithered over to our side of the fence. No-one questioned at the time the significance of the Night Owls agency supplying highly paid consultants to both the department and the main supplier Tex4Tex. Through the poor strategic thinking leading to the redundancy exercise, we had in the words of England's former Princess of Hearts, a third person in our marriage.

Night Owls were set for take-off. Although initially only a handful of staff, they expanded quickly and their significance would soon far outweigh their numbers as they saw both sides of the fence, had contacts inside both main employers, and the desire to exploit opportunities. It must have been easy money if you were shameless enough to take it. Night Owls consultants were being paid fortunes to carry out roles long-serving employees had performed only weeks before.

Understandably, the Night Owls became a target for knee-jerk resentments. The injustice which led to friends and colleagues losing their jobs to enable savings, only to be replaced by self-confident gobshites on vastly inflated salaries, couldn't pass unmentioned. There was no logic to it. The account couldn't be saving money this way, and hadn't that been the rationale for the redundancies? However, despite this seeming basic statement of the obvious our accusations were denied and countered. We were assured our resentment and fears were misplaced.

"Consultants are paid from a separate pot," Roger explained with absolutely no certainty at all he knew where the pot may be, or how we might climb into it. However well-intentioned his intention to pacify may have been, he didn't satisfy us. It was a paradox, while the headcount had been reduced to manage costs, the budget available for consultants seemed to be an infinite pit.

A few weeks later I became more confused when I entered the canteen for my packet of crisps and two chocolate bar lunch. As I paid at the counter, I identified a familiar figure sat alone hunched over a pie and chips meal. I approached him nervously because this was a sensitive matter.

"Hi Ralph, what are you doing here? Have they cocked up your redundancy?" I had a reason to suspect this, the payroll department had acquired a reputation for miscalculation. Invariably in the company's favour as luck would have it.

But no, Ralph Ebbrell shook his head. He looked embarrassed, not pleased to see me at all. He put his cutlery down, and I noticed expensive looking cufflinks. It was a new suit too, I'll wager. And then as I smiled and wondered what I might say as a follow-up, I noticed the tell-tale plastic lanyard hanging from his neck. He placed a defensive palm across his green contractor pass – 'Night Owls consultant,' it said.

Ahh! Those rumours were true.

"Living the dream," I laughed, "I'd heard Martin was calling you all the hours in a panic."

He just sat there still blushing, perhaps wondering if I might denounce him as a traitor in front of his former colleagues.

"In fact I think I witnessed Toby trying to make contact with you," I added to put him at ease.

And then as he composed himself, realising I held no grudges, he explained.

"Refusing to take that moron's Toby's call was the best thing I ever did. The release collapsed and the department went mad. I'd told them I was irreplaceable, and thanks to Toby I was." He smiled the smile of a man who'd proved his value. "A week or two later, Monk is begging me to return to work, he says he'll wipe the slate clean, but only if I repay my redundancy first. Cheeky bastard. I refused of course, why would I do that? I've already got my holidays booked." He'd put his cutlery down and was now savouring his last chips manually one bite at a time. "Later the same evening Night Owls called. They basically outlined my old job but for five times the wage."

"So why aren't you back with Martin's team?"

"I am but it is too embarrassing, pal. Embarrassing for both the company and the department if I sit at my old desk. What would that say about Martin? And others? It's not just him." He leaned forward conspiratorially, moving his tie to safety away from the remaining food on his plate. "You might not believe this but there's a bunch of old Tex4Texans hiring out an office in the shopping centre. I'm only surprised they don't ask us to wear a disguise when we visit you."

I was intrigued.

"So let me get this right, they dismiss you to save money, pay you redundancy, then pay Night Owls to rehire you at five times the rate performing the same role you had before?"

"No, that's not fair. They are also paying me petrol allowance, and of course they are providing a donation to the costs of the new accommodation."

Welcome to UK Government PLC everyone. Sit down and enjoy the show.

Part 2
Treasure Island

March 2005

Roger always had targets to reach and savings to make, and as we have already learned savings make profits and profits mean bonuses for executives, and further down the line bonuses afforded a present for the kids and a babysitter for the evening. It was the trickle-down theory of wealth in action. By tradition of course savings had never been good news for workers, it meant the hatchet man was forever waiting round the corner, but now in our upturned post-redundancy world it was re-packaged to us; cutbacks in expenditure guaranteed job security. Yes, 'your job's safer because we sacked the others. Hooray!' And so, in a similar vein we were encouraged to think job security could only be improved if we can think 'out of the box' and challenge 'accepted orthodoxy'.

As it turned out one of these exciting challenges to the status quo involved a further outsourcing of our security guards to a much cheaper alternative. It was of course a bold plan on the whiteboard, and although I doubt the guards had much input into it, I'm sure the decision-makers praised each other for their dynamic risk-taking. Not of course that the managers were taking the risk. It was the guards having the risk imposed upon them. Aye, if you bring in a bunch of gangsters to remove employees' job security, shift pay, overtime and pensions then the savings are virtually unlimited.

Marvellous!

Unfortunately, the bad news was that one of the completely unforeseen consequences of less security guards was less security, and soon the Shropshire underworld descended upon the site. Barely a week would go by without management issuing a memo reminding us to close our windows at night for fear we may arrive in the morning to find our monitors missing and our beloved gonks thrown to the floor. It was upsetting of course, no one mourned the loss of a monitor, but poor Harry Hairy, how could they do this to him? He deserved better.

Wiping tears aside, you or I may have pondered the possibility of perhaps increasing the number of security guards or taking the responsibility away from the gangster employers, but that was never going to happen. Such a move would involve acknowledging the mistake in handing out the contract to them in the first place and perhaps punishing those involved. And if there had to be a review of the path which led us here, then surely the same managers responsible for the decision to secondary outsource would be responsible for the investigation, and where would that take us? Yes, it was a conundrum all right. Riddle me this, exactly how do you fix a problem that didn't exist before the change creating the problem without changing the change, or acknowledging the error in judgment in making the change? Yes, there was plenty of blame to be shared around the whole leadership team, so it was best not to go there.

It fell to Roger to provide a local solution. He proposed a temporary additional insourcing alongside the outsourced outsource by means of a piratical vigilante. Simple – just think outside the box.

He pulled me to one side.

"Now then, captain, you'll be aware the criminal classes converge upon the site every weekend. You are also no doubt aware even now Telford's Mr Big is probably bouncing around the perimeter on his Space Hopper looking for weaknesses in our defences".

"Aye, I've heard – tap-tap, smashie-smashie. But so what?" I picked at my nails irritated, he was wasting my time. "The cameras surely pick them up."

"Well, it's interesting you say that, because unbeknown to you there's been a philosophical debate within the Security industry. You are clearly unfamiliar with modern thinking on the matter advising the best way to prevent crime is to outsource your guards, and then argue over who must pay for film for the cameras." He was right, he'd got my attention now, I wasn't aware of that. It was an update of the old story about having the cameras facing outward so you could see who was walking past, but not who was climbing in.

"But surely, stealing from a foreign multinational is a victimless crime? Pro-active redistribution of wealth I'd call it. A few computers here and there, a couple less ivory mouse-mats in the boardroom. So what?"

Roger leaned forward impressed by what he'd heard.

"Well, again it's interesting you put it that way, because it's an example of the kind of carefree reverse psychology prevalent in modern Security. At first, I had doubts when the idea came to me, but now I feel sure that you are exactly the resource I want guarding this site on overtime rates. Once we'd have a low-paid security guard, but now we've got a computer techie on double-time. God bless privatisation and its power to make a difference through innovation."

I caught his mood. Inspired by both his enthusiasm and the mention of overtime I leapt at the chance. It sounded like an easy 3-0 win-win.

"So, what you're saying is that I can put my feet up in the office for a few hours, basically doing nothing, and you'll pay me double-time."

"You got it, cap'n. Oh, but I won't pay you double-time out of my budget. By the miracle of paperwork, it will be cross-charged to Security, who will cross-charge Tex4Tex, who will then charge the department. Tex4Tex saves money and the taxpayer foots the bill. That's the way the system works."

"Great. Should I beef up my pirate regalia, and look extra frightening? I can put fireworks in my beard like Blackbeard if you like."

"Absolutely, you'll need a uniform."

"Can I bring some cans, and have a kip when I get bored?"

"Absolutely, I want you to fit right in, and uphold current high standards."

It was going to be a long night, and I was going to have to ration my energy between occasional bouts of stretching my legs. As I pondered how I might fill the thinking hours I reached for my pipe. No, not there, not in that pocket. No, not there either. I realised I knew exactly where it was – on the side of the basin at home. This was a blow. I wasn't going to last the night without a smoke. Therefore, my first task as temporary security guard was to start going through drawers and cupboards in the half-light attempting to find some sustenance. I had expected my night as a guard would be a quiet one and wouldn't involve theft at all, let alone with myself as the perpetrator, and I mused over the irony as I broke into to the top drawer of Tony's pedestal, turned the papers to one side before seizing on his emergency Rothmans. No one was around so I slumped to the floor and, holding a bin between my knees as an improvised ashtray, I lit up. After all I could always open the windows in the morning to clear the air.

As I rested, Rothmans in hand, I pondered the twists of fate leading me from idealistic young punk driven by modest public sector career ambitions to an ageing drunk in a pirate's hat playing guard on a mega-billion contract. And of course, that was the joke, I hadn't sought this excitement, I wasn't an adventure junkie like Indiana Jones, I'd just stood still while the world had revolved around me.

It was the world that had gone mad not me.

I sniggered involuntarily, and then laughed out loud at the memory as I remembered I'd heard Calum and Tony bickering earlier the same week. Calum had used the D-word, "Dinosaur", to describe us old civil servants. It was a word we heard a lot these days. Tony had of course reacted to the provocation, and a bizarre argument followed his defensive comment about people digging up two hundred million-year-old dinosaur bones, and making films about dinosaurs, but no-one ever bothered to make a film about the rats, weasels and lizards following them. It wasn't the emphatic putdown he'd hoped it might be, and the argument dragged on. Although the row never threatened to escalate into violence, it did become increasingly heated on Tony's part and I feared a temper tantrum, but finally it ended where all disputes between grown men should end, forty-five minutes later, in a search on the internet. Was Godzilla a reanimated dinosaur (Tony) or a radioactive lizard (Calum)? Tony sulked whereas Calum laughed out loud as he dropped the bait.

But whatever the rights and wrongs of latex dinosaurs I was attracted by Tony's romanticised view of our occupation. Just like weavers, chimney sweeps and rag and bone men, we were led to believe public servants were soon to be consigned to history. It played to all our egos if future generations would learn something unique may have been lost by our passing, and the progress which doomed us wasn't really progress for Britain at all. It gave me hope to think perhaps one day a thousand years from now a civil service computer nerd may be discovered buried like an Anglo-Saxon king inside a wooden single storage unit sarcophagus, and alongside the skeleton, a base unit, a phone charger, and a sheet of A4 covered in passwords.

As I ordered my thoughts, I was shocked when I heard an unmistakable tinkle as glass gave way. There were intruders clambering into the office, and torchlights flickered across the desks. Damn. I hadn't planned for this to happen. I had expected boredom would be my enemy. My throat was dry.

One voice surprised me though, it sounded familiar. That detail was comforting.

"No doubt the old lush will be asleep somewhere, if he even bothered to turn up at all."

It was Teflon Jake Megson, the overpaid, gum chewing Night Owls consultant slime bag currently attached to Movement, the team who delivered our PCs. Although Megson was nominally on a twelve-week agency contract with the department its rolling renewal meant he'd be on site plundering the account longer than many permanent employees. Christ, it wasn't a complicated equation, if Tex4Tex and the department had really wanted to identify savings, they should forget about outsourcing the guards and start by looking at that overpaid wage thief.

My fears evaporated. I wasn't in the company of a desperate criminal stealing to fund his or her drug habit. Opportunity had fallen in my lap. By chance it appeared fate had delivered a moment for me to set the record straight and strike a blow for real employees against the consultants. As I rose to my feet, I fumbled with matches to light the fireworks in my beard for the true Blackbeard terror effect.

"Ahoy there, Jake!"

The fireworks in my beard fizzled and popped as I advanced towards them, plastic cutlass drawn. I saw their eyes widen in disbelief when I loomed into range from the dark. The surprise was lost briefly because we three began coughing and spluttering as the smoke from my beard enveloped the darkened room.

Jake was as they say, temporarily gobsmacked. I think the full smoky buccaneer had really got to him. To be fair it was quite possibly the last thing he expected. He may have expected the police, or Security, but I bet he didn't expect an old man in a pirate hat to set his own face on fire. As Roger had said, the key to modern Security is reverse psychology, and the art of surprise. And surprise was something I'd delivered in buckets.

I wanted to stop and congratulate myself but whilst I momentarily held the upper hand, I was frankly unsure what to do next. I was never going to fight them or catch them if they ran, but I felt I needed to keep them there until Security arrived. In the circumstances I reasoned the unreality would help keep them confused and off balance, so I continued in similar vein. Besides my pirate identity gave me an unusual confidence, as though my outfit was casting a spell on me. I felt like a shy actor in a role of a king, gaining confidence from my disguise, enjoying a moment in the spotlight.

"Shiver me timbers, shipmates. Dare I venture this'll be a Black Spot on the Flagship Tex4Tex. Why surely there be many ways and means of stealin' from Queen and country but am a reckoning this'll be against all our master's wishes."

For dramatic effect I placed my plastic cutlass against Jake's chest.

Amazingly, he answered. He had always been a confident smart-arse. I think it came with the consultant job- description.

"Look, gimme a break, Captain Pugwash. It's a victimless crime." He pushed the cutlass away with his hand as he justified his actions. "The department pays for PCs to be installed, the more we install the more Tex4Tex get paid, so we steal a few to keep demand up. You should thank me. It's not so different to planting a bug to fail your own code so you can come in for a few hours overtime and fix it."

I must have grinned ruefully in acknowledgment through my smouldering beard, and he appeared to settle.

"Yes, everyone's a winner. Well, everyone except the department muppets who haven't worked out they've bought twice as many computers as we have people."

He snorted in derision, staring at me, awaiting a round of applause for his cunning. When he didn't get the response he expected, he shrugged and nodded to his accomplice who began to separate the base unit on Calum's desk.

Still in character I straightened and puffed my chest out.

"A crime without victims you say? Does yer captain's hairy ears deceive him? Be they playing tricks? Why I think Her Majesty shall wonder why Telford be so loose with her computers when she already pays the New World so much to take care of them?"

I pointed to Jake's silent colleague, "I think young Calum will wonder how he may work tomorrow with nothing but cabling?"

Jake smiled; he'd made his mind up. Frustrated, I became angry, my ascendancy waning as I reverted to the role of powerless employee. Before my courage finally departed, I swung round and struck Jake with the hollow blade across his face. He didn't seem hurt or even upset. He just stood there and jeered at me.

"You stupid old man, fuck off will you?"

I think he really thought this would simply pass, because Night Owls consultants were a protected species. He would see it through, and I would back down. Isn't that what we lower grades are meant to do? But then, before I could decide on the next steps, to my relief the corridors lights bloomed, and the sound of the tramping feet and grumbling voices of our pensionable real Security heavy mob grew steadily louder. As his mate climbed out of the window and back into the darkness I tried to cling on to Jake's sleeve until the wheezing guards arrived, but he pushed me away to the floor and followed his partner in crime.

I hit the desk with a bump on my way down, and I was shaken. Getting up is hard enough for a man of my age without hitting the ground by surprise. I don't think I passed out, and I'm not sure what the health and safety protocols are, but I was surprised to have a fire extinguisher blasted in my face. I was expecting a bit more gratitude. After all, I was almost a hero, and deserved a kiss from a grateful tear-stained damsel, not a wipe down from Stan's soggy hankie.

The good news was the break-ins stopped, and my night duties were needed no more. I received my first and only bonus for exceptional one-off performance in the field of Security. Although the culprits hadn't been apprehended, and there was no-one able to corroborate that one of them had been Teflon Jake, I had saved my employer money, and by saving money I had helped make money for a foreign dividend holder with a stake. Roger was also feted in despatches for his innovative leadership in recommending a man with my peculiar skillset for the job.

As for Jake, well he didn't work for Tex4Tex, and for that matter nor did the guards anymore. I was the only one prepared to give evidence against him inside the company. I checked with Stan and even though he confirmed Teflon Jake was discussed at length in his debrief, it didn't make the final draft of the report from Security. It didn't have to be this way, but contract politics had intervened and Tex4Tex had folded under pressure from outside. The gossip said someone well connected in the department had designated Jake a mission critical account asset, and remember, the customer is always right. Tex4Tex made a judgment call, the whole squalid affair needed an ineffectual light touch investigation so we could all move on. No one wanted to waste police time and risk a public statement. God forbid the involvement of journalists embarrassing the department.

Jake was suspended temporarily from the agency list. He would be back.

April 2005

Coalford – Coalport - Bedlam Furnace – Ironbridge -
The Wharfage - The Tar Tunnel - Coalbrookdale.

There are some places where you only need to read
the signposts and pause for a moment to understand the
history of the town.

Once this tourist trap at the edge of Telford New
Town was the soot-filled crucible of the British Empire,
but now two hundred years later with the gentle
assistance of public funding the dramatic history of the
Ironbridge Gorge has been rediscovered. Ruined
wharves and collapsed limestone kilns overgrown with
moss litter the bankside, and across the River Severn a
single-track railway has been replaced by a footpath
through the woods for dog-walkers and joggers. If you
follow the path on the Broseley side of the river after a
mile or so you reach the fenced perimeter of the
Ironbridge power station. Its cooling towers
incongruous against the natural backdrop; it looks like
a giant had dropped them there distracted by more
pressing issues. The closure of England's prettiest
power station had been foretold since the collapse of the
Miners' Strike, but still it limped along. I guess no one

had the courage to kill it off here in the birthplace of Industry.

On the Ironbridge side, the day trippers stroll from car parks to the world-famous bridge, only to mutter ignorantly 'is that it then? I thought it would be bigger," before dropping disappointed into the high street pubs and cafes for lunch. The Gorge's steep sides discourage a walk off High Street, but if you had the courage to change the angle, you'd encounter gentrification, well preserved 'workers' cottages' with their sidewalls knocked through, satellite dish accessories and polished cars parked outside. And this is Ironbridge – its history simultaneously preserved and erased, caught between a dog and a wolf – the Industrial Revolution as Disney might have presented it.

It was a sunny day. We were idling at the wooden trestle tables outside the Tontine Hotel, a place visited by one of those inbred Georgian monarchs while he ticked the iron bridge off his bucket list. The afternoon was a team treat. These days it was rare for all of us to be together away from work. Yes, comrades, things had worked out well for me getting a bit of praise from Tex4Tex, a bonus, and an 'Event' in my honour. I had originally offered to take Mrs P out with my bonus, but my lovely kept her feet firmly on the ground. "I don't want you taking nothing from that shower of shit" were the exact words she used to decline my invitation. It was the same honesty and bluntness which made her presence at the Tex4Tex Rattlesnakes Chilli family day so memorable. But that's another tale, so instead of my love, I pivoted and took the team drinking, and Roger, bless him, told us he'd find a suitably anonymous business code (we called them dustbin codes) to charge the time to so we didn't even have to take the afternoon off on annual leave.

I'm sure they were just being polite, but it seemed appropriate we were discussing my heroic defence of Tex4Tex property. After all, without my courage we wouldn't have been drinking together.

"Soooo, let's get this right then," mused Paula. She was in a playful mood, perhaps it was the wine taking effect. "You pulled your floppy little cutlass out of your trousers and slapped him across the face with it." Her fingers danced a circle around the edge of her glass.

"Be still my beating heart." As she spoke, Paula patted her chest and pretended to fan herself. "I love it when alpha males clash."

She sighed extravagantly and then continued.

"Mmmm, now then Pinky, can you tell me this? Do you remember if the fireworks in your beard burst into life because you lit them, or did they spontaneously self-combust in the sheer, gushing, passion of the moment?" Even I laughed as she savoured the punchline, delivered with a breathy girlie voice. "Did the red mist come down when you gazed deep in his eyes, and said, 'Jake, oh Jakie, is it the computer you want?' "She ran her hands through her red hair, winked, and then let it fall naturally across her face 'or is it me'?"

While Paula teased and supported in equal measure, Tony held pint after pint to the light commenting on the gravity and the cloudiness with the air of a Real Ale aficionado, one who wouldn't be seen dead drinking Wolvo estate pub piss-water the next day. That's when he wasn't responding to the barbs of Calum who always made sure he was sat close to either Paula or Roger and seemed a little in awe of them but took great delight in winding up the old guys. It was a good team to belong to and becoming kind of unusual these days. We laughed more than we bickered and despite all the change elsewhere the team had defied the odds and stayed together. Roger's 'if it ain't broke don't fix it' attitude didn't win him many career brownie points from above, but I knew I was lucky to work for a manager who was happy to leave us be so long as we delivered on time.

Tony was enjoying the discussion, and my discomfort.

"But what I can't get is this pirate voice. Honestly, do you know Shropshire is a landlocked county? It's all simply so weird. I mean what the fuck is it with you and pirates?" He slapped me on the back to show he meant no hard feelings but was merely curious.

"Yeah, come Captain Pinkbeard, tell us a tale."

"Well, I don't know really," I lied, modestly looking into my beer searching for inspiration. Except of course I'd rehearsed and told this story countless times, and often to Tony himself. He either liked hearing it or had never paid attention. "I guess I've always been a bit of a dreamer and I just started dressing in baggy Oxfam jackets supplemented by hats, waistcoats, belts, and boots when I was a young punk, and the look grew from there. It was other people who made a connection, I just let them think what they wanted. I was always a quiet lad, so it was nice to not feel invisible. But the funny thing is that as I matured, I learnt more about pirates. I liked the connection, I saw them as ordinary working people striking out on their own. Like punks weren't musically trained, most pirates were amateur seamen. I reasoned the pirates were like seafaring punks rebelling against authority and empire – the ultimate anarchists. The pirates worked together, they shared the spoils, they didn't need bosses or owners. Captains who didn't treat the crew fairly were replaced or were unable to get a crew at all the next time they sailed. Just think on it, a bunch of rum-drinking pipe-smoking pirates in the middle of shark-infested seas on a wooden ship loaded with gunpowder, but, and this is important – it was better than the life they'd escaped! It was like a big union, and no one could escape the boat when there was trouble. They seem so free, living for the moment, not needing to worry about tomorrow."

I laughed self-consciously, but as I did so I noticed the others were in rapt attention. It was unusual for me to speak for so long, and more importantly speak openly about myself. Once again it had been the pirate within who had freed my tongue, so I continued. I broadened my subject matter.

It was a stream of consciousness – how much had I drunk?

"You see history is rich people's history. History demonises the pirates, just like it ignores the working class and our many achievements. We should never forget we're the folks who really made things happen." I drummed my fingers on the table. "Look at the middle-class BBC – one period drama after another portrays our British working-class forebears as drunken cannon-fodder and no more, but if you look around Ironbridge you see the truth. For a hundred years or more, our ancestors were the most skilled workers in the world mixing cutting edge technology and brute force, and that's the real untold history of the British working class. The tragedy is we only see our forefathers through the bosses' eyes recorded in history, but they weren't the apes the modern world makes them out to be."

Rising to my theme, I continued. "Their work could have dehumanised weaker people, it would have been easy for it to happen. Twelve, thirteen, fourteen hours every day for a poverty wage and squalid accommodation, but at the same time, and this is their miracle, despite their grim existence those early generations of the working class created things of value outliving the centuries, not just bridges and railways, pistons and pumps for the Empire, but co-operatives and unions, to protect themselves and future generations."

I paused, I wanted this to sound prophetic, "You know it isn't just the Ironbridge which remains of them. It's everything."

I stopped suddenly, I realised I had gone too far. I felt embarrassed talking about something I believed in, modern society was too cynical.

Out of the corner of my eye I thought I saw Tony pass a conspiratorial wink to Calum as he lowered his grinning face to his pint. And what else did I expect? After all this was Blair's Britain, class warriors were said to have been defeated. It was an accepted fact people who thought like me didn't exist. We were told we didn't belong any more. It was as though we'd all thrown ourselves lemming-like down a disused mineshaft in the mid-1980s and the country had moved on without us. It crossed my mind again. Maybe I really was drunk, and I should leave before I accidentally dropped my guard and let slip how I felt about public servants working for a foreign multi-national. Who knows how many disciplinary offences I might be in danger of committing – careless talk cost livelihoods and don't forget it.

To my right I heard Tony snort, but I didn't look for fear of losing my temper.

Roger stepped in to save me.

"You know my Dad worked briefly at Longbridge in the Seventies. He was one of those blokes the newspapers blamed for the downfall of Empire. They said he had the British disease, always with his hand-up for strike action in those car park meetings. He told me the issue was always the same. It was class war. It was about stopping them bastards getting their own way. Sometimes it was the bosses, sometimes it was even the union bosses taking the coin. You stood by your mates. They call it dangerous Militancy now of course, and pass anti-union laws against it, but he'd call it Solidarity. It's how things always used to be. Everyone laughs now about those Sxties films with stereotypically gritty northerners trying to escape the certainty of their futures, but like your romanticised view of pirates, Jack, there's a basic truth behind them. You know just like in the films I was the first in my family to go into higher education, Dad thought it was a real achievement for the bloodline, like after two hundred years the workers had finally found a route to parity in the battle."

Roger took a moment to gather his memories. "In later life I used to rag him about those Leyland days, and you know he always had a comeback that I couldn't argue with. He'd say, 'my generation joined the unions, voted Labour, made your bosses grant pensions, built the council housing stock, took the Welfare State to every council estate in England, and look at what your generation has done. You're one of Thatcher's kids,' he'd spit, 'the worst generation in history, the first generation since the Black Death to leave your kids poorer than their parents. And you've given it all up for a CD player, a Sky Dish and Tony-fucking-Blair shaking hands with the enemy, and all because you wanted to compete with your neighbours and own your own home when you should have been fighting together for your class. I'll give you ten years and you'll surrender your free education and the Health Service too'." Roger stared down at his hands temporarily, as though he was ashamed. He had soft office worker's hands. Roger remained lost in thought reliving his father's life and words, but then he roused himself, and turned to address us all. "And basically, he was right of course, this generation after us are almost starting from scratch again. No overtime, weak unions, crap pensions, and no solidarity. That's how far backwards the working class has gone in only twenty years of thinking the battle was over."

His pint glass chinked with mine. "You would have liked my dad. People would say he was a dreamer too, but nowadays that's no bad thing." We both turned to stare across at the blue-grey girders of the Iron Bridge. Roger stood stiffly, and then moved a dozen steps to his right. A pint of Butty Bach in hand, he struggled to concentrate as he slowly mouthed the inscription across the arch – "This Bridge was cast in Coalbrookdale."

Constructed in its time as a glorious home-made tribute to an industry in its prime that the workers of the Gorge had passed to the world, the iron bridge reached across the eras of British industry. Sadly, it was only a brief period when Shropshire led the world – new factories and processes created monuments out of prototypes we created here, and the world leapt forward.

The mines and furnaces are long gone now, and here we sat a group of privatised IT workers discussing the endgame of the car industry in the West Midlands. Aye, history marches on and I could hear the band playing.

July 2005

Open dialogue between bosses and workers was of course a vital ingredient in the Tex4Tex recipe for success. We were told it was the healthy cross-pollination of ideas that nourished our Leviathan. Therefore, it was natural our freshly appointed Global CEO, Richard Richards ('TwoDicks' for short), a pink faced silver-haired Californian, communicated with us so regularly via the fibre-optic superhighway. In case of any doubt, we were reminded how 'innovative and 'ground-breaking' it was that we below decks could have the opportunity to take part in two-way communication with him. Of course, this wasn't to be direct conversation as he was much too busy, but we had the ability to reply via a designated email in-tray with his name on it. You couldn't expect a personal service in an organisation of two hundred thousand employees.

As his part of the bargain every few weeks an email arrived with the latest bloggings of our Commander-In-Chief to kick-start the conversation. Invariably Dick would have to send his ramblings in the brief breaks his globe-trotting schedule allowed. "I am dictating this sat on the crapper" was how Tony put it. My colleague did have a point, our Big Dog appeared to spend his entire life in airport departure lounges gladhanding his passage from one mega-deal to another; in Israel we may be discussing cyber-defence contracts, in China he may be preparing to reach untapped new markets. As for Russia, pragmatic Comrade Putin had seen the light, Moscow had 'top-class hotels' and was fast becoming a Western economy. Yes, the world was shrinking by the day; democratic governments and dictatorships alike had gone neo-liberal capitalist crazy buying and selling IT, all courtesy of a loan from the World Bank.

To summarise our global strategy for you – Tex4Tex sold cyber-technology to under-developed countries, and we sold cyber-security to developed nations to protect them from the poorer countries we'd just sold the cyber-technology to. I guess you'd say his monthly updates were harmless enough if you overlooked this undeclared arms trade or were unaware of the David Icke analysis arguing the world was run by shape-shifting Lizard Men flitting from one country to another plotting the enslavement of mankind. And yes comrades, thank you for asking, the postbox never replied to that piece of feedback.

TwoDicks said there was only one worry in the global marketplace, and it was standing in the way of a humble multinational's ability to own the planet – worldwide terrorism organised and funded by evil people. Like a playground bully Al Qaeda needed to be confronted, thrown to the floor, and put in its place. I kid you not, at times you could swear he was high on Boeing fumes dictating his latest fantasy about body-slamming Bin Laden as though it was Royal Rumble, and no-one in the Press Office had the courage to stop him from pressing SEND. According to my CEO well-intentioned international politics do have their rightful place opening doors and gaining access to new countries, but additionally everything has a business angle if only you could spot the gap in the market. And those visionaries were the real world leaders; the men who literally sold the world, men who didn't fret about the consequence for others, men who could cut through the sentimental crap about child soldiers or starving refugees, men who could see the profit in misery.

Allow me to digress. Batman for example, is not just a crime-fighting superhero but in the New World Order he is also an opportunity for profit squandered. In my CEO's head, Batman could still be fighting crime but would have stopped working unpaid for the Gotham police, and Wayne Enterprises would now be contracting security services at the market rate. Poor Commissioner Gordon would have been in no position to refuse given the parlous state of Gotham City finances, its total lack of cyber-security and dependence on the voluntary sector for crime-fighting. Yes, in the New World Order the streets of Gotham would still be safe, Wayne Enterprises would have a contract which writes itself, Batman could afford to do better than live in a cave, and poor old hapless public servant Commissioner Gordon would surely be a cost saving.

Ha! I'd better stop my flight of fancy here before I get carried away. Comrades, twenty years of outsourcing has taught us reality is different. Yes, in the real world of privatisation Batman would have downgraded the work to Robin, who would never have survived his tortuously long non-contractual apprenticeship scheme, and Penguin and The Riddler would have put in rival bids undercutting this poor-performing contract, and the chances are the bumbling oaf Commissioner Gordon would have become Consultant Gordon and been rehired on three times the salary. Progress for Gotham City, that's what they'd call it.

You see what mattered in our boardroom was a comprehensive approach to profit and responsibility which operated on the theory that every cloud has a silver lining, or hand me lemons I'll make lemonade. It was taking the positives from a negative, except that in a world of competitors one man's positive thinking is another's callous opportunism – every winner needs a loser, every seller needs a patsy.

Back in the real world there was indeed a global conversation triggered by the monthly emails, but it may not have been the one they expected. One memorable TwoDicks email ramble arrived within twenty four hours of the July bombings in central London.

"The prayers of our global family go out to the victims in London, and we will support them in any we can. As we saw in our own tragedy on September 11 when ten of our dearest colleagues lost their lives and left grieving families behind, Tex4Tex stands alongside you. At an emergency interactive online free-chat the board has generously extended our 911 fund for employees. We will make it available to all victims of the London bombings. And Tex4Tex will match every dollar you raise from company funds. I know we are in mourning today. But tomorrow we will back on our feet. We will not let terrorism defeat us. Now the civilised world needs to consider how IT may help prevent future outrages. We will talk to all interested parties and see how they may help us fast-track our Defense contracts through the appropriate departments. Soon the whole world can be more secure through the benefits of an association with Tex4Tex. We will not let terrorism defeat us. Tomorrow Tex4Tex Defense will be running a Video Conference with the heads of Europe, Asia, and Africa. We will cascade the information. Now more than ever it is vital we remember all the good we in Tex4Tex represent. Governments all over the world will surely be spending more on Defense and Military procurement in the next few years. We must make sure we are ideally positioned in the marketplace to win that work. And I know that we are. It could be an exciting time to be a Tex4Tex employee.

"Pray for the people of London. Like you pray for the people of New York," he finished.

It was unusual for Paula to swear but she was right to. It was fucking outrageous. Her husband was in the military, and like many directly affected she wasn't remotely grateful that our CEO saw the profit and opportunity in death. But it was young Calum who normally went with the flow who spoke up.

"I knew a few lads from school. We weren't friends or nothing, but fair play, they're out there now in Afghanistan, and you can't not think of them when the news is on. Does he think this is a joke? Talk about crocodile tears and matching shoes. He should get out there and tell them how exciting an opportunity for Tex4Tex this is."

"Yes, Roger, you should complain," Tony advised our startled team leader. And then by way of explanation he added, "You should complain about the fact Dick has jizzed his pants in response to the Euston bombs. We've got people dying here. Some blokes who Calum knew are risking life and limb and Two Dicks is travelling the Middle East selling our IT to the people who are probably funding the terrorists."

Roger was clearly embarrassed and on the defensive. "I don't think I'd put it that way."

"So how would you put it then?" Tony sensed our boss vacillating.

"Errm. Well, I don't know I'd bother to make a complaint. Americans say stupid things. One email isn't going to make a difference." Roger wanted this feedback to go away.

"But we're your team. We want you as our team leader to have two-way dialogue with these numpties. Make the complaint." Tony jabbed a finger at him. Roger looked at us, he saw we all wanted to complain, or rather more importantly we wanted him to complain on our behalf. After all we knew better than to put our heads above the parapet. Instinctively I knew Roger wanted to tell us to get back to work and stop bothering him but as a good manager and decent human being he needed to maintain the pretence that the opinion of employees may matter a fig.

Roger was clearly displeased, and I assumed he was just waiting for the day to end in the hope we would be moaning about something else tomorrow. He'd played that game before. However, I was wrong, he'd made the call it would be better for everyone if he wrote the complaint not us. He passed the afternoon drafting and redrafting emails trying to balance the angered sensitivities of his team with the gung-ho insanity of the business. As Roger put it to us, 'if my name is going at the top then I'm not going to use words or expressions like 'blood-money', 'red-neck', 'profiteer', or 'lunatic'." His reply to the CEO's sixty second brain-dump was a painfully precise and considered response, acknowledging the company's desire to support victims but asking for the tone to be reconsidered in future in the light of Britain's war weariness.

"Light blue touch paper and press Send".

It was disappointing to note that on the one hand Roger wasn't individually phoned by a profusely apologetic TwoDicks, but neither were we marched outside and denounced as traitors in the car park. It was all a bit flat, but offstage things had happened we hadn't appreciated. It all came to light when Roger passed us the email response. It was good they had replied, that alone was more than I expected. In fact, the reply was well considered. It thanked us for our interest, acknowledged our concerns, but reminded us that Richard was passionate about Tex4Tex and our democratic governments, and he was trying to convey his immediate thoughts to all employees but particularly the British ones at this difficult time.

Tony tapped his pen on the desk and gave his stock response, "Yeah, I said that would happen. I said it was all just a waste of time." I thought for a moment he might print the email if only to rip it up in Roger's face as a point of principle. Roger seemed quiet and resigned. I assumed he was hiding his real feelings, namely he was infuriated his experienced team had wasted an afternoon on an indulgence, and then not even had the courtesy to thank him for his effort. It was an hour or so later when a smirking Martin Monk came over that the whole sorry story came out. It was unusual for Martin to speak to us unofficially, so it made us all smile briefly to see him so chirpy.

"Did you show them it, then? Did you show them 'Dick's reply'?" He had his fingers in the obligatory bunny positions. We were momentarily baffled and looked to Roger for an explanation. We didn't need to wait, as Martin gleefully updated us. "You see Dick sends his email, and you get Roger to write back. Your memo goes to a mailbox. It goes to Communications Global, they send it to Communications UK, who pass it on to Comms in Telford. Comms in Telford drag Wiley in, Wiley screams at Roger for wasting his time in the leaders' meeting, and as punishment gets Roger to draft the reply to his own email issued on your behalf. The reply then had to be cleared with Wiley, Comms, Communications UK, and Global Communications. About the only person in the whole world who definitely did not see your email is Dickie." With that Martin departed to pass on his funny tale to everyone else, about how a poor leader of a team of whiney moaners got his come-uppance.

I looked over to Roger, and he just shrugged a reply. He'd taken one for the team – none of us had thanked him and he'd only been ridiculed for trying.

"Christ, he's a twat," said Tony shaking his head, but it was unclear whether he meant Roger or Martin.

December 2005

Faceless multinationals may demand employees live by imposed corporate values of respect and integrity, but the same companies have short memories if they are expected to live by their own ethics. By now it was widely accepted that the global redundancy round and massive job losses had not been inspired by a desire to take tough decisions and secure our long-term futures, but a desire to match the eye watering quarterly profit forecasts of the board. Our bosses had lowered morale, risked service, and almost burnt the house down, yet only months later the same bosses were playing with matches again. They just couldn't help themselves. It was the old one-two, the Ali Shuffle, the double-whammy, the private sector experience; record profits now accompanied by a pay freeze. Yes, we seat-warming button-pushers were getting our noses rubbed in it once again by the Dallas bean counters.

To hear the unnatural shrieks of outrage you'd have thought Brontogeek and Dorkosaurus were clashing at the tea-point. But when the anger and the hot air left the room, when the threats to resign and create a new career path had died away, we had to face the reality, the pay freeze re-enacted the scene in Jurassic Park when the helpless tethered goat is taken in one bite by the tyrannosaur. Except of course it was being repeated one hundred thousand times across the planet.

A global pay freeze may sound like the kind of approach to staff development Ming the Merciless or Fu Manchu might take but no Blair's besties and social partners in the private sector took this path to secure their futures. Now you or I would have thought record profits carried a kind of proof of our viability, and was all we needed, but that is of course Loser Talk. Promises to investors must be honoured, tough decisions had to be made. The path to global domination was never easy.

We were exhorted to follow the example of Lance Armstrong racing up Mont Ventoux, cancer-free testicles bobbing on the saddle, and marvel at the miracle of a Texan man of passion and commitment. He didn't sit there moaning about rising prices and bills to pay. And how did he do it? What iron-blood did he have coursing through his veins? We were advised he should be our role model because he never surrendered to the odds. Of course, Lance never raced to the top of the mountain to be told the prize money had been withdrawn either, but that's not the point. The point is, comrades, they stole our pay rise because the opposition was feeble. It was too easy. And so, while I stood dutifully for fifteen minutes alongside Paula in the foyer handing out union leaflets urging us to fight, colleagues trooped past, heads bowed. We had lost this battle years before it even began.

They were to be exceptions to the pay restraint of course, as even multinationals can see one size fits all won't necessarily suit all. While we were redoubling our efforts to control costs and cut investment in the established economies it would of course be foolish if Tex4Tex took a short-term view. Investment would continue to grow in the Far East where India and China were producing whole armies of graduate IT professionals queuing with diplomas in hand to replace us. They were the future. Yes, people younger, brighter, and better than me were waiting in the wings at the Tex4Tex University of Freedom Through Technology in Mumbai. Damn their talented poverty-stricken hides! Tony howled at the injustice of the company preferring to hand a pay rise to workers earning less than a fifth of his wage, but I wanted no part of his rant. In my mind it only proved globalisation on the bosses' terms wasn't the celebration of the Universal Bond of Mankind its liberal apologists argued. Globalisation set the poor of the first world against our potential comrades in the Far East, it was a provocation to racism and an attack on the worker's terms and the job security our ancestors had once fought for. It was going to fuck us all over just as surely as globalisation of farming had led to Mad Cow Disease, infected beef, foot and mouth and the genocidal slaughter of the ancient Shropshire herds. Aye, and that was a catastrophe met by real men's tears.

The story ran that many locals had life partners on those hills.

As if to rub our noses in it, a new performance system appeared. Yes, that's right, a new performance pay system unveiled in the middle of a pay freeze. Presumably, this was to give us all a dry run for a year when there was going to be some money in the pot. The new system was not just about performance though it was also about potential. Yes, cleverer folks than us had reasoned that providing a pay rise relative to how good you are at your job was simply too straightforward. What you needed to factor in was how good you should be at your job bearing in mind how long you'd been doing it. This involved a complicated equation, and no doubt a significant payment to the management consultant who hooked the big fish, but whatever the history this was bad news for long-serving steady-eddies like me. To all intents and purposes, I was never going to get a pay rise again because the outcome of the equation was inevitably that middle-aged workers who weren't running large projects were failures.

When Roger discussed my progress and potential with me, he said the equation indicated I was behind track, and maybe I wasn't even on the same track. Whereas others had careers racing like Seb Coe bouncing on a modern fast track, I was ambling gently on a crappy old cinder track of the kind Sir Roger Bannister used to become the first Briton ever to complete a mile without taking a fag break. As you can imagine the problem was that I wasn't sure how best to defend myself from the damaging accusation of loyalty, consistency, and competence over my career. I mused I could point out the whole aristocracy seemed to be doing okay, and they hadn't had a single direction change or promotion in generations. But what was the point? For me it was inevitable, you get privatised by Blue Labour and you get turned over. What did you expect to happen? At least this way I had the comfort of having ticked a 'I told you so' box in my head even though I was talking to myself.

However, across our bank of four desks Tony took the news badly. He saw himself as an undervalued asset whose experience had taken him to the brink of promotion, but had now been presented with another hurdle, a performance system directly discriminating against the same knowledge as a practitioner which was of course his strength. Following Roger's advice, he had been working all the hours God sends to try and get promoted only for Tex4Tex to move the goalposts. After years of good service, the company had designated him a failure.

"Of course, you are better than your colleagues," the company said, "you are more experienced than them, so what?" Whereas I left my conversation with Roger with a shrug, a crestfallen Tony continued his negotiation into team briefings. We were all going to feel his pain.

At the next team chat Roger congratulated young Calum on his advancement. He was no longer to be exploited as an apprentice, from now on he was only going to be exploited just as badly as the rest of us. It was good news. Tony however sat there harrumphing through the announcement.

"So, is he going to pick up the same workload as the rest of us then now he's the same grade? Do I still have to help him when he gets stuck?"

"Yes of course, we work together as a team."

"Bostin, just bostin that is. So, he gets the credit for the work I'm teaching him to do. He gets promoted and I'm a box three. I'm Mr Average and I'm carrying all the high-flyers. It's not fair."

"But I'm a box three as well," I added. I was trying to be empathetic, telling him there was no shame in being part of the crowd, but I had miscalculated his mood.

"You're a Box three?" Tony seemed outraged. "Look at yourself, Pirate Jack. You're a fucking joke!"

He jabbed his finger at me.

"Seriously, Roger, how can he get the same box marking as me?"

I didn't need to look. I could feel heads bobbing upwards further along the office in response to the increased volume.

To make matters worse Paula intervened. 'That's not fair, Pinky's one of us. You don't slag off your colleagues. Before you criticise others, look in the mirror yourself, why don't you?"

"Oh yes, I knew you'd defend him. Roger's blue-eyed girl. 'Hi, I'm Paula I'm as nice as pie, I care about everyone. Can I take some time off I've just had another baby? I'm sure Tony will pick up my work while I'm away.' Gimme a break!"

There was a pause. Faces were red with pettiness and rage. Tony had completely lost his compass. Roger looked completely lost as well. His easy-going laid-back style all at sea as his long-serving team rolled and capsized.

Things were quiet for what was probably only seconds, but it felt like an age.

Out of the corner of my eye, I noticed Martin Monk heading into Cliff Wiley's office. As I turned back, I saw Roger had witnessed it – his rival passing on the gossip.

The whole office was silent. It was waiting to see what would happen next.

"I'm just saying like, no offence pal, but Jack's a joke, everybody knows it." Tony was slumped like a sulky teenager turning the mobile phone in his hand.

"Tony, maybe you should leave for the day. Take the afternoon off. Don't come back until you've calmed down. We'll discuss your promotion tomorrow. Privately."

And as if on command, Tony picked up his jacket and with affected nonchalance strolled out of the office whistling.

Maybe his rage had been building up for a while. I didn't know. I felt guilty, as though I'd been letting my friend down when I thought I was only trying to survive in a hostile environment. I suppose I'd instinctively calculated by not pushing myself forward, by not competing for quality work with him, I was helping him get promoted, and he appreciated this. Obviously, I'd been deluding myself, Tony didn't appreciate this detail at all.

I looked to Roger, he caught my eye, and looked away. He knew something. It told me this wasn't the first time. Of course, I'd witnessed Tony's callous attitude to Paula over the nursery closure. I realised his outburst probably wasn't out of character, and he wasn't just a bit of a moaner. His desire for promotion from a remote employer had changed him into a fully charged twenty-four/seven resentful moaner. I was struck by how sad and pathetic it was that Tex4Tex had reduced him to this. Tony's lowly ambition and his frustration upon rejection had become an issue for all of us. He saw personal injustice everywhere and his moods and attitudes swung wildly. One day he'd be slagging off manager X, but the next he'd be in chummy conversation with the same manager in the lift whilst blanking his colleagues. It was both cynical and naïve. He wanted to run with the fox and chase with the hounds whilst being praised by both. He'd lost his solidarity, comrades.

"Tough day," I said to Roger a few hours later. And then I remembered what Roger had said to me and Tony about the nursery and repeated it to him. "Management is like a viper's pit, seething and boiling with personal ambition and vanity."

He nodded.

"A viper's pit in a shark-infested sea on top of the coldest mountain apparently. Anyway, I'm sorry you had to witness it. Tony gets too worked up about these things. Since Tex4Tex landed we're all getting brutalised a little more each month. The sad thing is if he just kept the noise down, and the scattergun criticism to himself, it would be easier to make his case for advancement at Ranking. Nonetheless he owes you an apology, and I'll talk to him again and advise him to smooth down his rough edges."

"Oh, don't worry I've known him for years. It's his rough edges I like. No doubt we'll have a pint in a day or two and have a laugh about it all. Blokes say stupid things we regret every week. He just explodes all the time these days and seems really stressed about the promotion. And to be fair he is better than most of the technical specialists above. I'm not sure what good it will do but I'd still take a pint off him and that's what counts, isn't it? It's Calum he should apologise to. His good news was ruined. He's a decent lad, he's now the same grade, and he gets paid less than I did ten years ago. I'd hate to be his age growing up in a declining world."

"Yes, well I'm trying to do my bit for him as well."

I was about to walk away when Roger called me back.

"Pinky, the stuff Tony said. He's not the only one making comments. You need to take care. Just muddling through isn't going to be good enough any more. They don't like those that don't fit in. Full stop. And they absolutely despise those like you who could fit in but choose not to. I know you're just doing your own thing, and you're much better than people think, but some of them are taking it personally and they feel like you're ridiculing them. Take care, captain, people are watching and identifying lists of scapegoats for future reference. Don't turn yourself into someone's project."

He swivelled in his chair and picked up his desk phone to end our conversation abruptly. I didn't know if Roger was threatening me or genuinely warning me. I wasn't sure how to respond.

And then I spun round in response to a commotion from Martin's team, they were laughing at something whilst looking towards me. Behind them Martin Sidepartin smirked as he leant against the photocopier. It looked like Roger was warning me. Wow, Captain Pinkbeard might have a higher graded nemesis. I was both frightened and flattered in equal measure.

August 2006

Like George Orwell and his bird in 1984 we all need a safe place, and the car park was ours. Despite the multi-faceted communication tools available to us, for sensitive issues we spoke outside face to face when we needed to. It was away from prying ears that appraised and judged, and away from the computers which monitored and tracked. A few years before car parks had been the sole preserve of lovers working out the mechanics of their illicit affairs. Nowadays all manner of staff trickled up or down the concrete steps connecting the cars to the building. Aside from the complexities of office politics and discussions on who was in and who was out, many colleagues felt the need to clear their heads by taking the air. They may have been divorcing couples continuing the row over breakfast, the desperately seeking credit brigade begging the landlord for more time, I remember Greenway the Grey perched on the passenger seat of his Nissan playing, or perhaps practising may be more accurate, the saxophone. But most of all I remember the men, it always seemed to be men, red-faced, middle-aged men, often sat gripping the steering wheel shouting obscenities at the windscreen. They were letting their frustrations run amok, shouting things they'd never dare in the workplace. Venting, I think they call it. Taking a rest from their powerless existence by acting the Angry King for the lunchbreak.

This was of course a paradox of life inside the multi-national. We were encouraged to communicate our ideas, but not to openly criticise or express frustration with either management or company. After all that would be negative energy, and negative energy drags everyone down – it makes Tex4Tex cry. That's what we were told. Over time we learnt to publicly share and emote whilst accepting the parameter this was the best possible of all worlds. It was a conundrum, we'd never had so many opportunities to communicate our feelings through team meetings and staff surveys, but many of us felt our most helpful contribution to the Big Conversation was to keep our mouths shut and our opinions to ourselves. Yes, nowadays meetings weren't for listening and questions, they were for insiders shouting 'Me, Me, Me'. They were for flattery and ambition and putting the Tex4Tex line more enthusiastically than the speaker before. Sometimes Tony and I left unit briefings and jogged into the car park as fast as our dodgy hips could carry their load before we exploded, laughing until we cried at the absurdity of it all. It wasn't the funniest line in the world, but Tony loved repeating it in his best high-pitched la-di-da posh voice,

"Of course, I'd love to see things from your point of view, Toby, but both of us couldn't possibly fit our heads up your arse."

Yes, if you wanted to go off message you had to go offline. Car parks were for conspirators, and that's what we felt like.

In the six months since I last updated you, to the relief of all Tony's promotion had finally arrived. He was now graded specialist; his role was to work with team leaders to ensure the correct technical decisions were being made, and to liaise with and support junior staff. Keep it to yourself, and don't tell him, but I was relieved, and a bit surprised, to see extra responsibility suited Tony. I'd witnessed many colleagues forced to wait years for promotion just like he had, only to begin mimicking the bitter and spiteful managers who had held them back. For whatever reason they distanced themselves from former associates, and then used their tiny platform to lecture the world on the benefits of tough love. Tony however, relaxed upon promotion, he'd found his level and rediscovered his solidarity. Now he could be his own man and revert to type – grumpy, sarcastic, and disobedient. He knew he would always be an outsider in their corporate world, and he clearly delighted in continuing to associate himself with lower grades avoiding the management cliques.

So far so good then, but the bad news was Tony's promotion had come under the auspices of a restructure program called Challenge, and such is the modern way of things, he had therefore been granted extra responsibility without the compensatory pay rise. As you can imagine he couldn't let the injustice pass by without a mention.

"They say I'll get a bigger share of the cake when the pay round is concluded. Yep, a bigger share of a fuckin' global pay freeze. Bostin, just bostin."

Yes, it was great to have the old curmudgeonly Tony back, trying to convince everyone he was the unluckiest man in the world. He'd been promoted, but he still had found something to moan about. It was a lose-lose only Tony could manufacture. The way he told it even his career uplift had been a management conspiracy, providing a kick in the teeth after he had jumped through all the hoops on a promise of jam tomorrow. I listened patiently. Whilst I recognised his pain, I saw it as a justification for my own passive resistance to the game-playing. I didn't need to say I told you, he knew anyway.

Calum and I were traipsing alongside through the car park to the social club because Tony said he had something important to discuss with us about the Challenge restructure. Something that would affect the future of the unit, something so precious it couldn't be shared in the office. Frankly, I wasn't interested, but you know, gossip is gossip, and you can't let a chance go by. "New restructure, same old shit," I'd yawned, but Tony insisted I should take an interest in this one, this was different, he said. He wanted to explain what the rationale of the re-org meant in real terms. Of course, an explanation would be useful. According to the publicity Challenge would improve competitivity through customer focus, dynamism, resolution, intuition, flexibility and all the other vague meaningless guff they say at these moments. I didn't believe any of it of course. It stood to reason, if there was any substance to the constant top-down initiatives then every boss we had must be so customer focused they must be following their departmental counterpart home and standing in back-gardens, binoculars in hand ,before preparing overnight reports for the sales team.

Yes, despite the rhetoric Challenge was not a moment of intuitive genius thrashed out in the boardroom. It was just like the last re-org and all those preceding, always wanting more from less, endlessly repeating the cycle from the time our Tex4Tex ancestors painted their first Buffalo hunting vision statements on the cave walls. Of course, it wasn't just Tex4Tex which recycled restructure programs. I'd been working for nearly twenty-five years in the public and private sector, and never once had we re-organised with the rationale we could slow down, pat ourselves on the back for a job well done, take a break and chill out for a bit.

A tense Tony continued marching myself and Calum to the peace and quiet of the social club staring into the weather on the border of our territory, a hundred yards or more from the main building. One entrance faced towards our own main Tex4Tex car park, and there was another smaller entrance facing the outside world via a small visitors' car park. The additional entrance had a purpose – it enabled visiting darts or snooker teams to play their matches without the hassle of the paperwork and security passes accompanying a formal visit to the site.

The club was perhaps the most significant loose end of our privatisation. Technically it belonged to the social club committee and remained outside the grasp of the employer that was nonetheless compelled to pay an annual fee for its upkeep. Despite the financial guarantee, the club had fallen on hard times. It was best to forget the days when it was the crisp and beer- fuelled hub of an unhealthy workplace. Yes, despite the investment lavished elsewhere modernising the site to corporate standards, the social club remained impervious to the benefits. It was like a wilting houseplant dying of thirst while the storm crashed against the windows, a sanctuary for wobbly tables and creaking chairs which lay scattered around the room with no sense of planning or design. The groaning, tired furniture had largely been gathered intermittently in ones and twos by members of the committee as personal favours when friendly porters could be persuaded to make an unscheduled detour to the bar rather than reach the loading bay for disposal. However haphazard and unattractive it may have looked to the dispassionate, lately I found the décor comforting as it had begun to resemble a civil service time capsule – a little walk back into the 1980s, the previous time the site had been refurbished properly.

Admittedly the company had honoured its agreement to underwrite the club, but the subsidy had stood on mark time while the cost of living was inevitably taking its toll. And when the ruling came from Dallas the social club was part of Tex4Tex and should reflect a non-alcoholic, smoke free workplace it condemned the club to a lingering death. Nowadays it was an empty shell of its former self. But on some days, a bit of the old excitement returned. To Tony's frustration we weren't going to be alone.

"Makes you wonder how much more efficient we might be if we piped *Test Match Special* over the tannoy," he commented as I parked my stern between him and Calum. He may have had a point, already an impressive array of cricket fans had pulled the green plastic seats from where they were stacked against the wall, and they crowded in front of the drop-down screen to watch the Test match.

Once settled I took a slow panoramic view of the room, and realised I was surrounded by strangers, new recruits I barely knew. This was happening to me with greater regularity. I'd been on-site twenty years and sometimes I strolled whistling into a meeting calm and settled only to realise with a jolt I had become the outsider. My comfort zone was in retreat. I hardly knew anyone any more and had become a stranger in my own land. Of course, there'd been the redundancy round to speed up the process, but nonetheless us old codgers were still quietly disappearing one after another. I imagined one day Human Resources would come for me and I'd be handed a P45 and politely shown into a *Logan's Run* style waiting room for the Rapture with the others too old and tired to carry on.

"Hey Paula, since when we're you a cricket fan?" Tony joked as Paula arrived to make the last invited participant to our impromptu meeting.

"Well, if you think I'm going to cover the phones while you three dossers are sat here watching telly you've got another thing coming," she replied in kind. "Besides, Roger's working from home today. He says he's practising delegation by leaving us to cope without him, and it will take him all day to do it properly."

We all gave knowing smiles – "working from home" – the weakest excuse in the leaders' lexicon. Working from home was our managers' perk. They owned it and were reluctant to share with others. At first home working only applied to those senior managers who lived down South but stayed in Telford hotels during the week. They styled themselves as some sort of work hard, play hard, brigade of corporate funsters that the rest of us should aspire to be. Ha! Maybe, but maybe not. In my circles, we called them TWATs because they only attended work on Tuesday, Wednesday and Thursday. It was funny 'cos it was true. But by 2006 working from home was an accepted unofficial account wide leader's perk. Almost all team leaders, including Roger, would work from home on Fridays, but I didn't join in with the moaners to complain about the injustice of this term and condition apartheid. After all management's absence meant the site was like a ghost ship once a week. It was my favourite day.

"I cast no aspersions here, but haven't you noticed he always works from home when there's a Test match," Tony offered in a disinterested matter-of-fact kind of way.

"The cheeky B, the last time he worked from home he claimed overtime as well!'

"Typical,' moaned Calum, "he tells me I'm not entitled to overtime even when I've been working all weekend. I wish there were a union to look after me." He was winding up Paula.

"Why don't you try getting your mates to join it?" answered Tony flatly, ending the conversation before introducing the reason he'd insisted on our presence. He said the company propaganda on Challenge stated there were no substantial changes and the restructure only meant those of us with experience would help others out wherever needed, but Tony added gravely he had seen through the lies. All technical staff were going to be pooled. He spat the word 'pooled' out. It sounded like waterboarding the way he said it. Pooled was of course a duplicitous corporate term –it sounded like we'd work together like a typist pool, but really it meant separation, sold on an internal market, and working away from each other on different teams. But interpreted by Tony, worse was to follow. There would only be one role for the team leader as the teams were to be merged, and Martin Monk would be competing directly with Roger for the role. The two managers were like chalk and cheese, Roger tried to limit corporate influence, if anything Martin seemed to get off on it. And if the last few years had taught me anything it was that the company advanced their own above others. And secondly, I knew I didn't adapt well to change. This wasn't good.

Five minutes later and Tony was still excitedly jabbering away. He'd heard consultants yakking that Teflon Jake was not only back on site but due to be seconded to the team, and he would work directly to Martin. Apparently, Jake had been overheard crowing he'd been instructed to clear out the cobwebs.

This was double-plus un-bostin.

As the conversation strolled into other areas, I rested my head against the back wall and drifted, hoping against hope Tony was succumbing to one of his traditional bouts of workplace paranoia and it was all nonsense. In the next twenty minutes deliveries turned into overs and batters came out wheeling their arms, later trudging resignedly back again to the pavilion swearing under their breath, and the room began to thin out as people remembered they had jobs to do.

Suddenly Tony leapt from his chair pointing at the screen, breaking up the chatter. "Did you see that? Did you see that?"

We all faced the screen as Tony demanded a replay from the broadcaster, and as if in deference to his higher grade, one arrived. A bowler, a batter, a diving fielder crept by in slow motion, and then a ball crossing a boundary. But we had no interest in them. We were drawn towards the celebrating crowd, for there partly hidden beneath a pair of comedy breasts and a distressingly low top was Teflon Jake Megson, and beside him with a bushy pink beard and a silly pirate's hat was Martin Monk. In fact, there were half a dozen leaders dressed as either pirates or wenches. It was the world's first and worst Captain Pinkbeard tribute act.

Tony patted my back.

"Blimey, some men want to be you, and other men want to be women that want to be with you. You've got something, I'll give you that."

I kept my thoughts to myself. Tony didn't understand. If he was right about Challenge then these comedians were my new bosses, and they were having a twenty-four hour joke at my expense. As my workmates pointed towards me laughing and cheering, I thought I had better simply suck it up and take it on the chin the way blokes are meant to. Make some daft comment like 'they got me there' and convince myself this was a kind of bizarre flattery – a bit of banter, some harmless macho bravado, a joke we were all in on, but inside I was churning. I wasn't in on the joke, my new bosses were laughing at me, and there was no getting away from it. I was a worker just like them. Better than most of them in fact. I may dress differently, I may not be career minded, but these dullards didn't have the right. The public image belongs to me.

Paula tapped my arm, 'wankers' she mouthed silently, "leave them to me". She then rose and straightened her top in a manner distracting the men's attention away from the cricket.

"Now where was the Test match? Nottingham? I suppose I better get the forms ready they'll be wanting to claim travel expenses. Are you coming, Pinky?"

Once said she offered her arm for me to take and walked me from the room with two dozen jealous eyes on me. I was feeling better already.

And she really did it, my friends! Each of the Pinkbeard impersonators received an expense claim form copied to Cliff Wiley, and a polite enquiry if they were on company business. She got replies by breathless return – half a dozen leaders had remarkably all forgotten to put their leave sheets in, and they now wanted to correct the minor oversight and apologise for giving the erroneous impression they were watching cricket on company time.

Cliff was delighted, he'd got one over the managers beneath him. He called Paula to his office to thank her and tell her of his appreciation. Paula told me later she'd asked if he was going to do anything about higher grades taking the mickey out of lower grades, technically it was bullying. She told me he gave a broad grin.

"They were on their own time, and if they want to dress like pirates, what can I do?"

Part 3
Fighting the tide

2006/7

You'll remember of course, a while back I told you the secret to good computing was cohesion, unity, and a naval discipline enabling a workforce to ride on top of the highest waves whilst maintaining a true course. Computers are complicated beasts, I argued so keep it simple and think in straight lines.

I think we can agree privatisation had tested my argument. Nothing ever seemed simple or straight-forward any more, but Tex4Tex ploughed on regardless. In the contract's early days our bosses had made reassuring statements that our relationship with the department was still close. One hand washed the other. They said it was more than just a business partnership – it was a marriage where the whole was greater than the individual parts. That's what we were told, and maybe it still held true, maybe it was still a marriage. The only problem was that it was now a loveless marriage, a marriage where the partners had grown apart, a marriage lacking trust where one partner withholds vital details before three days of rowing starts. Yes, that sounds about right. A marriage, but an empty shell marriage – a marriage doomed to fail.

What's the expression? Marry in haste, repent at leisure. If only there had been a quickie-divorce available for the department then perhaps they wouldn't have casually plotted their way into a long-term relationship of suspicion and contempt with Tex4Tex. Unfortunately, they were held in a python's embrace. Tex4Tex held a binding contract clarifying that the department could only seek separation after ten years and you could bet divorce wouldn't be cheap. No one likes it when the lawyers get involved. Aye, financial penalties on top of financial penalties.

What an expensive pre-nup clause that proved to be.

So how did we get here? How did our marriage fail? Well, I'm glad you asked, every month the government's computers were in the hands of Tex4Tex the relevance of the department's in-house knowledge subsided and every month the mistrust grew a little. The department had created a problem they couldn't publicly acknowledge. They had privatised their computer brain, and thanks to outsourcing they no longer knew how their own taxpayer-funded multi-billion-pound computer systems worked. They were sure they were being duped, but they couldn't prove it. You see the department which was tasked by government to make decisions on Tex4Tex worthiness for this or that project depended on the same Tex4Tex to supply the evidence for their informed decision. 'Like shooting fish in a barrel' was how our gleeful sales team put it. In desperation the department realised they needed to wave the big stick, make the threat to send work elsewhere, and remind us that every decision they made had profit implications for Tex4Tex. Now I'm sure this played well to their own gallery and scored them some points, but the sad thing is no one considered that only a few years before we'd all been civil service colleagues playing on the same side. Thanks to privatisation, trust and respect had disappeared, and an open confrontation rose in its place. They thought we were liars, we thought they were fools, and we were probably both right.

Over time, the department demanded Tex4Tex hire more and more exorbitantly priced consultants like Teflon Jake and Night Owls to provide a supposedly independent viewpoint of our performance. The theory was this would help direct future strategy. It was a whiteboard idea, another one designed to impress a Minister – 'we're paying a fortune so the advice must be good.' But it was also a desperate argument, one a techie like me would have known to instantly discard. After all the consultants worked for agencies and it was no surprise if they invariably delivered reports suggesting greater use of consultants. It must also have been like shooting fish in a barrel.

To make matters worse, in what turned out to be its last days, Blair's government had also caught the corporate bug for pointless change. Departments were merging and splitting with alarming regularity while for legal reasons contracts had to stay resolutely in place. Multinational beasts reluctantly fought for territory in the blurred margins of the departments, and this chaos was hilariously interpreted as competition and therefore good for the public purse.

To top it all one Spring, an email arrived proudly proclaiming our newly titled departmental ecosystem. Our ecosystem was apparently a carefully crafted technology rock pool; a myriad of employers harmoniously working alongside Tex4Tex on the public payroll. It was greeted with incredulity by Tex4Tex staff for we knew the truth about contract politics. We knew the crooked path we'd taken and why it had ended here. It was the truth that when you saw a new face you first grasped their security tag to see who they worked for. If you knew who they worked for, then you knew what truth to tell them. Yes, we knew the absolute truth, our harmonious ecosystem was paper-thin public relations, and nothing more. Unless of course, they had seriously meant to compare our ecosystem to a tropical rock pool – one of those Attenborough visits where every critter tries to eat the other.

Straight lines, isn't that what I said? By 2007 the department had consciously taken a decision to move away from hearing one voice and opted instead for a discordant cacophony of self-interest. It was yet more greedy mouths competing for the public tit. Yes, outsourcing, secondary outsourcing, supposed progress and competition had led to a situation where simple fixes to minor problems often needed the consent of a dozen employers, and arguments about blame and responsibility ran into the early hours. Who paid for the fix? Who was responsible? Which name goes in the press release? Those were the critical arguments and often delayed the fix itself.

It made me smile to think of those unenlightened dark ages in the civil service when I could pick up a phone and ask, "Yam, do us a favour?" Sometimes it would cost me a pint and a bag of Scratchings. God bless my acid-lined stomach it should be preserved for the nation. It must have saved the taxpayer hundreds of thousands of pounds back in the day.

March 2007

Although it was only a short walk across the room, I felt like I was crossing a border into a foreign land, and I couldn't decide whether it was a short step into a Dickensian past or towards a tormented Orwellian future. Nonetheless Martin had taken a special interest in me and had decided my rightful place was seated directly across from him in our bank of four desks. After decades of service, I had finally graduated as the naughty boy in class.

Yes, comrades, my Roger-sized safety net had been removed. As Tony had predicted in our social club discussion, thanks to Project Challenge Martin had been handed a decisive victory in the interminable leadership wars and his rival had been driven from the field. Roger was facing exile, and my old crew had been swallowed up. My former leader was still employed of course, but he was the one being pooled, unattached, without a team or a desk, sold every month across the site's internal market drifting from one short-term secondment to the next, fully occupied (on a repeating temporary basis) clearing up the mess the more ambitious, more destructive, higher regarded managers created.

"Bandages for the Tex4Tex working wounded,' was how Roger described the role in his customary deadpan manner.

Surely, he deserved better than this? I think we can all agree on that.

For the foreseeable future, or at least until the next reorganisation, what was left of Team Roger had been integrated into the flourishing twenty-strong Team Martin. At the far end of my office, our youngest Calum had long passed his probation, but he was seated with the apprentices waiting for them to catch up. Just like Roger, Tony was often seconded away to other teams, but by his moan-a-thon standards he seemed content as he was now getting the recognition, if not the salary, he felt he deserved. He was also designated to firefighting duties as the computers creaked under the squeeze for greater profitability. However, he took on this burden magnanimously as it highlighted his experience as an invaluable commodity again. He felt vindicated, he had aged alongside the computer system, and he instinctively knew why it worked the way it did and where the anomalies were. One afternoon he confided in me.

"You see we old guys have one big advantage, we know where the bodies are buried," and then after a reflective pause he added with a wink, "after all we put them there."

Paula was the only one of my former team remaining in the same place, now alone in her window seat at a bank of four desks with her back to the rest of us. Martin seemed a little afraid of Paula's certainty – a woman with an opinion and a union badge was a thing to be feared. He was surely contemplating a Keep Away sign to pin on her back. The lucky woman had inherited my old dead-man duties. It was ironic my friends, Paula was doing work I wanted to do and I was doing work Paula wanted to do. A simple swap would surely be the solution? We were convinced Roger would have allowed it, but Martin refused. He had no interest in sticking with a successful team, and in what would become a familiar defensive posture interpreted our suggestion as a challenge to his authority. He had a team of twenty to manage, and he wasn't going to indulge the experienced staff, that would lead to double standards. Martin was in charge; we would do it his way.

Paula responded to her enforced isolation by personalising her desk to an alarming, mothering extent. It was as though she was creating a shrine to remember who she was, and what we once were. Taking precedence, she had placed family photos across the horizontal. Behind them were team awards and training certificates she'd received from the department before we were privatised. And here and there as a spicy topping there were union stickers, a dozen of them she'd squirrelled away over the years now attached to mouse-mats, trays, drawers, and phones. It was a fact, she said, "Union stickers cast voodoo on the evil spirits that plague us." I didn't believe her, but I knew what she meant so I took a few. Better safe than sorry.

As you can imagine, there was an enormous contrast between my old team and my new one. Under Roger there was little fuss, except for Tony's occasional amateur dramatics, we just did our job and went home. For his part Roger kept things ticking over, shielding us from Tex4Tex. It was only now I was beginning to gain an inkling of the so-called progress I'd managed to dodge that I genuinely appreciated what a good job Roger had done. You see it wasn't to be low key and steady as she goes under Martin. He informed us that we were all catalysts. We all had to contribute. We all had to get involved. There were short meetings, long meetings, daily meetings, and those meetings needed agendas, they needed note takers agreed in advance, the notes needed to have their actions confirmed in writing by three. There were performance reviews every month; feedback needed to be obtained as evidence and training needs had to be identified. Even personal skills databases needed to be completed and kept up to date, rather than ignored until forgotten about which is how I'd managed them before.

Under Martin's leadership it became tiring just standing still going nowhere. All told it was no wonder we were encouraged to find shortcuts to our daily tasks as presumably this would enable us to squeeze in more time for meetings. Aye, on Team Martin we spent so much time being participant employees we barely had time to focus on the day job any more. There I was a middle-aged man who hadn't had a pay rise in two years, and was unlikely to ever receive another, thinking this was all wasted energy. I remembered with a bitter grin that we had supposedly been privatised to free us from civil service bureaucracy and focus on our core duties but now my day-to-day priority was to keep Martin busy filling in his forms, completing his spreadsheets, and ticking those management boxes. We'd swapped one bureaucracy for another. Yes, I imagined our team looked hard-working and productive on the unit whiteboard, but it was patently obvious to this grizzled old mutt Martin prioritised his own weekly targets over the smooth running of the computer system which ultimately paid our wages. Martin didn't appear to be reckless, but nonetheless he had found it personally advantageous to abandon the wheel assuming the tides would always be in his favour.

Don't worry everyone, help was on hand.

You will be aware of course nature abhors a vacuum, particularly a power vacuum, and into the breach stepped Teflon Jake. On the face of it his attachment to Martin's team was an unlikely appointment – a pairing of a moralising Roundhead and a flamboyant Cavalier. Maybe Wiley thought one would complement the other. Or maybe he didn't think at all. He'd introduced Jake, an apex predator, into our duck pond.

Jake was on the face of it a contradiction. Although years of contracting inside the public sector had made him a rich man he would still try and present himself as a working-class wide boy giving it large to all and sundry. He would swear at the computer, abuse junior staff, and play practical jokes on the older ones. Remarkably he maintained continuous one-sided exchanges of banter with Martin. It was odd to witness, Martin was the manager and nominally in charge. He would be strict with fellow Tex4Texans he didn't trust, or he thought were challenging his authority, but at the same time he seemed to quietly defer to Jake the consultant on everything no matter how undermining the banter became. Honestly, I hope I don't sound jealous, in fact the truth is that part of me wanted to congratulate Jake. The manipulative swine was 'managing up' in a brutal fashion. It was almost a daily occurrence when he would remind the team Martin had no technical IT skills and couldn't write code like we could, Martin was 'just' a manager, Martin was totally dependent on techies, and Martin wouldn't know a computer if it fell out his arse.

Our man in charge, Martin, retreated behind his screen, and this is how it happened that Jake, an outsider, was allowed the de-facto running of the crew. He had grabbed the wheel Martin abandoned and was now steering us chaotically into rocky shallows. Where Martin concentrated on his costs and budgets and interminable profit and loss spreadsheets Jake used his freedom to create a toxic boys club atmosphere with some of his young favourites. I'd often witnessed the bravado of male office workers overcompensating for their emasculating jobs before, but this seemed without the usual boundaries. Whereas offices are normally quiet except for the hum of the computers and the conversation, here there was shouting and swearing, football banter in abundance, whooping, catcalls and high fives when a shortcut worked. Most of us hoped Martin would show some leadership and intervene but when that didn't occur, we kept our heads down waiting for the noisy boys to go away. The problem was they were hard to ignore when they tagged their puerile jokes to group email distribution lists. On other occasions we knew if they'd worked late because they left subtle signs – abandoned pizza boxes on desks and discarded cola cans on the floor where they'd been trampled and kicked in midnight office football. They were Jake's Alpha Males, and they weren't going to clean up. That was for others lower down the pecking order, and the hardening pizza stayed on the desks until the cleaners started their shifts at five p.m. You see Jake's arrival wasn't like Vikings raping and pillaging, but it was a harbinger of things to come – the consequences of the lowering of standards. We oldies would scratch our heads when we received emails politely reminding us not to vandalise our own toilets, or when we saw the signs in the tea-point requesting we resist the urge to throw hot coffee out of the upper floor windows.

Funnily enough we'd never had the urge until the company suggested we shouldn't do it.

It seemed like Jake was in the vanguard of this new madness. The charge sheet against Tex4Tex was lengthening, and Teflon Jake, a Night Owls consultant, gleefully added to it. In each team double standards, resentments, distrust, and personal debris were piling high. Every decision the managers took was interpreted as fragmented and self-serving. Standards didn't matter so long as teams ticked the boxes and hit those weekly targets.

For example, theft from a shared fridge may never get on *Crimewatch* but it does upset colleagues when they learn to distrust teammates. Normally staff rant and rave for twenty-four hours, or until people stop listening, and then they shrug their shoulders and carry on to the next day's grumble; after all it wasn't as though our felon was stealing wallets from coat pockets. But Maggie Something-Something didn't calm down, she'd worked on the team for years and held a position of respect unrelated to her low grade. Fair play to her. She pointed the finger at Jake's overnight gang and submitted the written complaint – theft of personal property re: M&S lemon drizzle cake. There was no evidence to back up the accusation of course, after all it had presumably been consumed, and the matter was quietly dropped by unit leader Wiley after an email to the teams asking them to respect other people's property. A week later Maggie left her daughter's home-made chocolate cake in the fridge overnight. In the morning there was a footprint in it. Oh, how they laughed! She requested a transfer which Martin granted the same week. He said he didn't want to keep people from pursuing their career path.

It was about eleven a.m. a day or two later, and I found myself sharing a coffee moment with Jake in the tea-point leaning back against the shiny magnesium counter staring at the scene of the crime. If Jake was relieved Emilia Fox wasn't here testing our shoes for cake dna then he hadn't let on. And of course, if there had ever been evidence of cake dna, the chances are Jake's acolyte, fat Toby Mullett, would have licked it off for him.

"One less ugly whiney bitch" was how Jake summarised Maggie's departure. Our conversation continued in the same charming vein. Now you'd have thought Jake might resent me for nearly derailing his gravy train when I caught him red-handed stealing laptops, but bizarrely I had inadvertently only enhanced the legend of Teflon Jake. He himself saw the upside, which was of course that it was public knowledge someone high-up in the department had declared him mission critical. It was the people's perception Jake could do what he liked, and Tex4Tex couldn't tear up his contract even if they wanted to. To make matters worse, they'd even placed him with Martin, a non-technical manager who couldn't understand Jake's role even if he explained it. Jake had become Untouchable No.One and on balance seemed quite grateful for my part in defining his aura. His influence was rising alongside his confidence.

"Some of your young lads, they've got some talent, they could go far." I apologise for that my friends, but I thought I should at least make the effort to get along with Jake, and to be fair, away from the pack, most of them were sound.

"Some talent?" He wasn't interested, he was poking at his mobile. "Trust me they're fuckin' useless, cap'n. They won't survive their probation I promise you that," and he tapped my wrist with his empty cup.

"And why do you say that?" I was surprised to hear it. "Surely it'll be your job to nurture the youngsters and help them along?"

He turned to me and smiled, rolled the gum around his mouth, and gently pulled my arm in,

"No way. I'm a consultant for Night Owls," he proffered me his green site pass as evidence, "you Tex4Tex eejits are not my problem. Your male apprentices need to learn to sink or swim without me. They're to be a dying breed anyway."

He smiled as his final throwaway comment caught me unawares. He knew something I didn't. "Haven't you heard we must recruit more young women into IT? It's your own company orders. Yes, we must do our bit to recruit more totty onto the team to correct the gender imbalance. Wiley has set the unit recruitment targets and bonuses on the orders of those HR feminists. The unit needs to be totty-fied."

He sniggered as he finished and pulled me close invading my space. Beneath the coffee I could smell last night's whisky on his breath.

He rasped, "Don't tell anyone." A throaty hiss followed. "Jakie's gonna build a fuckin' harem." On that bombshell he sniggered once more, rubbed his hands together, spat his gum in the sink and left.

Well, at least he seemed to be enjoying himself.

August 2007

Martin informed me when I first joined his team that he felt Roger had disregarded me, Roger had let me down, he said. Ominously by explanation he stated Roger had encouraged me to work in my comfort zone. This comment he added as though it was a crime. But what's wrong with working within my own boundaries? It didn't bother me. I liked my comfort zone, it made me feel...comfortable, exactly like it should. However, Martin did not accept my lack of ambition, he was going to drive my career forward. He promised to give me exciting new challenges; he was going to stretch me; he was going to force me on; he was going to improve me whether I liked it or not. As you can imagine I was horrified! Under Roger I had an informal agreement with the company to stay in my comfort zone for the rest of my career, and this was how they rewarded me! It was outrageous. I felt betrayed by my employer. Again.

In more serene moments I would later write these days off as karma, as though this recent change in circumstances served me right. You see I had never really given Martin a second thought before. We'd been only a few feet away from each other for three years or more and yet I had never taken the trouble to get to know him, or picture him and work him out. I'd just written him off. I knew nothing about him, and it didn't bother me. When I thought about it, I don't think I'd ever heard him speak about anything other than work. I didn't know if he was single or married, or even which football team he supported, and let's face it for a bloke that is base camp one. He just seemed to be one of those anonymous managers with a yard brush up his backside, not a bad person just a dull one, a joyless company automaton. Unless I was alone in a lift with him, my ignorance had never mattered to me – he was the dullard over there doing Roger's job on another team, and that's all he was. In the coming months I would pay for my failure to build a bridge or pay attention, the problem was of course that I was as distant to him as he was to me. Like a pirate ship on the horizon, I was an unwelcome sight in the morning.

You see I hadn't expected Roger's easy laid-back attitude when I settled in, but at the same time I wasn't prepared for the considered and deliberate nit-picking. Martin was constantly chipping away, hour after hour, day after day. On an ordinary day he would gaze impassively at his PC for a coffee or two before unleashing instructions or comments and then exiting the room without allowing time for a discussion or explanation. It felt like unrelenting petty point scoring, all without a comforting pat on the shoulder to show it wasn't personal. He wasn't rude or abusive but there was no sensitivity either.

"You've never done this before? Surely you must have. All the lads on my team must be able to do this." Or sometimes he'd say, "That's the old way, Jake and the lads have developed a shortcut that's far more time efficient." These pronouncements were made to me but were also loud enough to provide entertainment for the rest of the office. And then he'd be off and out the swing door again, as if he had somewhere better to be, and all the team would turn and briefly stare at the old codger they had to carry before swivelling back to their PCs shaking their heads and muttering.

This was embarrassing. I wasn't the bad worker he tried to make me out to be. It was just he was giving me the wrong work! He'd given my work to Paula. Why didn't he see that? Why couldn't he acknowledge my achievements? After all, for twenty years I had muddled through. I could pride myself on an exemplary record of being bang average. And remember, comrades, average is not bad, it is not failing, it's mid-table, it's satisfactory, it's okay. This was unfair. No matter. I guessed I'd squeak through again just like I had always done before. I assured myself every morning and every lunchtime I just needed to keep my head down and persevere through these awkward months until events took over and the happy day arrived when Martin inevitably chanced upon another scapegoat. Yes, I thought I just needed to show some patience and hang in there until the opportunity arose to worm my way to the safety in the centre of the herd, but life didn't work out that way. Even when other teammates made mistakes and I reasoned my ordeal may be coming to an end Martin remained doggedly on my case like an anchor dragging me back and hindering my escape.

I didn't realise it there and then but the years I'd hid behind my beard and waistcoat were coming to an end. I had been undermined. This was my dark age; stress was eating away at me. At night I would stagger home from the pub raging loudly to the walls in frustration, enacting fanciful arguments with Martin, and then I would crash out fully clothed on the sofa. Usually I would wake up tense, grinding my teeth at stupid o'clock, and my stomach would heave as the Colgate passed my lips in the morning. My chest fizzed like it was full of eels when I hobbled into work, my knees creaking with each reluctant step. Every working day I became so frightened of making mistakes I lost the confidence to take decisions, and I would pass the time trying to retrace lost blacked-out hours from the previous day. The next day would be the same. And the day after that. Each week I survived hoping the next would be better without ever taking the chance to change my circumstances.

Martin was successfully turning me into a poor performer.

I was fifty for chrissakes, people like me didn't get treated like this. The company should be leaving me alone so I could prepare for retirement – I was meant to be winding down to take my pension and head to the sunset. It's an absolute sociological, biological fact – middle-aged white men are the kings of the jungle. We don't get bullied or picked on. We're not victims. Statistically, this couldn't have been happening to me. Yet it was the only conclusion I drew. I may have hoped a chance to prove my steady-eddie value would arise, but it hadn't so far. I felt I was past my sell-by date, I remembered Tony had told me once the problem with modern IT was that computing was becoming too easy, and now I understood what he meant. Time and again, grinning apprentices half my age were teaching me how they did the job their way. They were pushing keys, even though they didn't appear to know why, because they didn't need to know why. It seemed like computing whac-a-mole – one problem would go away but then the next day another would arise close by.

Now don't get me wrong, in our upturned profit-driven world their short-termism wasn't a bad thing. Far from it. Lurching from one crisis to another looked impressive on the performance charts, because it made the team appear to be dealing with record levels of problems. I'd go as far as to say the underlying problem was that this haphazard crisis management wasn't acknowledged as a problem at all because it was mistaken for productivity. There was no desire to let an old man use a couple of days to find the root cause and a lasting diagnosis, and why should there be, after all the company made an easy profit just treating the symptoms every day.

History would prove a wiser management would have sensed danger was just over the horizon– behind the ocean swell, hidden in the fog. The signs were there, Tex4Tex contract with the department was heading straight to the iceberg. It was inevitable, just a matter of time and luck. But I was no hero. I kept my opinions to myself. I didn't want to appear negative and provide Martin with more ammunition against me.

However, the strategy of keeping my head down failed. Over the weeks Martin's frustration with my detached air continued to grow. He started calling me at short notice into private rooms, briefly asking me if I was okay, looking me up and down, and then unleashing another forty minutes of criticism over this or that. He would always end by checking his watch and finally, after consulting his notes, he'd confirm I could always approach him for support. He was following a HR script, and there was still no emotional connection between us. He seemed easy with that. There was a clear message underlining our meetings – he had a revolving door just waiting for me to utilise, I only had to request a transfer. If I chose to stay, he'd let fate take its course.

To be fair it wasn't as though he wasn't giving me advice along the way.

"Your appearance is the door our customers walk through. It is our customer's first impression every day." Now my appearance hadn't changed for years, yet

Martin was concerned that looking the way I did was another signpost to yet another slippery slope. Whereas Roger had told me they couldn't sack me for looking like a pirate, Martin chose a different tack. Piracy suggested poor behaviour and poor behaviour led inevitably to poor performance. Yes, his analysis was that I would have been able to adapt to the new work quicker if I didn't look like a degenerate. It should have been laughable, but he was deadly serious about the dress code. If I didn't act or look like part of Tex4Tex, then I was deliberately letting our collective high standards drop. He was the innocent party; I was forcing him into action was the way he interpreted events.

I would lean back in my seat as I listened to him lecture me and smile at the irony that we both agreed the unit's standards were dropping.

By maybe our fourth or fifth informal but stilted chat I had become bored of constantly hearing him icily recount how my appearance underlined failures in performance, attitude, and behaviour. He sat there ready, impassive but expectant, pen in hand waiting to note down my reply. He wanted my agreement. I'd been waiting for this moment. It had been building up for months. Both of us had been waiting.

"You see the thing is jockey, you've got a team that shouts and swears all day long, and Christ knows what they work on at night. I mean I know what they're doing, but do you?" I looked at him, but I couldn't read him. "You should try asking Jake," I spat. "What about their attitudes and behaviour? How can you overlook Jake and the lads publicly appraising women in the room? Where are their company values? You tell me about the lads and their shortcuts, but I ask you can they do the job properly? Why do they keep having to fix the same basic problems? Or do they only know shortcuts? How is it you're such a stickler with me, but you let everything else go? How can you be a pedant on demand? Answer me that."

I was trying to provoke him just to get a response, he must have been furious as I had hoped he would be, but he still offered no sign of passion. I gave him my best Paddington hard stare, but he still wouldn't be drawn.

"Okay, let's have it your way," was all he said as he carefully folded his papers. This time he left without assuring me I could always approach him if I wanted to. I gathered a coffee, 71 with extra sugar, and returned to my desk. Martin wasn't there, the whiner had already gone through to see Wiley, but when I flicked open my email there was a note purporting to be a report of our meeting, and a formal memo he must have written in advance which placed me Under Supervision.

He was proposing to monitor my performance and behaviour for the next two months, and I would be tasked to submit evidence I was 'achieving against my goals' in anticipation of weekly one to one meetings where the evidence could be reviewed. Here, if needs be, I had the opportunity to request more help from the boss who said I wasn't good enough, and by doing so, provide him with evidence I acknowledged and accepted my failings. It was the performance Catch-22. Support, that's what he called it. It was comical. There was nothing left but to conclude as I was perceived to be struggling, I was to have extra meetings in addition to my daily meetings, and to help improve my performance and detached behaviour I would be placed under the direct threat of dismissal. If I hadn't been struggling before then I surely would be by the time Martin had finished supporting me.

The next day I had a chat with Paula, my local source of wisdom, to see if there was an easy way out of the cobweb I was tangled in.

"He's a petty little man," she advised, "if he can sack you for looking like a pirate he will. Your appearance is the crack letting the demons in. He's not looking to develop you he's trying to put you under pressure so he can harvest your fails and then make a case to dismiss."

Paula's honesty was a little demoralising, and she told me nothing I hadn't worked out for myself. Nonetheless, reluctantly taking her advice, I started keeping a diary of little incidents that may help me further down the road. According to Paula I was preparing foundations before building my walls in anticipation of their assault on my employment status.

That didn't sound good, but I guess she knew more about these things than I did.

Along the way she taught me so much more. When I proudly showed her my notes from my previous meeting where I had given Martin a few home truths, I had hoped she might pat me on the back or throw her arms around me and give this brave bashful old fool a peck on the cheek, but she didn't. She sighed, a frustrated irritated sigh, before she dropped back automatically into her union mode.

"Pinky, I know you're angry and frustrated, but you need to stop this self-pitying passive aggressive nonsense and start playing to win."

When I stared back at her blankly, she continued,

"He may appear it, but Martin is not a fool, he's goading you. Stop rising to the bait." She wagged her finger to emphasise the point.

As I screwed my face up and reluctantly granted an acknowledgment of her analysis, she advised me to 'flip the issue,' and lay a trap for my manager.

"Pretend you respect his opinion, and you want to impress him. If you were going for promotion, you would email him and offer to teach the apprentices to do their jobs properly, and you'd notify Martin about Jake and his poor behaviour. That is what company values tell you to do. Use them to your advantage for once. Company values instruct you to grass up your colleagues, why not these colleagues? Force him to ignore you. Keep a written a record, it's money in the bank for later."

Then she progressed to my biggest fail – my fingerprints on the murder weapon – the bushy beard and unconventional appearance. Now if Martin and I had been able to talk to each other like adults then I wouldn't have denied my own stubbornness had contributed to this crisis. All those months ago Roger had told me my appearance was okay but marginal. I should have listened to him when he said I needed to take care and keep tidy, but I'd allowed my appearance to drift from the time Martin and others mocked me at the cricket. I decided that as I'd tried to smarten myself but they still took the piss I wasn't going to bother making the effort. It had become a matter of honour for me. My hair and beard grew uncontrolled because I wanted to defy him, and bedwetting dullards like him. I was reluctant to stop dyeing my beard red let alone shave-off my pride and joy just because my imbecilic team leader was now trying to prove an arcane point about tough love at management bun fights.

Worryingly, the serious aspect of the charge was that Martin had emphasised in conversation it wasn't Tex4Texans who were complaining about my appearance. The complaints originated from inside the customer, and remember, a customer complaint has a potential financial consequence, and it is a weight on the scales of company justice. Somewhere out there a voice unknown was taking the time and effort to grumble about my appearance and behaviour, but not caring to copy me in, or approach me for a discussion.

I didn't know what to do about the tittle-tattle, but fortunately Paula had a plan to confuse the enemy. She suggested we should play invisible before and after. On the following Friday afternoon when the Tuesday, Wednesday And Thursday gang were working from home, and Jake and his posse had disappeared God knows where, Calum brought his doorstep-sized camera in so Paula could photograph me. This development baffled me, but intrigued, I tagged along. We found an empty meeting room, AbDab1, in the AbDab corridor, named in honour of Telford's first family of Iron Mastery, the Abraham Darbys.

After initial uncertainty and stiffness, I grew in confidence adopting my best if limited range of modelling poses. Calum and Paula offered instruction and encouragement. They were trying their best not to laugh, although they soon surrendered to the struggle and their further guidance was delivered with giggles and occasionally gales of laughter.

"Pout!" I puckered my lips.

"Thrust!" I put my hand on my hips.

"Give me anger.," I gritted my teeth.

"Give me contemplation at the tea-point." I stroked my chin.

"Roger Moore," I raised an eyebrow.

"There's a ship on the horizon." I raised my arm and pointed out of the window.

"But it's your ship, someone's stolen it."

"Huh?"

"Okay. Give me loss."

I removed a hankie from my pocket and wiped away an imaginary tear. My paparazzi clapped and cheered as the camera clicked. I posed and then strutted an imaginary catwalk between the whiteboards. And then as I sat down breathing heavily after my exertions, grinning, and smiling, relaxed for the first time in weeks Paula snatched the camera off Calum and took the few final pictures for my portfolio.

"I tell you what, if you do get sacked, don't take up modelling. The women of the world are simply not ready yet for a Shropshire Valentino."

It was the first time Paula, Calum, and I had been together in weeks. It was great to relax and simply enjoy each other's company again without the management overseers draining the spirit. Intriguingly, Calum also dropped a morsel of gossip that some of Jake's boys were also grappling with their probation. A few weeks before, I would have muttered the kneejerk grumble-guts response "and so they should" but now I offered to help. The realisation they were struggling as well didn't significantly help but I felt better for not being alone.

Silliness aside, Paula had a plan she hoped might satisfy my bruised ego and Martin's too. Each week I was to make a minor adjustment to my appearance to be recorded by the loving camera of Calum. On week one, I rolled my sleeves down to hide the tattoos, the next I may remove a ring or two, tone down the earrings, wash and comb the knots from my hair, whilst letting the dye come out my beard. We recorded each minor change and over a period of weeks I slowly transformed myself from nautical punk to something off-beat but acceptable by our calculations within the dress code guidelines. There was no mathematical formula for us to follow, but we hoped this would be enough.

I embarked on my next schedule of review meetings with renewed confidence but despite the alterations to my personal appearance, according to Martin, the regular complaints about me continued unabated. He or she or they hadn't even noticed I was changing. It was frustrating, I was trying to adapt but they were still hitting me.

"I'm sorry but I'm going to have to extend your period under supervision for another two months." I thought I detected a grin, and then after a pause he added, "This is your last period before we make the decision to discipline you."

Now pardon me but shouldn't it have been whether to discipline me?

Apparently not. Bless him, Martin Sidepartin was probably working on the paperwork already. I briefly pictured him rocking excitedly in his seat while he gleefully practised his signature for the dismissal letter.

"Really?" Paula asked when I gave her the update the next day.

"Yes, really!" I was angry at myself for listening to her. There I was following Paula's advice on jumping through the hoops and it was getting me nowhere except another week closer to dismissal. I was a cute kitty with its neck in the jaws of the Lurcher, and no matter which way I twisted and turned it patiently continued to squeeze.

"Really? That's interesting." Paula's dispassionate union crap was not what I wanted to hear. "No, it's interesting because you're hitting their targets, but they insist you're falling short."

"Don't you think I don't know that?" I was exasperated with her. The world was against me, and here was the proof. I wanted my union rep to bang the table and tell me OJ's lawyers had taken the case. Or at least she could provide a bit of tea and sympathy, but no, she was treating me like a specimen in a test-tube.

"Listen Jack, do you trust me?"

I shrugged. I was feeling sorry for myself, but you know the way I saw it I was designated the weakest reindeer in the herd and Rudolf and his mates were leaving me behind for the wolf pack. 'Rather you than me pal', they said. Yes, at least Paula was here and this was a crisis, so it still made sense to stand by those who stood by me, even when she was pissing me off with her stupid useless advice.

And so, reluctantly, disconsolately, there I sat in one of the familiar impersonal Darby rooms the next empty Friday afternoon, on an isolated chair with a cotton bed sheet across the floor. Calum cheerfully took pictures while Paula shuffled behind me, a pair of clippers in her hand. My head responded to her ministrations, moving down to watch my mane drop onto the cotton sheet as she shaved my head.

"Now let's see if your stalker notices this," she said when the grisly barbaric task was complete. She walked me gently towards the black reflective screen of a disconnected PC, and I cautiously bent down to take a view at what I hoped would prove to be a career-defining haircut. As I nervously peered in, I could see she'd kept my beard in place, but tidied it, and both the beard and modest earrings stood out proudly against the pale shaved uplands of my dome.

I looked to Calum. He was grinning. "Cool," he said, before looking at Paula and nodding. She was smiling too. And then I was laughing. Cool? I loved it.

Pirate no more, now I looked a bit like a Viking. It could make all the difference.

November 2007

Paula became a union official because she wanted to make a difference. I wanted her support because I wanted things to stay the same. That's why I paid ten pounds a month subs to the union – to try and make the clock stop. It was all I asked. The working class would have to throw off our chains another time. For the moment I needed Paula's undivided attention, she had my job to save.

We were seated in the AbDab Rooms, the place where Martin had lectured me, and the same place my hairdressing sessions had taken place. These soulless, unadorned working rooms had become the backdrop to my life. Although there were seats and computer points for twenty, we four decorated one corner. Jack and Paula sat at the edge of the short end, and at ninety degrees there was Martin and Gloria from HR. Gloria was here to ensure fair play and the right result, for the company I guessed, but Team Pinkbeard was confident. 'Hair today, gone tomorrow,' we'd giggled on our way to the supervision review meeting. Our hopes of avoiding a formal disciplinary meeting now rested on the shaven head that we considered acceptable under the professional attire provisions of the dress code, but ironically handed me the intimidating presence of a fifty something hard man you would dread to encounter invading your space in the queue.

Cool.

I ran my hands through my non-existent hair, and then gently tugged my beard for comfort. My nerves were beginning to make themselves heard despite Paula's calming presence at my side, and yes, it was a comfort to have someone alongside who had probably witnessed more disciplinaries than the young HR manager. It gave Paula a gravity the rest of us lacked. Notwithstanding Paula's experience and Gloria's expertise, Martin was nominally in control of the meeting. HR's presence had turned his booster on, and rather than the churlish uncommunicative soul I encountered daily he made small talk and even shook hands with Paula which was a surprise as he detested, and maybe feared her a little. I smiled inwardly, I bet disciplining staff and obtaining a 'fair outcome' would usually be far easier if my 'bloody union woman' wasn't there.

This could be a contest for him. Fortunately, he had his paperwork, his laptop spreadsheets and HR for comfort lined up against my pocket size force of darkness, who was in turn aided of course by my recently shaven head.

I jogged through my mental notes, trying to ensure all the relevant details were close to my lips, ready for production on demand. Throughout our preparation meetings in the intervening fortnight, Paula had explained to me that as proceedings were now formal, Martin had to share his evidence and stop simply making uncorroborated accusations. In her mind moving from informal to formal was therefore a good thing. But that was her opinion my friends, surely this was glass half-empty, glass half-full and to my anxious state of mind the formalising process also took me one step closer to a possible dismissal. I gulped and took a drink of water. This meeting really mattered. Mess it up today and the next stop was Trouble.

Ignoring my fears Paula assured me the real politik was if you can do your job then you'll get the benefit of the doubt, and I'd been doing just enough for years. She made it sound so simple. It was part of the game you see, he wanted to sack me for looking like a pirate, but he needed to prove my degenerate style had affected my work, and consequently threatened the company bottom line. I briefly perked up realising how tenuous and vindictive Martin's case seemed when Paula put her slant on proceedings.

Game on.

After Martin ran us through the introductions for the record we began in earnest. I tried to answer his questions as best I could, and I quickly realised the value of having followed Paula's advice to keep a diary of incidents during the last quarter. Each time Martin put an accusation on the record, I had a primed response.

I gained confidence as I quickly realised the preparation had worked, and Paula's insight had helped me anticipate his questions. I was doing the best I could hope for, because I could see I was better prepared than he was. This time, for the first time in months, I was putting Martin under pressure, as it dawned on him this may not lead to the slam dunk celebration he'd expected.

And he was being beaten in front of an HR audience. It was a comforting thought. Maybe he gets disciplined for not being able to properly discipline me. Surely a failed disciplinary is a waste of everyone's time and money. Maybe next week he'd be in my seat, perhaps I could make it a personal goal on my mission statement. Ha! Wouldn't that be an irony? At the point of dismissal, Martin had finally managed to motivate me.

To frustrate him more and pile on the pressure I simply kept returning to my notes, and as Paula would say, I played the game. No opinion, no temper, just the facts. On the twenty-fifth I would have told him server twenty-three was down if he hadn't gone to a meeting after pressing send on the email. On the twenty-eighth ASMS was in quarantine so I couldn't work for two hours. On the thirtieth Jake's boys had disappeared, and I had to cover their phones as I have to every Friday, as he would have known if he attended work on Fridays. And here are the emails I sent you, explaining this. I pushed over the freshly printed evidence to Gloria not Martin.

Gloria leaned forward. She took an active interest for the first time,

"Are you saying that Martin ignored what you told him?"

"No, what I'm saying is that he's my boss, and all he does is email me instructions and then disappears to avoid having a discussion." I held her gaze as Paula had advised me to. Nothing says innocent-like eye contact, and consider this, I had worked longer on this site than Gloria and Martin put together. That must count for something, surely? Despite my difficult circumstances, as I looked across the table corner part of me sympathised with Gloria, having to deliberate in this inconsequential row between grown men who should know better. My mother would threaten to 'bang both our silly heads together'. Different times. Gloria held my gaze for a moment and then returned to her own notes.

So far so good, but then it was time we came to the real meat of the meeting. Paula had only taken notes so far, she was about to take a leading role. Whilst I felt we'd proved my work was up to standard regardless of what I looked like Martin began his comments and complaints about my appearance with gusto. We showed our pictures in response. Gloria's eyes arched at this strange turn, and she looked quizzically at Paula, and then at my bald head.

I thought I detected a smile of acknowledgment.

Martin had complaints about my appearance, and we had an audit trail of photos which we claimed would disprove the detail of the accusations. Paula's strategy had turned the meeting into a debate about what I looked like on what day. Now as I sat there listening in, I was struck by the thought a better manager, one not emotionally charged, would have realised it only really mattered what I look like now, and taken the credit for the change, but Martin couldn't help himself. He had to prove Paula wrong. She'd goaded him. Paula had barely spoken but she'd goaded him with her presence. I remembered the previous encounter between the two of them, maybe he'd carried this frustration since we humiliated him in the Values Training, and perhaps he thought this was a chance to settle scores, put one over on the union, and score some Tex4Tex brownie points.

"But these are complaints from the customer," he protested, as though a customer complaint was a sacred text from an angry god. It had to be acted upon, it didn't matter if it was a lie. Perception is reality, he argued, and sometimes the truth must take a back seat if the customer complains.

It was a weak argument. Martin was shifting in his seat I think he wanted Gloria to intervene and help him.

Gloria sat still and said nothing. I'd like to think she was enjoying the contest.

"Where do the complaints come from? Are they dated?" Paula asked. She was cool and level-headed. She was winning – taking charge.

"Some are in writing, but they're mainly verbal reports," he said before emphasising the words, "from the customer."

"Verbal? Well, that's unfortunate. Non-evidential verbal complaints? That is really, really, unfortunate." Paula stopped smoothly after saying it. She didn't need to embellish her sarcasm. She'd all but called her direct line manager a liar to his face in the presence of HR.

There was no bridge to compromise from here.

I was uncertain for a moment. I guessed this wasn't the end, but it felt like the meeting had ended. Gloria shifted in her seat, a slim young blonde I'd be attracted to under different circumstances. I remember thinking eye contact was good, but I really should stop staring. No matter, Gloria began talking, it was her job. This meeting had to end, she needed an outcome otherwise she'd be back here again next week.

"You say these are the pictures dating Jack's change in appearance?" she asked rhetorically. "Perhaps we can compare your timeline of Jack's appearance to Martin's schedule of complaints to HR."

There was a sigh from Martin, I bet he hadn't expected to have his evidence challenged.

For the next ten minutes Paula and Gloria chatted amicably together as each photograph was placed directly against the nearest dated complaint. There was no match-up. According to Martin someone was even complaining about my wild hair long after I'd cut it off. There was another stating I'd been drunk on a call, when I hadn't even been in the office that day. It was all a fabrication, just one-man, Les Reivers, whoever he may be, making a series of petty complaints about me. I thought I knew most on site, but I had never heard of him.

"Who is Les Reivers? Does he even exist?" Paula asked.

"He's a customer, of a sort," Gloria replied. "Not the department though, he's a director with Night Owls."

Jake's agency! Night Owls! The devious conniving bastards! Was Jake trying to take revenge on me after all this time? Empire building? Trying to create space for his proposed harem? Whatever the motivation it was clear to me Martin and Jake were using the special weight attached to customer complaints to conspire a disciplinary against me. Had they really got nothing better to do with their time? Was I that much of a threat? I guess I should have been flattered.

The meeting still didn't end there though. Gloria and Paula continued their dialogue patiently noting one inaccurate, dishonest complaint after the other. I relaxed for the first time in months as I felt the tightness in my chest evaporating, and knots of stress unravelling.

Breathe, Captain Pinkbeard, breathe in the air. I glanced up, caught Martin's eye, and smiled.

Paula and Gloria worked to end the meeting as professionally as they could while Martin filled the time checking his phone, and then rechecking or doodling in the corner of his meeting invite. One empty triangle after another was created before they were coloured angrily in darkest Biro black. Ignoring Martin and talking direct to Gloria, Paula's conclusion was that I should be removed from being Under Supervision, and Martin and Jake investigated along with Les Reivers for malicious false accusations. Gloria replied coolly confirming a decision on my status would be made in the next twenty-four hours, and what Tex4Tex did with the managers and consultants was none of the union's business.

We sat there silently. I looked to Paula, she looked to Gloria. There was a pause as Martin finished shading his latest Biro triangle. Gloria tapped her pen impatiently on the table.

"Would you like to bring the meeting to an end, Martin?"

January 2008

My friends, just like Barry Manilow, I'd made it through the rain, and the complaints against me had evaporated. There was neither an apology nor an explanation, only an email from Gloria copied to myself and Martin making it clear I had met the terms of the process and I was no longer Under Supervision.

It may have been low key, but it felt like a victory. By way of thanks, I forwarded the mail to Paula.

I bumped into her an hour later at the tea-point.

"Are you going to let it end there?" she asked incredulously. "You have momentum, you should strike while the iron is hot. Raise a grievance, teach them a lesson. Stop them doing this to others."

She shook her head in frustration and tapped her clenched fist against the vending machine when she recognised my blank expression. She'd expected more of me, but I was prepared to let her down. Of course, I would have liked this part of my story to end with me dancing a jig and firing my pistols in the air like Yosemite Sam, but I felt I owed it to myself to move on. Sometimes when my head hit the pillow and I passed judgment on the good, bad or pointless working day just gone I was attracted to the idea of fighting back and being a *cause celebre* for the union, I loved it in fact, but I didn't like what I'd seen to be the reality of union involvement, namely months of stomach-churning stress and shuddering mood swings. No, I just wanted Martin's special attention to end, that would be enough for me.

Paula however was genuinely annoyed, and my personal gratitude wasn't enough for her. I was abandoning her battlefield. She had been so calm and supportive when I needed her to be, but now she seemed passionate and angry. She wanted a favour in return.

"Stop them doing this to others," she repeated as she pointed an accusing finger at me. "You'll regret it when this happens to others."

It was like she had a plan of her own and I was thwarting it, but I knew this wasn't a moment for curiosity. I'd made my mind up, I didn't want to get involved, as a union member her support was my entitlement, it didn't work both ways. After all they weren't the Teamsters, if I chose not to repay the union a favour, I wouldn't wake up with a horse's head next to me in the bed. She had no claim on me. I intended to reset the clock, let bygones be bygones, and let the water flow under the bridge until the next time I needed the union.

Aye, I looked forward to getting out of getting involved.

It was a complicated situation though. By making my decision to not pay Paula back with my support, I'd falsely assumed because Paula had helped me, she would automatically help others in trouble. Yes, naïve though it may seem because she was a union official, I'd imposed assumed stereotypes upon her. You know the ones – union officials were always forgiving, liberal softies, they were the sentimental bleeding hearts of the world. In my imagination my union rep lived in a house held together by protest posters and overrun by three-legged vegan dogs passing their time chasing one-eyed cats. The kind of pets that others turn away from at the rescue centre.

Paula was to prove me wrong – she was a mother, a wife, and a worker. She had a belief system it didn't pay to cross. She proved this a few weeks later when she demonstrated that she wasn't the charitable workplace angel of my imagination. You see, I always thought Paula would help Jake's apprentices, but she refused. They hadn't joined the union. It wasn't her problem, she wouldn't lift a finger, and they would be dismissed.

"These are the facts of working life," she said. "Don't waste your time helping non-members unless you want someone to practise on."

It surprised me she took that line, and I tried to reason with her. I explained to her that Jake had told me at the tea point a few months before his lads were never going to survive their probation. I passed on my gossip, the throwaway comment I hadn't taken seriously at the time. Jake had his own plans – he wanted to build a harem.

I hoped this information would concentrate her mind, and maybe I succeeded, but I had only made things worse.

She fired comments and questions at me.

"He told you this, and yet you did nothing! You knew this, and you still couldn't be bothered to raise a grievance, or even get the apprentices to join the union? All the time I was supporting you, and you said nothing."

It was just one true statement after another delivered with her precise but exasperated tone. I stood there praying for someone to come and interrupt her flow as she forensically continued to dismantle me one question at a time.

"What did you say when Jake told you this?"

"When he said he was going to totty-fy the office, did you laugh along with him? All the boys together?"

"What exactly did you say to him?"

"What were the exact words you used?"

"Was it a good story to tell Tony in the pub? Is that all your women colleagues are to you?"

And then as someone else finally entered the tea-point to relieve the siege, she ended with her gender's catch-all dismissal from before the dawn of time.

"Urggh!! Men."

There was one last look of contempt before she turned her back on me to signal the conversation had come to an end. This wasn't the first time, and it wouldn't be the last time I had misjudged long-standing colleagues. As I watched Paula's back disappear around the corner heading back to her desk, I was dumbstruck. I'd let her down lots of times before, and she'd never reacted like that. What was up with her?

On a historic level of course, Paula was right. My friends, non-members are little more than parasites leeching off the achievements of those paying the union dues, but at the same time I was also right, these were children barely out of school; they deserved a second chance. They were bright young lads with a decent future, but innocents in the ways of the workplace. Yes, it was their misfortune to be raised at a time when the Labour Party in government had been hijacked by public schoolboys conveniently preaching the class divide had been overcome. Our supposed one-nation politicians had indoctrinated a generation of school-leavers to regard themselves as neither bosses nor workers. A fine thing to be sure, but remember my friends, you don't abandon the class war trenches for a kickabout in ones and twos while the other side is still shooting. Aye for all their youthful gobby confidence, today's non-aligned young workers stand in no-man's land with targets on their backs.

A week or so later, despite Paula's reservation about the apprentices and their unwitting role in undermining two hundred years of trade unionism I still wanted to help. I agreed to witness Luke's probation hearing with Martin and Gloria reasoning I had spent so much time in formal meetings with Martin that, rest assured, I had probably picked up more information than 'you might think'. After all, it wasn't as though union officials were trained like barristers. Yes, I was sure I could wing it and help Luke.

Besides his exploits appealed to my sense of mischief. Luke was one of four apprentices from the unit called into formal hearings after achieving notoriety in North Wales. The boys had gone away on an Outward Bounds teambuilding expedition in Snowdonia under the control of the Inspiration team. Now to my mind, Inspiration was an odd bunch, they supposedly fostered unity and team spirit by harnessing youthful positivity but in the main they ran around yelling 'Hooray for Tex4Tex' spending corporate money like it was on fire and urging us to celebrate the pay freeze. But lads are lads, from one generation to the next, and Luke and his fellow apprentices had shown a bit of risk-taking initiative I for one cheered and applauded. The story goes that whilst their mentors in the Inspiration team were no doubt keeping out the cold by singing the company song on the freezing slopes of Snowdonia, Luke and his mates were sensibly down in the village pub drinking themselves to sleep in front of the fire. As I said, lads will be lads. Perhaps it could have been managed quietly, but the innocents had gleefully posted their drinking pictures on the internet. That had made it a public indiscretion, and a stick to beat Tex4Tex with in the light of our failing systems and deteriorating relationship with the department. A customer had seen them and made the complaint.

The complainant was of course, Les Reivers, yes him again, Jake's mate, Mr Night Owls. Nothing passed his all-seeing eye, whoever he may be.

I spoke up in the meeting and pointed out this coincidence to Gloria. We'd been here before.

"But the pictures are on social media. It clearly shows him in the pub, and not with the Inspiration team, and," she paused to pick her words, "each complaint must be treated on its merits."

"But he's barely old enough to drink."

"Even more reason why he shouldn't be sat in a pub wearing a Tex4Tex Inspiration sweatshirt having his picture entertaining the global superhighway." The pen in her hand tapped against the table. I'd seen that unconscious sign before. Gloria seemed angry, perhaps frustrated, almost as though she was pleading with me to find the right arguments, but it wouldn't happen. My cupboard was empty.

To make matters worse, Luke and I were relying on a previously unblemished past record and good relations with Jake to see him through. We hadn't taken the time to prepare and build up our own evidence because Jake had assured Luke that he didn't need to waste time when there was real work to do. Jake had said he only needed to put in a good word for Luke. It was a five-minute job. Yes, Luke had been relying on Jake intervening on his behalf, and so he sat there dumbfounded as Martin read out a series of criticisms from Teflon Jake and Martin himself.

"Jake never told me this. Nor did you." Martin didn't bother to respond.

"I haven't been warned before. They're both lying!" Luke pleaded to Gloria.

I was hopelessly out of my depth – a witness not a representative. I wished I hadn't been there.

This time Martin was smiling at me. It was a smirk saying, 'not so clever without your union pal,, captain'. I turned my head to the side as I sensed Luke shift, I didn't hear him crying but there were tears rolling down his face regardless. He knew what was coming. He'd been stitched up by his managers, and I hadn't found the advice or the words to save his job. I thought I might be able to wing it, but I'd been underprepared. I'd let him down.

Luke and the other apprentices wouldn't be sacked, but their probation was ending instantly without a permanent job offer. The effect was the same. Reivers's complaint sealed it. It was just too easy for the company. The Tex4Tex machine chewed up the apprentices and spat them out. I had no doubt that within a month there would be another fresh set of young bucks queuing round the corner anxious to take their first steps into the world of work. Ha! Welcome to the Hamster Wheel.

There was only one thing left to do. Paula had told me in a conversational olive branch that if she was losing the hearing she would always let the members have their say.

"It's their meeting. They'll have a lifetime to resent you if you try and stop them saying something that may be important to them. Some just gabble on to delay the inevitable dismissal," she added in her pragmatic cold-hearted way.

I knew it wouldn't work but I didn't intervene. Luke leaned back in his seat and reached into his right trouser pocket. From inside he produced a crumpled handwritten letter. It was a note from his mother saying he was a good lad who loved working at Tex4Tex, and surely, he deserved a second chance. Gloria winced, as his tears flowed openly now. Briefly, I hoped she might relent and realise they were using the full weight of the company to dismiss an apprentice, a child no less, for acting his age.

"Thank you for this, we'll definitely take it into account," Gloria responded, and gently pulled the letter from his hand, and as she did so I noticed Martin roll his eyes and stifle a yawn. What was wrong with him? No empathy at all. He leaned forward to show he was taking charge again.

"Thank you. Can you send the next one in please?" He turned his head to Gloria, and consulted his list, "I think it's Luke."

Gloria looked aghast.

"No sorry, my mistake everyone," he laughed. "You're Luke. It's Darren next. Send him in on your way out please."

I felt numb, I thought of all the stupid things I'd done at Luke's age under the influence of youthful high spirits. I'd only ever been shouted at and instructed to apologise, and invariably the boss doing the shouting would be the first to buy me a pint at the Friday lunch session. All this talk about cutting red tape, and introducing the right to manage, and this is where it's led England, dismissing daft teenagers just because we can.

After I'd walked Luke to the gates and wished him well, I thought of those conversations I'd shared with Tony where he proffered his opinions on the opportunities and security that we old civil servants had lost through privatisation. I realised that there was a nuanced further truth Tony hadn't acknowledged because he was too blinkered and narrow-minded to see, the biggest victim of privatisation had been the generation of workers following in our footsteps.

March 2008

This is how the trestle table became smoke free.

It hadn't been part of the designated smoking zone and was therefore off-limits, but nonetheless we smokers had tried to appropriate it through mission creep. Initially we had dropped our jackets and laptops on it, we then progressed to nonchalantly resting against it as we chatted, until finally we rested, and using improvised ashtrays made from saucers stolen from the canteen we took control. Briefly, we were regaining territory from the corporate machine, a small victory, but our strategy only worked well for a month or two until the tell-tale fag end debris resulted in non-smoker tittle-tattle and a warning sign threatening disciplinary action. That was all it needed to discourage us, and from there on we remained within the freshly painted yellow line borders of the smoking zone.

I had no doubt the society of smokers considered me a traitor to sit in disputed territory without a pipe in my hand, and I was sure I would be sent to Coventry until they next needed a light, but I liked the isolation, and I wanted to be alone. After all I had some thinking to do, I was still cursing myself for failing Luke by not preparing either of us for the meeting with Martin and Gloria, and of course for letting down Paula by not sharing Jake's plans or raising a grievance.

Martin and I hadn't kissed and made up if that's what you're thinking. The company processes expected me to move on, but it hadn't been easy to forgive and forget that my boss designated me unfit for purpose and had tried to dismiss me. We barely spoke before but now there was no pretence of establishing a working relationship. The decision to remove me from the disciplinary process had not been an end to the bad blood, and I never doubted he would try again if a chance presented itself. My workplace personal diary was accordingly updated daily. I felt like a soldier placing a Bible across the heart when I jotted down my notes at the end of every day. Just in case.

I was spending as little time sat opposite Martin as possible. Sitting for hours on end, barely feet away from a man I had come to detest felt oppressive, and I feared the day would arrive when I lashed out. My raging daydreams carried a fanciful notion that a Western-saloon style fight with my team leader, across tables and floor, smashing chairs over each other's heads would prove emotionally liberating, for me at least.

It seemed reasonable therefore to think that escaping the office was probably in both our interests. Like a break in the battle that perhaps only I was fighting. A sunny Spring morning presented the opportunity to sit outside at the tables dropping bread on the floor to feed the pigeons feeding furiously at my boots. My laptop was open, I calculated this gave me a pretence of working, and I made sure my fingerless gloves responded when the email pinged.

I was burnt out. I rubbed my eyes. I needed a break. I felt shattered, bewildered by the recent turn of events. My survival, Luke's dismissal – two working class generations, the two different outcomes; Paula working amicably with Gloria as they organised the photos; Martin's smirk while Luke cried. These snapshots of the past weeks flickered across my mind.

If I turned to my right and looked back into the office, I could capture Martin and Jake studying me through the window. One of them, presumably Jake, may well have been providing a running commentary for the team as I detected heads rising and falling in the shadows of the background. Pulling up my collar I prepared to receive a reception of oh so clever comments when I returned.

Even as I sat here alone, Martin Monk and Teflon Jake's distant presence had embarrassed me. They were inside my head messing with my brain. With a sudden cold-blooded chill, I became self-aware. 'That's why they were staring,' I realised with a thump. I felt sure I had been seen conducting the orchestra again – waving my arms, shaking my fists, pointing fingers, and shouting at the clouds. I was mortified colleagues had witnessed my weakness, my lack of control, but I wasn't sure how to control this recently acquired combustive rage. It was like the red mist dropped out of a clear blue sky, and one vague harmless memory would trigger a reaction and connect me to darker ones. Within seconds I instantly transformed from placid autopilot into the world's angriest sleepwalker with no route home while I was entranced. It was like being on public display like an animal in the zoo.

By now I realised one mistake I'd made was to assume the relief I'd first felt when Martin's direct supervision process collapsed and would sustain me over the winter, but it hadn't. My period of calm and vindication had been short lived. It flickered briefly to be replaced by this uncontrolled black angry depression vented upon myself and others. In middle age my innocent childhood dreams of escape from small town England had grown ugly, twisted horribly out of shape. Nowadays I didn't plan to leave for the Big City seeking fame and fortune like Dick Whittington. No, these days I just wanted to stay where I was and for everyone else to fuck off. They can escape. I only wanted to hibernate and wake up again when the seasons were more fortuitous. It was my earnest hope winter would cleanse the world of my enemies without my intervention. I wanted them to feel my hurt.

'Cool down, captain. Count to ten think you're a tree.' In fact, think about anything other than work. Shift mental tracks.

If I looked away from the office, breathed deeply, and calmed myself, I could see folks going over footbridges into the town centre. Well, we called it a town centre, in truth it was just an indoor shopping centre that had been constructed in brown fields when Telford New Town took shape on modern roads, uniting the dying mine and foundry settlements of East Shropshire. Cold but functional, appropriate for the cradle of industry.

They say somewhere near here, possibly under the retail centre car park, or maybe over there towards the dual carriageway, is the lost battleground of Cinderloo. Never heard of Cinderloo, comrades? Don't worry, few people have, but on this ground in 1821, or maybe on that ground over there in 1821, the Shropshire Yeomanry were ordered to open fire on unarmed striking miners who were protesting with their families on slag heaps and passing the time pelting the local militia with lumps of stone and coal. The miners' poverty pay had been cut on the instructions of the cartel of rich East Shropshire mine owners and they took the only action open to them. To strike.

The bosses called it sedition, and of course the authorities agreed with them. Together, working in partnership, they organised the violent response. Two were murdered at Cinderloo, others arrested, imprisoned, and in one case executed.

The reason I bring this up is that in the last forty years Telford has spent enough public money building its museums to venerate those cruel mineowners and foundry masters but there is nothing to commemorate the brave miners. Nothing to educate the present about the past, their story is gone for good it seems. Buried, possibly deliberately. Yes, better keep our history to the one looking good in the brochures and doesn't risk upsetting the wealthy descendants of those men of iron and coal who resorted to murder.

Of course, I admired the martyrs of Cinderloo, and I was ashamed of myself by comparison. They stood up for what they believed in, and they were even prepared to die for it. They didn't worry about all those know-it-all dementors sucking the joy out of the air telling everyone how difficult this or that was, assuring the room all militant opposition was pointless. Just like we do, those miners must have stressed and feared for themselves and their families, yet they avoided the soft option and bravely tried to take control over their destinies and make a difference. 'At least they tried, Captain Pinkbeard, at least they tried'. I punched my temples in frustration.

Paula had been right of course. I should have raised the poxy little grievance against Martin when I had the chance, and when it might have made a difference. I knew that now. I should have tried to clip his wings. In the wider scheme it was no sacrifice at all, it was insignificant. For years I'd crashed around in my rebel's coat mouthing off about solidarity, but when push came to shove, I'd been found wanting. I'd been presented with a chance to make a small difference but had declined the opportunity, and in doing so maybe I had cost others their jobs.

I sat there berating myself. Now I was unashamedly recommencing my conversation with the pigeons and the hedge, listing the crimes against my former teammates. What if I had raised a grievance against Martin, or had reported Jake's plans? Maybe Luke and the other youngsters would still be in work, and I would have achieved something to be proud of. What if I'd recruited them into the union, maybe Paula would have saved their jobs? She would surely have done a better job than I did, she couldn't have done a worse one. And for that matter, if I hadn't taken him drinking on his first day maybe Calum wouldn't have been held back, and if myself and Tony hadn't been so intent on damaging our livers over the years then maybe Paula could have been promoted instead of wasting her time covering for us. As for Tony, my closest friend and drinking partner, he finally had to disassociate himself from me before he could make a successful case for advancement. And Roger, protecting me, shielding me from the employer, creating easy hit tasks for me, helping me when the management soft option surely screamed to pass me on to someone else. He had probably knowingly put his career on hold for me, and in return I had taken his good management for granted. It was only now I had a lousy manager that I finally appreciated all he had done for me.

How bad was that Captain Pinkbeard?

My head was thumping, and my hands were moving freely again. I saw things clearly now – I was a conspirator in my own misfortune. I had always been proud to say I hadn't adapted to life inside the multinational, I thought of myself as the rock facing into the storm – whoever said no man is an island had never met me. Yet the price of my isolation was that I expected Paula, Calum, Tony, and Roger to talk to the world for me while I sat quietly in the corner thinking I was above it all. I must have been working with my eyes closed all these years. The world had turned, and because my support network had disappeared, I had missed it. I was a man out of time. My new colleagues were strangers, I knew nothing about them and my lack of curiosity was killing me.

While I stood still proclaiming my personal rebellion real life had been happening around me. For all my fancy analysis on the state of man versus corporation, prior to Luke, I had never actually lifted a finger to help. Whatever crossed my mind had rarely passed my lips. Without realising the irony, I'd outsourced my battles to friends and colleagues – they were fighting them for me. You know I used to joke I was the nightmare employee from corporate hell, and I'd tip my pirate hat in accompaniment to my own back-handed compliment, but a nightmare is what it seemed I was. A nightmare to work with if you have an ounce of ambition. I realised that now. Somehow, quite unknowingly I'd had a negative effect on all my colleagues' careers. Momentarily appalled by myself, I tapped my temples again, hoping it would concentrate my mind and help me snap out of this self-destructive train of thought. I was thirsty for a drop of the reckless courage of Cinderloo.

While I fought my demons at the trestle table, mulling things over, promising myself not to stand idly by in future, hoping to somehow reconnect with the man the youthful punk had once expected to be, Paula wandered over with a couple of coffees balanced precariously on a hardback training guide. She carefully placed them down before sitting across from me. I hoped they were a peace offering, and if so, I appreciated the gesture, but I should have been the one apologising to her.

"Calm down," she said. "The way you were going at it I thought if he carries on like this then I'll have to start following him around with a defibrillator." She winked at me as she said it to show she was just teasing. "What's up, captain?"

"Just things piling up is what's up and it's getting me down. I've been passing the time ghost-dancing – summoning up the spirit of our ancestors. "

"Oh aye – did they help?"

"Sort of. They haven't obliterated my enemies, but they've given me a sense of perspective."

There was a pause, as I guess Paula struggled to work out where this odd conversation could lead. I didn't offer a way forward, so I think she just said what she came out to say.

"Don't be so hard on yourself. Take my advice. You should talk to yourself less and the rest of us more."

I grumbled a response. I knew she was right, but I was in a huff, I couldn't bring myself to agree with her. Paula was undeterred, she was going to mother me whether I liked it or not.

"You know you did your best with Luke. It's just the way things are. At least we know that all the complaints are coming from Les Reivers, whoever the hell he may be. That's useful to know. We know Night Owls are making complaints about the team, probably at the direct request of our own managers. I mean like Kate Bush – wow, amazing – think about that, two sets of managers from two different companies conspiring against us, and we wouldn't have had this confirmed if you hadn't represented the apprentices."

I did feel a bit better for hearing her words, it sounded like I'd played a positive role the way Paula put it.

She picked up her coffee, blew on it and took a sip. "So, promise me in future, don't blame yourself, blame them." She flicked her head towards the office to show me direction. Her hand snaked across the table and gave mine a comforting pat. "HR give the managers a dozen options every time they get to the table, they're the ones choosing to go down this route. Sometimes we can persuade them but most of the time we don't. Win some, lose some, jockey. I can guarantee they don't feel half as bad about Luke's dismissal as you do, and that's what makes you the better person. What's important is that you witnessed it, the truth about management, just by attending you didn't give them a free ride. They know that you know what they really are. It makes you a danger to them."

Dangerous. I liked the sound of that. Paula had a way of finding the right words. We chatted amicably for ten minutes before she tapped her phone and showed me pictures of her son Liam in a West Brom top.

I instantly felt the blood of my yam-yam ancestors rise when I saw it. I just blurted it out.

"Raising a dingle? You bitch."

After a shocked pause, I smiled to show I was just winding her up. She calmly brushed me aside.

"And that's the thanks I get for asking you to talk to me."

Against my mood, I giggled my response, and then we sat there silently for a moment enjoying the sparrows fighting in the hedges.

"Football, bloody football," she sighed. "Britain's opium. The poor's great distraction," she blew on her coffee again. "The workers divided will always be defeated," she added before she took a sip.

May 2008

Of course, it had to happen sooner or later, but preferably later, far, far later. Like sewage polluting a river, the dysfunction we lived through every day corrupted and eventually overpowered our computer system. Despite the profits, or perhaps because of them, the contract had been spiralling out of control for months now. It was only a matter of time and luck. A 'computer crash' that's what the papers called it, the source of the story came courtesy of a leak inside this 'high profile and controversial privatisation'.

Crash – that's a strong term. It conjures up a moment of juddering finality. When a pigeon hits the window pane maybe, or perhaps some muggles might think a computer crash would be like one of those episodes of *Star Trek* where James T and the crew stumble from one side of the bridge to the other while the red-light flashes, the alarm blares, and the camera spins. But that's not right, what they usually term a computer crash isn't so dramatic. If you want to visualise a failing computer you should imagine crawling traffic on the M6 at Walsall when the road network is overloaded – don't get angry, you'll be here for a while so cut your engine and lower your expectations. Yes, just like traffic at rush hour, the computer was performing all the tasks exactly as it should, except it was performing them very, very, slowly.

My indignant colleagues were furious, the media were stupid, this wasn't a crash at all, technically the computer hadn't failed. What comfort this conclusion offered the end user as they gazed at their frozen screens was questionable, but it was important to us. If our computer system had failed and crashed it was surely our mistake, but if it was overloaded then maybe we were working to the wrong specifications, and it was doomed from the start. More importantly, if the specifications were wrong it could be the department's fault for providing them.

It was a matter of principle for employees. For my employer, it was a significant financial penalty that comes with a seat on Her Majesty's Government naughty step. Officially in response to the leak in communications which enabled the media to get hold of the story, Tex4Tex and the department issued a rare joint statement acknowledging teething problems on the latest software release and providing the assurance we were working to bring back full service. Presumably this clause was added just in case the end users were thinking otherwise. From there on it was no comment all the way.

Off the record it was a different story, and both partners were using respective press offices to brief against each other. Behind the language of co-operation, the employers were only united by the desire to identify and punish the perpetrators of the leak. Finding the source of the leaks prioritised discovering the cause of the service failure. On the day the story broke an email from Communications appeared referring to data theft and the Official Secrets Act. Some phrases were underlined for emphasis, we were prompted that sharing information about a misfiring taxpayer-funded contract was not a matter of public interest whistleblowing but an act of disloyalty to our Tex4Tex colleagues. We were left to think of the consequences if the journalists phoned.

However, as I've said before, there are always opportunities created through every disaster, and isn't that what makes corporations so resilient? Due to the 'unprecedented situation' the company now reminded us of its search rights over our workplace belongings and personal computer files. The culprits of the leak must be apprehended, disloyalty must be punished, and Tex4Tex middle-management cadre gleefully directed office gossip towards their usual enemies within. To my immense relief I was not one of those identified as a potential source of the leak. Perhaps the sight of me arguing with myself at the trestle table weeks before had removed me from the list of suspected workplace criminal masterminds. It was ill-informed speculation of course but it served a wider purpose, the managers assumed union officials served two masters and therefore warranted further investigation. At ten a.m. the staff witnessed Martin, Jake and Terry from Security standing over Paula demanding she open her drawers and cupboards for them to inspect while the rest of us pretended to work around her.

"So you think I secretly accessed confidential files, surreptitiously forwarded those documents to the press, and then stupidly printed off the email, and hid it in my drawer?" asked my bemused colleague.

Later they answered her in their own way. When she had left for the afternoon school run Martin and Jake returned to cheerfully peel the union stickers off her desk. After pausing briefly to admire their handiwork they swept all the family photographs and mementoes decorating her workstation into a black bin bag which they dumped unceremoniously on her chair. Task completed, Martin returned nonchalantly to his desk opposite mine, and pressed, with a Liberace-like flourish, the SEND key on his computer. My email pinged in reply, and I viewed my screen to read the message. In response to the system failure and our loose-lipped enemies within, all private possessions were to be removed from desks. The unit was to have a Clear Desk Policy. There was to be no personalising memorabilia, except those celebrating our role as employees of Tex4Tex.

We had taken another step on the road to dehumanised workplace. I swear they'd replace us all tomorrow with donkey robots if they could.

A few days later there was a team meeting. Surprisingly perhaps for some of the site's superior minds, removing Paula's family photos hadn't fixed the computer system. So, the good news was Paula's children were in the clear and thank God for that. However, the searches hadn't identified the leak and Gloria was back again. HR's presence is never a good sign, and we appeared to have one on tap these days. She read a prepared statement 'for internal use only' referring to the computer failure stating the employers were addressing the problems over the lack of capacity, but progress on one problem was leading to other failures. As she finished speaking, she folded her print-out to indicate she was going off script. I was experienced enough to know HR would never go free-lancing, and this was the critical part of our internal message, the part which absolutely couldn't be transcribed for fear it might be released into the media by our enemy within. "Undocumented changes,," Gloria said, and she shook her head sadly for effect. Tex4Tex had discovered colleagues providing accurate fixes but not completing the documentation to inform other teams of the changes. In other words, the computer didn't look like our records said it should, and if it didn't look like it should then every release we'd worked on from the moment when we failed to properly complete the documentation was guesswork.

Oops!

I nodded as I listened, this outcome gave me a moment of private vindication –"I hate to say I told you so." Gloria saw my movement but appeared to ignore it.

She explained our immediate task as employees was clear. We in Tex4Tex needed to restore our own confidence in Tex4Tex, but without the customer noticing our embarrassment. Gloria promised an amnesty for anyone with information on the computer failure, other undocumented changes, or the sources of the daily accusations of mismanagement being reproduced by the gleeful media. Apart from my nodding head she was looking at an office of stony faces as she completed her hopeless task. After all an amnesty was a fine idea in principle, but every employee knew better than to make accusations to HR in front of their own managers. It didn't require brain surgery to understand the reticence. It was management's fault that we had dug this hole. They were the ones stood in the background passing the shovels and giving instruction. Where were the risk assessments? Where was the Emergency Recovery Process? Why hadn't the managers insisted on checking audit trails? Shortcuts you see. It was a deliberate act. Most of these safety tests had disappeared for more efficient use of resources, and for greater profitability no doubt. Shortcuts mean risk-taking and rewarding risk-taking sounds great when millionaire financial chancers talk to politicians about it. They make it sound almost patriotic, as though working in the City gambling other people's pension funds is an act of public service. Yes, everyone wants to jump on the risk-taking bandwagon, that is until they get caught taking a stupid risk. It's only then it becomes irresponsible.

It was no surprise me when the meeting kept its thoughts to itself as Gloria finished her statement. After all, we employees had to balance the stupid risk of using a shortcut with the stupid risk of speaking out about it and taking ownership of the failure. This wasn't a time for heroes. After fifteen seconds of silence Martin coughed as though he was about to move the meeting on, but Gloria intervened,

"Jack, you're an experienced employee. You seem to have an opinion on this." She smiled so sweetly, she hit the target. It was the HR honey trap. I was twice her age or more, and yet still desperate to impress. And she was right I did have an opinion on Tex4Tex failings. It was a speech I made several times a week in front of the bathroom mirror liberally soaked in swear words and finger-pointing.

"But…" I stammered before finding a suitable form of words. Instinct told me I should know better than to contribute. I was afraid everything I said would have a Disloyalty Alert attached but nonetheless I felt a primal compulsion to accept her challenge.

"I don't know about the leaks, but from what I can tell the leaks are coming from someone with knowledge of both the department and Tex4Tex." I looked up to see if people were listening, and caught Teflon Jake's eye. Was he smiling? I pressed on regardless,

"As for the computer things have been wrong for a while. It seems like we never say no. We just cash the cheques and make promises regardless of whether we can fulfil them." I took a deep breath, even for an experienced worker moderate criticism of bosses is a scary business.

"Sometimes it's like we don't respect the computers any more. Everyone's looking for easy answers. We cause our own problems. It's as though our bosses think we can flick a switch or push a button, and every shortcut must be explored. Anything is possible, and if this short-cut doesn't work then we simply try another one."

"Yes," Gloria said urging me on. I sensed other team members' eyes boring a hole in my head as I inadvertently denigrated their capabilities. Martin was angrily staring too. He was probably unsure what was going to come out next, and frankly, shipmates I wasn't that sure either. I hadn't intended to speak. I just didn't want to let down the pretty girl or myself either. After all I'd promised myself while I chuntered away at the old trestle table the winter before that I wouldn't sit and stare in future. I wouldn't let things wash over me. I realised I now expected more of myself than to simply witness injustice, I wanted to make a positive difference and connect to my colleagues.

Perking up, feeling more confident as I grasped that I was doing the right thing for myself, and maybe for others too, I let the words roll.

"Making sweeping changes to old computers is like telling an elephant it doesn't need a trunk any more. You might be right, but you wouldn't just cut its trunk off and tell it to adapt to using its nose." I heard others giggle, and even Gloria smiled, no doubt it would be another funny story to recount to her middle-class uni chums. But I continued undeterred, I didn't care about impressing Gloria any more, I just wanted to impress myself.

"The point is, if you were starting from scratch, you might not want to create a twenty-first century elephant with its big ears, long trunk, and dodgy knees, but that is what an elephant is." I emphasised the point again, "You must acknowledge the elephant for what it is, evolution has made it that way. On its own level it works. It may not be a gazelle, it may not have the pace, grace, and dexterity you'd like but it works to its own standards. The elephant is a strong, resilient beast and it should be respected for those achievements. It's the same with our computers, some of our systems predate the internet, and yet they still work, and like the jug-eared elephant tramping the same paths since before the dawn of Man, to abruptly promise radical change without careful consideration is not a good option."

Martin again tried to move the meeting on, but Gloria said she thought I had something more to say. She was leading me on again, but I was stuck on my metaphor.

"The thing is you must respect the elephant. You might not like it, but this is where we start from if you want to adapt to the modern world." I repeated myself for effect, "You can't wish away history. We can't pretend to start with a blank sheet of paper. These old robust thick-skinned computers are where we should start from if we want to sell something to the department."

I had hoped what I'd said had sounded emotional and passionate yet clever and profound. Sadly, as I finished and looked up, others were clearly at the point of bursting into laughter. Jake leaned forward,

"Oh, Confucius, please tell us what's next master?" He held his palms upright together in mock reverence. Others giggled, and then he spat out the words.

"Computing elephants, for fuck's sake." He was drumming a hand on the nearest desk as he let out that familiar hissing laugh.

"Can you answer me this, Jack?"

Jake paused, enjoying the moment, keeping us waiting for the punchline. "Won't their feet be too big to press the keys?"

Initially even Gloria laughed, and to be fair Jake made a good joke at my expense. Everyone was laughing hard except Martin. Impassively, he looked at me, as though he was considering retribution when Gloria left. To his side Jake and Toby impersonated great elephant feet stamping the ground, and it set off another gale of laughter, and then placing his arm stiffly across his face to replicate a trunk Toby twisted his frame, bent his head, and tried to type at a nearby keyboard.

I saw Gloria nudge Martin to indicate this had gone far enough, but he was not going to intervene and save me from my embarrassment. As far as he was concerned, they could keep howling till midnight.

From my left I heard Paula whisper. It was only one word,

"Offshoring."

It was a prompt intended to save me. Angrily, I grasped at it, and then I lashed out verbally.

"You see Jake and the boys are phoning the Mumbai Help Desk overnight to resolve problems that neither they nor the Help Desk understand. You see they don't know the computer's history; they haven't grown up with it like I have, they need to take time to learn," I gabbled. I was agitated, I resented being simultaneously the longest serving employee and a figure of amusement. I continued.

"Mumbai can patch problems, make them go away for a while, but you know Gloria, they never really fix anything, because they're always taking these shortcuts, and as you now know they're working without proper documentation. And this is because our line managers

253

are always teaching us it's never cost-effective to take time and do the job properly."

The laughter stopped when Gloria turned to Martin.

"You've given Mumbai access to the database?"

"No, emphatically no." Martin raised his eyes to the ceiling, hoping Gloria would feel his frustration. "Typically, Pinkbeard is misleading you out of spite. Mumbai allows us to offer twenty-four support at minimum cost. They don't access the database, we just give them cuts to test their solutions on, and then patch their fix in."

"Okay, and this has been documented and approved? It's in line with our customer's data protection policies?" Gloria continued to press.

"Yes." Martin looked to Jake, who shrugged and blanked him. I could hear Jake's brain repeat the consultant mantra, "I'm not Tex4Tex it's not my problem."

I felt Paula pat me on the back.

"You see," she said later over a coffee (65 no milk), "I knew you'd hold it together. You don't say much, but people listen when you speak. Martin may target you, and sometimes people may laugh, but you're the only one he hasn't been able to move on. It gives you credibility for standing alone and surviving."

I blushed at the compliment.

October 2008

I'm trusting to memory here, but I think I first spoke to her on a lazy Friday chatting with the crowd at the smoking shelter. She wore knee-length leather boots, tight jeans, a plain black t-shirt underneath an unzipped leather jacket, and as she talked, she twisted the cigarette through her varnished nails while the men gathered to offer a light. If something amused her chestnut eyes shone through immaculate eye make-up.

She had a hijab on her head.

I liked Farah, she was stylish and effortlessly challenging – one foot in the sands of Arabia, the other planted firmly on the concrete of Birmingham's Bullring Shopping Centre. She was who she was, and it was up to the rest of us to deal with it, confronting racists and narrow-minded dimwits simply by being herself. Yes, I liked that about her. Most important of all Farah became my first attempt in years to connect to someone outside my narrow circle.

My friends, Farah was one of several women recruited onto the team by Wiley's unit to replace the male apprentices who failed to complete their probation. This was exactly as Jake had promised me. She and her fellow new arrivals had an instant impact on the team's behaviour. The women created a brief but welcome desire to impress. Food wrapping started finding its way into bins, swearing decreased, and generally coming to work was an infinitely more pleasant experience. Shameful though it is for me to admit now, I did agree with Toby when he commented the workplace had gone from 6.0 to 8.5.

However, it wasn't all sunshine and roses, I for one noted with bitter irony the dress code didn't apply to lovely women the way Martin had tried to enforce it upon me. Women seemed to wear what they wanted, and no-one complained. Far from it they received the opposite reaction – my infantile shipmates stared in reverence when they passed by. It seemed like double standards, but I wasn't going to break my self-imposed vow of silence with Martin to raise the injustice. No good luck to the women I muttered through gritted teeth, their gorgeousness had helped them dodge that bullet.

I did mention the double standards in passing to Paula though, but I was wasting my breath, she wasn't interested.

"Leave them be. Trust me they've got their own problems to deal with, they don't need you adding to them." And there she was, wagging her finger at me again as if I'd done something wrong. "Take my word for it, being an attractive woman is a mixed blessing in this workplace. And besides, now you've brought it up, do you seriously think you look like that in a t-shirt and jeans?"

She'd finished her lecture, she didn't need to add more detail to her comparison, it might only hurt my feelings, and of course she was right. Young women could do smart casual – they looked modern, attractive, feminised, and empowered. Exactly the way the male, balding, overweight, middle-aged company powerbrokers wanted the Tex4tex workforce to be seen. Yes, on balance Paula was right, I decided to hold my tongue for now. It probably wasn't a winning strategy to make a complaint and push my luck with the keepers of the dress code again. This door was closed to me.

Fortunately, one consolation of being considered too old for courting was that Farah could relax around me, and over the weeks we bonded and soon established a rhythm of smoking together, gleefully taking every opportunity to swap stories about our mismanagement team of Martin and Jake. I'm sure you'll agree there is something very liberating in finding a new confidante to share a private joke at your manager's expense. My best intention had been to warn Farah about Jake's plans for women employees, but surprise, surprise it appeared Jake had already beaten me to the punch and my heads-up was unnecessary. Whereas Martin had been his usual self-contained discouraging self to the new starts, Jake was over-compensating. He was attentive, if anything too attentive, constantly offering her help or tuition – offering to mentor her. Farah joked he was going to mentor her brains out if she let him. And then one day as an illustration of Jake's approach to supportive hands-on management she showed me a text message as we stood there.

"u luk sexy toda."

Another message arrived while I was reading its predecessor,

"got a hard on, meet me in car park. 1 Wnt u on bck sit. gonna rip ur hedscarf off."

I raised my eyebrow and handed her the phone back, giggling as I did so,

"I think this must be for you."

Farah smiled patiently and rolled her eyes as she read it. He was 'pathetic'. She offered her comment as an explanation as though she was sub-consciously attempting to downplay and rationalise his behaviour. To my eyes, she appeared surprisingly calm, almost as though a nine to five nuisance at work was normal and expected, a female rite of passage you might say, but I thought I knew differently, and I could see these messages were beyond the boundaries of the acceptable. I was sure the company would act to stop this behaviour. You'll have to forgive me, comrades, but in line with my recently acquired policy of trying to make a difference, I breached Farah's confidentiality, and spoke to Paula the next day seeking advice.

It was a simple instruction she gave, 'bring her to me on Friday'.

I don't know what my new friend expected as we chatted and joked our way towards the AbDab rooms, but personally I was surprised to see Paula surrounded by a reception committee of half a dozen women staff members waiting when we arrived. Louise, Jenny, Ruby, and Clare I recognised, and Maggie Something-Something was there, I recognised her face, but I still couldn't remember her name. The other couple were new to me by sight, and then, quite bizarrely it seemed, Calum sat grinning sheepishly at the end of the table.

"Hi Farah, come in, come in," Paula urged us. She was beaming but agitated, like a host at a house party, she darted past to close the door, briefly looking outside to check the coast was clear. Task completed, she turned satisfied, and made her way back to the desk, her laptop already open.

"Welcome Farah, and everyone, to the Teflon Jake support group." She followed it with the instruction. "Ladies, open your phones." It was apparent the support group had been running for a while, right under my nose, and I hadn't even caught a sniff. Every week the women gathered to share their stories about Jake. I quickly gathered he was continually texting almost all the women who were still on probation asking them for sex. And not just them, but as far as we could tell there were dozens of women colleagues receiving his requests. He was spread betting – a serial pest, who cast his net far and wide on the off chance someone might say yes. Of course, Jake was arrogant not stupid, so his text messages were always couched as banter, quite ludicrous banter in fact, but persistent and outrageous.

And plain irritating.

Distracting. Pressurising.

Unilateral, unrequested.

And time-consuming. Very time-consuming.

Sometimes it was hard for the women to get any work done when Jake wanted to play. There could be dozens of messages a day. It seemed the women couldn't initiate a single interaction with Jake on a work issue without a corresponding question on their availability for a fumble. Some like Farah would receive daily comments on her clothing, speculation about her underwear, and comfort requests. Ruby had been asked to plead on her knees when she requested time-off for a training course. As for Jenny, she once had the audacity to wear a short skirt, and Jake promised to throw his pen on the floor and crawl under her desk if she wore it again.

"At least I could kick him if he did."

The support group was extraordinary to tired male eyes. It was a helter-skelter of emotion, one minute the women were crying and hugging, the next they were swearing like troopers and laughing uproariously at the ridiculous situation the Men in Charge had put them in. Perhaps it wasn't the angry response I had expected but I reasoned that knowing they weren't alone gave them solidarity, as well as personal confirmation Jake was indeed the horny loser dickhead he appeared to be. Yes, they could take comfort from the support group, it wasn't just their individual opinion he was annoying and should be stopped, it was the whole of Tex4Tex womankind, they'd had a vote and it was agreed.

But the women needed an outcome. As Paula sat there patiently typing her notes, asking them for proof of this conversation or that email or text, there was debate and disagreement on the next steps. Paula wanted a formal complaint against Jake, but the women were anxious about the consequences if they were perceived to have rocked the boat. Some of them had to balance doing the right thing against the contractual uncertainty of their probation status. They were after all only too aware of what had happened to the previous year's apprentice intake. In short, the women were concerned Paula would cheerfully burn all their bridges on a principle which might yet cost them their careers.

It was a mess, the like of which I didn't think could have been possible in the old days. Individual pay and a secret ranking process had handed our rotten officer class a full deck of cards. The managers held all the weapons. Us old dinosaurs from the '70s could pontificate on the mistakes of modern workers all we liked, but the young women of the twenty-first century couldn't avoid the fact they needed their harassers' approval to get a permanent placement, let alone a pay rise, or a transfer. Paula kept her opinions to herself as they spoke. I'm sure it was to her frustration, and my astonishment, that Jenny and Farah had both already broken ranks, followed corporate doctrine, and shared their concerns informally with their line manager Martin, only to be dismissed in a moment when he said it was between them and Jake. Frustrated, they compounded the mistake and sought an audience with unit leader Wiley, but he also wouldn't get involved beyond 'having a word' with Jake. The young women saw their management chain turning a blind eye to Jake's behaviour, and understandably demotivated they doubted they would ever be supported inside Tex4Tex.

The support group discussion lasted for over an hour moving back and forth across facts and feelings. In those occasions when the chatter drifted off topic, Paula stepped in sternly, and showed the objective, focussed, forensic side I'd witnessed, and eventually learned to admire, when she had supported me.

"Jake is a well-known figure with a powerful contact network. Unfortunately, this won't be the shoe-in it should be. If I were to represent him, I'd say his first line of defence when he bends Wiley's ear is that this all banter, you were flirting and encouraging him, and no offence is intended. His second line is that this has been going on for months without a formal complaint. You must consider that every week passing muddies the water and weakens your case, unfortunately you're a victim of your own professional attitudes trying to make things right and tolerating the unreasoned."

It was as close as she came to criticism of the women, but then perhaps realising she'd briefly lowered the mood Paula introduced Calum, who as the meeting's grand finale read out Toby Mullett's *Ranking List of Top Females*. Fair play to the big lad, he'd kept it up to date, every week a new comment on the appearance of women in the office. If only he had been this dedicated to his work reports. Who'd have thought it? Independent beauty analysis from a fat thirty-year-old man-child who spent most of the working week shovelling cake and crisps down his throat. It must have been hard for the women to respect their critic's opinion.

"I'll never wear that bloody skirt to work again," promised Jenny after hitting the top of the charts.

As Calum passed me the email, I first checked the distribution list. I was pleased to see The Mullett had removed my name as I'd requested and I was now out of the chain, but most of the men in the unit were still being copied in, including Teflon Jake, Martin Sidepartin, and there at the bottom, unit leader Cliff Wiley. Hypocrites the lot of them! All the compulsory training on values and ethics and here the men were rating female staff on their looks. FFS! I couldn't stand my employer, but even I understood the HR policies better than the managers.

After the meeting finished, I hoped that a change might come to resolve the discontent, however the following weeks would only show Teflon Jake's lucky reputation remained intact. The underlying problem in the unit appeared to be that while the women may have rejected Teflon Jake's advances, the men were swooning over him. Despite the tentative airing of the accusations by Jenny and Farah, Wiley and the unit leaders failed to move against Jake. Week after week, we all witnessed Jake's vulgar behaviour and how they went unpunished. Everyone on the office floor saw Jake dominating and undermining Martin – we watched as the consultant took decisions on Martin's behalf and assumed his responsibilities.

"It's just his way," Cliff Wiley had said to Jenny. "They both get on fine," he added as if Martin's feelings were her concern. And every morning we saw Jake entering and leaving Wiley's office laughing and joking like we were riding the crest of the wave. All that Blairite Tex4Tex equality box ticking, all that middle-class HR 'Women into Management' bollocks, it all meant nothing. With men like Wiley still in control the basic career advice for women remained unchanged from the 70s – girly-girls still needed to man up if they wanted to get on. Aye, no-one loves a tittle-tale.

My faint hope of a coming change was soon put to sleep. It felt like Wiley was in denial. His unit had accepted complaints from Night Owls about me and the male apprentices at face value, yet complaints about Night Owls by his own staff were rejected out of hand. Yes, aside from the continual nuisance texting and Jake's trouser-bursting management style, another problem the women identified, perhaps a more significant long-term one, was how a temporary consultant had become the most important employee in the unit. Jake was the man the technically incompetent managers leant on, the manager they trusted to speak to the staff in their own language. With the contract struggling and the computer systems failing, Teflon Jake was deemed business critical. He remained untouchable and out of reach.

Aye, no wonder the women were concerned about the consequences of action, and perhaps Paula was wary of pushing them too hard. Everything seemed to be heading unsteadily towards the decisions on probation and the subsequent individual salary review, and then afterwards if all went to plan, the women would follow Paula's advice, make their complaints, and hopefully escape the madhouse.

It was a considered strategy, except that office politics is like those shifting tectonic plates. There's always something bumping together or moving apart, and though unseen there are always consequences. None of us can stop the world turning, and time was not on the women's side. Teflon Jake had his own plans, and then one afternoon he tried a different approach with Jenny, explaining how he was working away from home and missing his wife. He needed a shoulder to cry on, and if he should happen to cop a feel while he was there, then what harm could it do and who was to know?

Whatever excuse he provided on whichever day the fact is his relationship with the women intensified as the probation review drew nearer. It was to be their moment of truth. The good news was the support group had succeeded in bonding the women together. As Paula had advised, the women were now not only rejecting his advances they were insisting he stop them. He was pushing them, and they were pushing him back.

It led to the familiar cocktail of male self-pity and menaces.

"So, you don't want my help then? I'm trying to help you through your probation. Why won't you help me in return? Lol. Show some appreciation FFS!"

Undaunted, the women stuck to their guns, quietly requesting feedback for their reviews. All the while Jake persisted with his game-playing. When Louise was working alone one afternoon he arrived at her desk.

According to Louise, Jake had placed his hand on her shoulder and leaned over.

"I know things about you, and this place, and what's going to happen next, things it would be useful to know." And then, she said he gave her a wink, drew a zip across his mouth, walked back to his desk and texted her again, this time on her private mobile number, the one which the unit kept for emergency purposes.

And then a few days later he crossed all the red lines. Maybe it was banter, perhaps he didn't think through the consequences, but it was received like a threat. He texted Farah and asked what her husband would think if he knew about 'them', Jake finished with a 'lol, xxx'. Just for good measure, and presumably to make it extra funny, he added her emergency contact number, her husband's mobile, to prove he had the capability to carry out his threat.

Now in these days of supposed political correctness gone mad, you'd have thought Cliff Wiley would explode into action and there would be blood on the walls when Farah's complaint went in, followed by the others. But no, perhaps because the informal approaches had given him a warning, perhaps because of his own dependence on Jake, perhaps because of Cliff's own presence on Toby's distribution list of the emailed Ranking of Top Workplace Females (a further upgrade), or maybe for other reasons not yet known to grunts like me, Wiley appeared to be playing for time.

After Paula had left for the day, one by one he called the women in for a private chat about 'these serious career-threatening accusations you're making' and making them aware of the grave consequences if the accusations weren't upheld. At the same time, he insisted he was magnanimous enough to declare his responsibility to take the complaint seriously for everyone's sake and 'put it to bed'. He would launch an investigation and make some enquiries. His stated aim was to keep everything informal and low-key, and that's why he didn't want the union involved,

"Because if you involve Paula, then I must involve HR. And you see, Jenny, this whole thing just gets bigger and bigger. And by the way, sweetheart, while you're here, how do you feel your probation is going? Martin says you're doing quite well, and they think they can recommend you if you maintain your current performance and keep away from bad influences."

Wiley's supposed investigation would drift for months while the complaints remained unaddressed.

There was one consolation, perhaps it was Wiley's intervention, perhaps it was a coincidence, but Jake found himself seconded to the joint employer team looking at the consequences of the recent computer failures, as well as the leak still dripping kryptonite poison to Parliament and the computer press. So, whilst Jake hadn't been suspended, for a while at least he was working away from the unit.

It was a curious kind of stalemate. Although Paula was frustrated the complaint was getting kicked into the long grass, the young women seemed pleased Paula had created the quiet space and the solidarity enabling them to cope under pressure.

It had been a team effort. They would now be able to complete their probation in peace.

January 2009

The world's economy had plummeted into recession. We knew this because the world's leading economists, the same ones who failed to predict the downturn told us so. Yes, despite their outrageous profits, banks had managed to place themselves on the brink of bankruptcy, and not just here, but here, there, and everywhere.

You see they had spent our savings on Toxic Debt, and it did exactly what it says on the tin, my friends. Yes, they had invested heavily and had spent so much money supporting bad debtors that they were never going to get it back, unless of course, they first continued to lend the debtors more to help them avoid insolvency.

Aye, it was like lending your junkie neighbour fifty pounds for food and water to straighten themselves out, and then wondering why they return two days later looking worse than ever and asking for a hundred pounds.. Now you or I would never make such a mistake twice, but our financial institutions kept repeating the error. They were like gamblers on a losing streak without the courage to break from the game, but hey, at the end of the day it wasn't their money, so what the hell.

To make matters worse, just like our own Tex4Tex a few years before, the world's financial institutions had been systematically ransacked by their own executives. As a result, they didn't have a penny in assets to honour the bills which arrived for their ruinous greed and incompetence. Fortunately for them, it wasn't all bad news for the bankers, the one thing they hadn't squandered was a firm control of the Stock Market and a clear understanding of how to use the power. In the City of London, hedge funds and institutions held thirty million workers' pensions hostage as a bargaining chip in their negotiations for a taxpayer-funded bailout. If we fail, we'll take their pensions with us, they said. It was an act of kidnap, they should have been arrested and imprisoned, but the Labour government paid the ransom and let the bankers go free. Whisper it quietly, our civil war was over before it started – the banks were now running and ruining the country while Parliament dutifully passed the cost onto the taxpayer.

Embarrassingly, as if in tune with the national and international crises, our computer systems continued to creak and splutter apologetically. Although the nationals soon bored and stopped covering the 'crash', the leaks to the MPs and the specialist media continued unabated. Somewhere in our midst we still had a treacherous songbird chirping through the chaos, and it was a painful song to hear. It was a tale of loss and regret. Once Tex4Tex were invincible, our contract had been the fearless corporate flagship, our double-digit profit margin made us the king of the ocean, and yet over a few autumn months the same contract had transformed into Turner's *Fighting Temeraire*, days of trade and Empire over, slowly getting towed to dock for break-up.

Our computers were broken. The customer had lost confidence, the staff had lost confidence, the markets had lost confidence, everyone who might have mattered had lost confidence. I don't know how they measured such things, but I didn't doubt it was true.

Yes, Tex4Tex had squandered our brownie points, and now our contract with the department and our individual futures were as secure as those sets in *Prisoner Cell Block H* which shook with every actor's tread. If we were a football team, we'd sack the manager, but we were a corporation so we could guarantee the approach would be more considered – it was the managers who would do the sacking.

And yet, despite their energy, remarkably neither Tex4Tex nor the department had managed to identify their enemy within, and if anything, the leaks were becoming more precise in their detail to taunt them. Yes, it was symbolic of how shambolic things were, even the team investigating the leaks was leaking off-the-record briefings to the papers and politicians.

The consolation was that this was good news for me and other workers, whoever the traitor was, he or she was well connected, the likes of us wouldn't have access to the secret information now being shared. 'I can't leak it cos I don't know it' I overheard Paula say on a call to the national union.

To make matters worse, at this time of crisis the Tex4Tex financial results were published. I'd venture it was perhaps not the best time to record another year of logic defying record profit, but that's what the bean-counters had promised investors, so of course that's what the accounts delivered. Yes, who'd have thought it? You replace old, experienced but expensive workers with youngsters on lousy terms, make them all eat a pay freeze so the best one's leave, and you make record profits. Outstanding! Bravo! And you lose your most able employees and in response your contract fails as the service disintegrates. Shame! Disgrace! Yes, who'd have thought it?

The profit figures amid service disarray meant Tex4Tex had handed the department a stick to beat us with. A mighty stick with pound signs on no less. For years we had held the upper hand in negotiations but now finally we were walking around with Kick Me Hard signs on our back. It was surely too good an opportunity for the department to waste.

For my own part, I didn't want to be seen to gloat while others worried over their futures, but between me and you, I was riding the collapse of capitalism with a song in my heart. After all my long-term career goal was to get made redundant on the most expensive terms available, and this outcome now seemed more likely than it had done for years. It was all there: A global recession, an angry customer, contractual uncertainty, and a failed attempt to dismiss me. Reading the runes on redundancy wasn't an exact science of course, but cross my fingers, I felt I was ticking every box.

Yes, I enjoyed Tex4Tex's recently acquired notoriety. Every setback and media dagger blow looked a kinder cut than the last. It didn't bother me that these days I was learning more about our collapsing contract from *Computer Weekly* than attending work and listening to my bosses. The search for information only added to the thrill of the chase.

For example, I hadn't realised until I read *CW* that Teflon Jake's lucky reputation remained justifiably in place. We'd assumed Jake had been moved downwards because of a harassment complaint, but he'd now landed on Experience, the high-powered joint working group consulting on plans to right this listing Flagship contract.

Experience was to become one of those sub-committees that starts low-key but then assumes powers through mission creep. At first it was set up to investigate the computer failure, but then it assumed responsibility for the leak enquiry, and within weeks it was involved in orchestrating a future direction for the Tex4Tex 'partnership' with the department. It now incorporated past, present and future, and all decisions now needed its ratification. How Jake, a consultant, had advanced to become such a corporate insider no-one knew at this time. To be honest we were not interested, we were only grateful he was no longer attached to our team.

His new assignment left his partner-in-crime Martin isolated, but I doubt it bothered Martin, he was born isolated. He remained detached, the only time I heard him raise his voice was when the Movement team blocked his application for the ultimate management status symbol, a single occupancy office. Martin could see the door which should have his name on, but it remained tantalisingly out of his reach. That fact infuriated him, for the rest of the day he was controlled office rage personified, tutting and sighing, slamming doors and phones, out of all proportion to the perceived snub. Part of me wanted to go to his side of the desk, grab him by the shoulders and yell, 'get a grip man, we're relying on you' Hollywood style, but I didn't. I was enjoying the show too much. To my mind it summed him up. No doubt when the Red Army smashed into Hitler's bunker to end the war there was probably Martin's Nazi equivalent surrounded by rubble complaining to the canteen manager about the cauliflower cheese and berating him for letting standards fall.

Gloria's weekly HR visit arrived with a sigh and a coffee. The days of two-way feedback were ending. Each meeting the same, she read a script, we listened and shrugged, and then we went back to work ten minutes later. If Gloria was bored reciting the same corporate script repeatedly to team after team, she never let on, she always appeared sharp and attentive despite the circumstances, but still it must have been demoralising for her however positive the body language.

As she entered the office, the worn copies of *Computer Weekly* scattered across the desks told their own story. We knew what she was going to say, we'd already read it. Thanks to the leaks, we'd all read Gloria's top-secret confidential announcement a few days ago. It read that in response to the contract's poor performance the computer would be shut down for seventy-two hours from Friday lunchtime. This would give Tex4Tex the time we needed to put the Domestos Extra into the system and clear out the bugs and glitches once and for all. The search for a scapegoat had now been dropped from the script, and Tex4Tex, whilst still protesting our innocence, would pay compensation and accept a commercially acceptable sized chunk of the blame. Yes, our bosses agreed it was best all round if the company agreed to scapegoat its own employees for the meltdown, after all there are other government privatisations to bid for and a prolonged stay in government contract detention did not favour the company's strategy. Additionally, as a sign of good faith and in anticipation of further changes recommended by Experience the company was considering a rebrand of its UK arm. Henceforth we may be repackaged as tex4tex, the lowercase to show our humility. Yes, that would be the humility Texan multinationals are famous for.

Apparently, the proposed rebranding woud come at a cost of several million. Aye, comrades, I know what you're thinking – and they laughed when I spoke about the elephants!

Of course, at the time of Gloria's announcement, we barely heard beyond the first sentence. It was like they were promising to create a new school holiday for adults.

"You will be granted ten hours leave on full pay. We will shut down on Friday for seventy-two hours, to enable us to overhaul and rebuild the system over the weekend and bring it all back on Monday. The department has agreed a financial package with Tex4Tex." Even I gasped, the company had blundered and here we were being rewarded with time-off courtesy of the taxpayer. We couldn't believe our luck.

Whatever plans people hastily drew up, and whatever good intentions we had to utilise our fortune wisely, on Shutdown Friday Tony and I decamped to a packed Wetherspoons for the afternoon. As he was now on the first rung of management, I insisted he bought the first drink. He seemed chipper, and so did I. The economy may have been collapsing, the contract faring worse, but for the time being we'd bettered Martin and got rid of Jake, who knows we might both be weeks away from a big cheque to leave, and here I was down the Wetherspoons on company time. What wasn't there to celebrate?

My friend was as ever full of opinions, but these were now better-informed opinions and no longer the usual unsolicited hindsight which had been his stock-in-trade. Because Tony was now a low-level boss it was his duty to attend unit ranking sessions and provide input into even lower graded staff reports. Really, he shouldn't have been sharing the information with me, but I guess that maybe he wanted to impress me, or bless him, more likely the noisy gobshite couldn't help himself, but I loved the gossip. Tony's promotion had raised the quality of our drinking chatter.

According to Tony, despite his Night Owls employment status as well as the still unresolved harassment complaint, Teflon Jake had been drafted into staff ranking sessions to lend his expert opinion on the women's performance.

"When your team are discussed only Jake spoke, and he seemed to think his role was to slag off everyone except his drinking buddies. According to Jake, the young women are not team players and complain even when people are offering to help them. Martin who should be making recommendations says nothing, he clearly has nothing prepared, and Cliff Wiley just sits there grinning smugly like Nero at the Colosseum about to give a thumbs-up or thumbs- down.

"Now let me summarise for you," Tony said before he raised a beer to his lips. "Trust me, pal, your girls were right to complain, there was never a chance of getting a pay rise out of that set of bastards." After he'd finished draining another glass Tony explained that when the women's in year performance was being discussed, a few childish managers openly commented on the women's availability for extra duties due to likely pregnancies, and then to the sound of their own hilarity they speculated on the likely candidates to do the impregnating.

Tony told me Roger had tried at several points to intervene and raise mitigating factors to give balance and complain about the standard of discussion, but the others united and portrayed him as a bitter manager, jealous of Martin, and in the pockets of the union (Paula). But none of what Tony said explained what Jake was doing at Ranking in the first place. Ranking was our Tex4Tex corporate inner sanctum, outsiders and particularly competitors like Night Owls, were forbidden. Everyone knew the quarterly Ranking Sessions omerta code meant chippy, spiteful, petty bosses could use them, could use them to quietly settle scores, and then return three months later and settle them again, ad infinitum, but none of this included a standing invitation to Jake and his Night Owls pals to pop in and fill their boots. The Experience sub-committee was spreading its tentacles everywhere, influencing events and writing its own rules as it went.

As our discussion flowed back and forth Cliff Wiley staggered over from the interior where he'd been drinking and jawing with fellow high grades and cronies. He had the pink-faced leer and bright shiny face of a man out of practice with the rigours of afternoon drinking. Poking his head in over my shoulder he hailed Tony, before stepping back wildly as he faked shock at recognising me. Moments later as his drunken stagger overbalanced, he fell against me, before finally propping himself up against my back, and grasping my shoulders to stabilise as he invaded my space.

"You still here then?"

Apparently, it was a joke so funny it was worth repeating.

"You still here then? I thought we'd sacked him," he said to Tony gesturing to me by way of explanation. He was laughing at his own remark, as if the conspiracy to dismiss me had been a hilarious game between grown men and I accepted it on those terms.

Never mind, better luck next time, old bean.

"You still here then?" His hands were still grasping my shoulders as he pressed against me. His grinning pink face rocked forward over my shoulder, and he puckered his lips to give me a peck on the cheek to show it was just a joke. A horrible joke. I kept my head down even though I was sorely tempted, I knew one move from me could send him crashing across tables and to the floor.

"No. He's here," Tony replied coldly. His eyes caught mine. "Wiley won't be here long, tolerate him and move on," they said.

279

In this instance Tony was wrong. Cliff pulled up a chair and positioned his frame between myself and Tony, leaning across the table to exclude me from the conversation.

"This is management stuff," he glanced at me as he said it by way of explanation, as though he expected me to leave the adults until he clicked his fingers and called me back. I stayed there sipping my pint, staring at the back of his pink head. From what I could gather, there was nothing new in what Cliff said. It was just the usual office politics garbage about who's trying to do what to whom, and why it should be supported or stopped. I could see Tony showing signs of frustration, his eyebrows furrowed; a sure sign his countdown had begun.

Five minutes before, we were having a quiet pint setting the world straight, and now the world had turned up to turn it back to crooked.

Wiley turned again,

"You still here then?" I wasn't sure if he was still referring to the comedy gold of my near dismissal or his attempt to talk to Tony alone. He turned back to Tony again, and shook his head as he spoke,

"It's funny. All those people worried about being made redundant, and we could save ourselves thousands by sacking the pirate anytime we liked."

Tony looked furious. I was so proud of him. Wiley continued,

"It's funny, I was so sure we'd sack him. I can't think what Gloria was thinking in letting him off." Cliff turned to face me again and grabbed me firmly by the wrist. "Aww, but it's nice to know we didn't sack you captain weirdo." He had that familiar smug grin, "you're like the cost saving and staff vacancy I'm keeping in reserve."

He laughed again, and then finally letting go of my wrist, he reached up and pulled my head forward, and then using it as a fulcrum levered himself up to full height before focussing his best concentration on the bar and lurching on unsteady legs towards his destination like Frank Bruno had just hit him.

If only Frank had.

Tony and I took a deep breath, nursing our pints as we sought to resume our earlier conversation. Tony apologised but there was no need. It wasn't his fault. This was the state of things – the unit and the contract were imploding, staff were worried about their futures, and the managers responsible were drunk in the pub alongside us. These things happen.

We continued to chew over the implications of recent events. It was instinctive behaviour; we were IT workers – solving puzzles was our job. There were certain things we knew to be true. First,, it was clear to us our Tex4Tex managers Cliff and Martin took no interest in the unit they were responsible for. Perhaps they were demoralised as well, but to be honest I don't think they ever saw beyond the end of their own in-tray. If they had ever looked up, they would see what we saw.

Secondly, Night Owls seemed to be involved in everything bad; the offshoring of the work, the public embarrassment, the victimisation, and harassment, the disciplinaries, the poor behaviour, the failed shortcuts, the Experience sub-committee. A few dozen Night Owls seemed to be everywhere. It was like the cuckoo was bossing the nest.

As far as Tony and I could discern Night Owls appeared intent on undermining the unit, the contract, and the company. Service was at rock bottom because of badly planned shortcuts, morale was flatlining because of Jake's behaviour, and in Les Reivers, they had an employee inside our customer drafting complaints to order, gleefully highlighting the problems they themselves were initiating.

Yet none of this told us the Night Owls' motive.

"Fireships!" I blurted out excitedly in a moment of inspiration. Tony gave me a baffled look. It was a look I interpreted as saying, 'oh go on then explain it to me.'

"Fireships. It's an empty wooden vessel loaded with gunpowder and slow fuses. The Elizabethans sent them into the heart of the Spanish Armada as it anchored in port. "

Tony stared patiently at me.

"Kaboom!" I added by way of explanation. "They cause mayhem to the enemy at minimal risk and cost. That's what Jake and Night Owls have done."

I waited for Tony's response but didn't need to wait for long. He pressed his hands together and raised his face to the ceiling.

"You see that, my Lord. Beam me up, jockey. That's how bad things are. The crazy pirate is talking sense these days."

But it was worse than that – more complicated. There was still something, a knot, we couldn't unpick. Some Night Owls contractors worked for the department, and some Night Owls contractors sat with us. How did they all benefit by the collapse of the contract? How can the parasite benefit through the death of the host? It was the question which needed to be asked. What was the Night Owls' motive?

And if we could recognise the problem how did our managers miss it? Our managers should have been trying to fight against Night Owls, to save the company's reputation and future earnings. That's the way we saw it. Our management should've been up in arms, Night Owls were running rings around us, making hay as the team and the contract struggled, yet nothing seemed to happen by way of punishment.

Furthermore, Jake's involvement on the Experience sub-committee seemed to vindicate what we assumed to be their strategy. Yes, if undermining the contract was the Night Owls' plan it had clearly worked, whatever the solution to the contract's difficulties, by gaining access to Experience it appeared the department and tex4tex had now given Night Owls a foot in the door, and a say in future strategy.

"And Experience was meant to investigate the press leaks. Who benefits by the leaks? Not the department, not Tex4tex that's for sure." Tony sat back and took a healthy draught in admiration of his own problem-solving skills. Management politics suited my old friend. I was pleased for him.

"I bet they never searched Night Owls PCs or ramraided their drawers for stolen documents or evidence. It's not Tex property, they wouldn't be allowed. It's too easy for them, the department and Tex4tex burn to the ground while consultants Megson and Reivers just sit back on either side of the fence laughing and feeding the media fire, taking advantage of the crisis they manufactured."

"But why? How do they benefit?

"Let's find out." Tony abruptly picked up our empty glasses and headed to the bar. It was Tony's nature to seek revenge for what happened earlier, but I wasn't going to stop him. He barged between Wiley and his latest drinking buddies and stood there gesticulating at him, moving from one foot to another. He stood over the Scotsman, looking down and poking his finger inches from Cliff's face. I couldn't hear what he said, but I could guess the gist.

Another manager stepped in to try and calm Tony down as others moved Wiley to the safety of the concrete beer garden.

"Having fun?" I asked as Tony returned with our pints.

He smiled, but he'd completely forgotten about the intended purpose of his discussion with Wiley.

"Bostin, bostin. Don't worry about me, pal, my promotion was countersigned by Cliff." He smiled, "I just wanted him to thank him personally and make it clear I have as much respect for him now as I ever did."

"Cheers!" Our pints clinked.

We carried on drinking and talking about the Wolves, and other life stuff more rewarding than work. He told me, the elephant comparator was a one-week toast of the site. Not everyone understood it, but that's what made it so true to those who remembered there had been a time before privatisation.

"It's your brain, cap'n. I swear it can shoot around corners." Our glasses clinked once more. It was so good to be back in the old groove again that I'd temporarily forgotten about the unpleasantness with Cliff Wiley until my unit leader returned. Naively I thought he was here to build a bridge or two, surely no senior manager worth his salt would want to be seen in a drunken argument, but I was to be proved wrong. There was never a chance of an apology.

Cliff Wiley stood wobbling patiently by the table as Tony and I carried on talking and ignoring him. After all this wasn't the military, we didn't have to salute the officers. Besides, our officers had all but lost the contract from an impregnable position, so they didn't deserve respect.

"Yeah, what do you want Cliffie?" Tony broke the stalemate.

"Nothing," said Cliff grinning, and wobbling as he played with his glass, I noticed someone had stuck a pint of orange juice in his hand. Thank God for that.

"I just wanted you two smart-arses to know I've stitched you both up good and proper this time. And those whining women, and that little pest Paula too. Finally, I'm washing my hands of all of you." He motioned to metaphorically wash his hands but spilt the orange juice on his shirt, much to our amusement.

"You'll see," he said as he placed the empty pint glass down and wiped the stain with his cuff. "You'll see," he repeated and slapped a wet palm on the table. And then with a tired, heavy sigh, he reached into his trouser pocket and pulled out a handful of notes and coins he'd no doubt been collecting as change through the afternoon drinking session. After carefully sifting through, he dropped a crumpled twenty pound note on the table.

"Enjoy yourselves, lads. For old times' sake." And then he left us.

Part 4
Mutiny

February 2009

It's strange how something as insignificant as one email amongst hundreds can change your life. The wording dispassionate and non-committal, the font and format adjusted to prescribed company standards. Yes, nothing to see here, move along please madam. Now you might expect some emails to come with clashing symbols, or thundering drums to help you attune to the drama, but they never do. Where is the *Jaws* theme when you need it? Dark and insistent, unsettling, menacing, telling you this was an email you couldn't ignore – giving you a heads-up there's bad news coming. But no, there was no warning. This was an email the same as any other. Mind you, having said that, the title was obviously bad news for some poor sods, and then, after I sniggered and clicked on the link, I realised one of those poor sods was me.

"Staff transfer to Night Owls Consultancy Services
The Department and Tex4Tex are pleased to announce a strengthening of our relationship with Night Owls Consultancy Services in line with the recommendations of the joint working group, Experience. It has been agreed that part of Cliff Wiley's

TSDB Team will be managed directly by Night Owls on a four-year contract initially valued at two hundred million pounds. All the staff on this distribution list are to transfer to Night Owls to manage, support, and develop the work.

"This promises to be a challenging new development for all of us and we trust all of you will do your best to make it a success."

At the bottom of the email were the two signatories: Les Reivers, Night Owls Customer Manager, and Cliff Wiley, Tex4Tex Relationship Manager. In addition, there were multiple attachments; a list of teams and individuals involved, a proposed management structure, a welcome pack, a Q and A. There was also a timeline for consultation, as if there was a point to staff consultation when they'd already tied up the key details with a ribbon and a bow.

Perhaps I imagined it, they say in times of stress it's easy to delude yourself into seeing or hearing what you want, but I could have sworn I heard a collective frustrated groan of disappointment rise from the workplace. There it was the unmistakable empty numbing feeling as bad news settled. Maybe it was the sound of pennies dropping, or careers being put on hold.

I flashed back to Wiley's drunken jeer in Wetherspoons the month before. He must have known then, surely the transfer had been in the pipeline since autumn. He'd stitched us up just like he said he had. Of course, at the time he pretended he was the puppetmaster in control of destinies, although it had been his politicking that enabled Night Owls to take a fifty million pound per annum bite out of Tex4Tex. He'd been outmanoeuvred. Yes, it was Wiley and Monk who had brought Jake into the inner circle of office management, but Jake had played the double agent. Jake had plans of his own. With Reivers's assistance, every petty-minded unit-sized failure became an amplified detail in the wider conspiracy between Night Owls and the department to undermine the Tex4Tex contract. It felt like checkmate.

In other professions, in different eras, workers may have dropped their tools to the floor and streamed out of the building as an instant protest to our treatment, but we were IT workers, and this was information overload. It was in our DNA to keep following the email links, to keep reading and not thinking, to try and solve the puzzle the employers had set us. We immersed ourselves in the detail and ignored the big picture, frantically we clicked from one connection to another, sucking it all in.

Just like my shipmates I wanted to learn as much as I could. To work out if there was a way to escape the trap which would only show itself to me. After a few minutes I gave up. I had to resign myself to the fact that once again I was to be a chattel in a staff transfer. If there was any doubt, the chance to transfer to Night Owls was an offer we couldn't refuse. The answer to final Question 23 of the Q & A made it clear.

"If you reject this opportunity to transfer you will have been deemed by Tex4Tex to have resigned."

Damn them! Damn them all to hell and back. Whoops, there goes your redundancy Captain P. Yes, there goes my pipe and slippers early retirement with the TV remote on my belly and chocolate digestives by the side. I sat there quietly raging, I felt like I was the unluckiest worker in the world, my golden Wonka ticket was blowing down the road again.

Yes, I'm not sure if he even remembered, or maybe the alcohol had wiped the slate clean, but Wiley had told us his version of the truth in Wetherspoons that drunken afternoon. It was possibly the only truth he spoke when he accidentally tipped the drink down his shirt. He was washing his hands of all of us. That's what he'd said. We were the Tex4Tex dirty dozen– Tony the serial moaner, Paula the quiet troublemaker, Pinkbeard the oddball, the women always complaining and wasting his time with their guilt tripping, but also other high maintenance staff Cliff viewed as not being worth his valuable time and energy.

I calculated it was safe to assume Tex4Tex had thrown a mega-deal sized hissy fit at being outplayed and losing work to Night Owls. Employer partnership and contract ecosystem be buggered, no doubt Cliff Wiley had been sanctioned by Tex4Tex to try and score some revenge points. He retaliated to events by jettisoning the staff he considered added no value to his own career. Yes, he was using the transfer to Night

Owls to throw out the trash. A bargain at fifty million pounds a year. Christ, if they had that much money to play with and I was such a nuisance, why didn't they just stop the game playing and make me an offer?

Perhaps I should have been kinder to him, even offer him a round of applause because I suppose this transfer demonstrated Wiley's progress. Once he'd been part of the flotsam and jetsam of the original privatisation, but now he'd manipulated his way to the point where he was now one of those controlling the fate of others. Although still on the scaffold, he'd graduated from condemned man to hangman. I guess he saw it as a worthwhile achievement.

As I mused at this day's turn of events and pondered my limited options, I decided I needed a smoke to break the madness. I lit up at the smoking shelter and Farah came out with Jenny. Jake was already texting them again saying how keen he was to have the 'girls working under him'.

Yes, I bet he was.

If transferring me was an act of spite on Wiley's part, then transferring the women was an act of criminal negligence. Their transfer to Night Owls came with a virtual guarantee of harassment and victimisation. The women were contemplating resigning, all of them, *en masse*. As I listened in, I was struck once again by how my generation had frittered the union's power away. Bad bosses needed to be confronted, not left for others.

Why should the women resign? Surely there needs to be justice.

"If you're happy and you know it, clap your hands!" I turned surprised as Tony appeared at my shoulder, that familiar silly grin on his face. "We should be flattered. It's like the Great Escape where they put all the awkward sods in a POW camp in the middle of nowhere." He slapped me on the back, his gallows humour a brief but welcome distraction to our negative train of thoughts. Whereas I agonised over the exact advice to give the women, Tony spread it on with a paint roller.

"The union has to fight, and Paula has to do what we tell her. If we don't want to transfer to Night Owls, and we don't, then she must come up with a plan to stop it. That's the way the game works, and it always has."

Inspired by Tony I returned freshly optimistic to the office only to see Paula surrounded at her desk, besieged by desperate members, and cheeky, hovering, non-members listening in. She had been trying to get someone from union HQ who would take her call, but she was alone; the lazy bastards had gone to ground. No doubt they would issue a press release in twenty-four hours calling for the contract to be renationalised, and then pop to the pub to pat themselves on the back for completing a tough job well done.

Ironically, the only positive from the announcement had been that the transfer was bad news for Martin because he wasn't to be a part of it. While the rest of us wanted out, he needed to be in. His small people empire would disappear overnight when the transfer went through, and with it his prestige and credibility, or at least the prestige and credibility that travelled with being a bad manager of a poor performing team. From his desk opposite mine, Martin spent his time launching trips to Wiley's office and sauntering outside holding his mobile to his ears. He had thought he was a corporate insider, but he'd just learned the truth – there's a difference between an insider and a sycophant.

Yes, Martin had served his purpose as a patsy for the schemers, and it was time for him to move on or accept diminished responsibilities. Finally, after months of directions from off stage, it would be confirmed Jake was to be our future team leader inside Night Owls. By the morning's end the porters brought the crates in one by one, Jake was moving into the same single-occupancy room Martin had tried to obtain for himself. Each clatter of the hardened plastic crates was a noisy reminder of Martin's lost opportunity.

I had always found it so hard to recognise his moods, but I suppose Martin must've have been angry and disappointed. Perhaps that's why he tried to break-up the noisy, distracting conversations taking place at Paula's desk. He marched over to confront her.

"We still have work to do. Get back to work or face the consequences," he reminded everyone.

Paula was waiting.

"It says here in answer to Q13 – 'our disciplinary records don't transfer'."

"Yes. So what? So? So?" he smiled condescendingly at the union dinosaur. Paula just smiled back sweetly.

"So, fuck off then!" she replied to loud cheers as he stormed red-faced back to his desk.

Paula was right of course. we didn't have to hide our feelings. She had given me an idea. Martin couldn't harm us any more. I know, comrades, cruelty is not usually my way, but I couldn't resist celebrating. The way I saw it this leader had dragged me down to his level, and I had come to detest this childish point scorer.

I broke our man-silence and shouted a loud girlish whisper above the hum of conversation and computers.

"Martin... Martin..." despite his bout of deafness I persisted. "Martin...perhaps you could ask your friend Les Reivers to make a complaint for you?"

He didn't look up or reply, the top of his head was partly hidden by the screen between us, but I saw it was shaking as though he was talking to himself, and I could hear the angry clattering of fingers on computer keys. Within thirty seconds my email pinged. I'd finally provoked him after months of trying.

"I hope you and that bitch Paula are happy working for Night Owls. The same for those tarts dressing like whores and complaining when men fancy them, Lol!

Ha!

I savoured the moment. Gotcha! I thought. Gotcha! Finally, I gotcha. You pedant bastard. I gotcha. I wanted to punch the air like I'd tapped in a sitter from five yards out. It was too easy. I simply followed Paula's advice from my own disciplinary troubles. My fingers danced in delight on the keyboard.

"Martin, I am disappointed by the tone of your email towards my current and future colleagues. Whilst I am sure you're frustrated to not to be part of this exciting new challenge, I hope in your own small way you will overcome your personal disappointment and try your best to make our endeavour a success for Tex4Tex."

I gleefully copied the email to Paula, Wiley, Roger, Tony, the women, the teams, and finally Gloria in HR. She can deal with his sexist attitudes.

In a better mood I stood to leave for another smoke and to quietly celebrate my moment of victory over him. I would be able to gloat properly alone. Only briefly though, I texted Tony to ensure I could repeat the pleasure of gloating alone, but in company. And later I would repeat the process with Farah. Desperate though the announcement was, I felt no pressure, I wouldn't have to face my new employer for a while yet. As far as I was concerned the period of consultation constituted an unofficial holiday period. There was no benefit in working hard for a departing employer. I may as well chill out and make the best of it.

Opposite me, Martin had read my email and he also stood to leave, probably to get some fresh air and contemplate the cost of his error. He followed me down the room almost pace for pace one step behind. It was creepy – we would go on shunning each other to the last. I opened the door for him. "Thank you," he politely replied on autopilot.

Together we tramped silently down the corridor until we reached the foyer and left the building via different exits.

March 2009 (day 1)

First impressions are important.

You'll remember when I was privatised management convened a shiny Tex4Tex gathering at the Telford International Centre. The meeting provided an opportunity for my new employer to strut its stuff in the shop window – 'hello small town civil servants, welcome to the twenty-first century'. No expense was to be spared, and nothing would be allowed to go wrong. Fair play, they had made every effort to impress – flashing lights, Tina Turner, gizmos, cameras, wandering microphones and best of all a buffet. A grand one– sandwiches, rolls, sausage rolls, quiches, and there were cakes too, cakes that needed slicing, cakes which got trapped in the beard, cakes that got messy. Yes, real cakes not just the usual defrosting buns sealed in plastic. Not that I was tempted but there was also fruit! 'Froot for the La-deez'. It was all very sophisticated and high class.

Now this commitment to excellence in the field of buffet may not have persuaded me to surrender my heart upon privatisation, but I appreciated the effort to win me over. It made me feel wanted and temporarily forget I'd been forced to transfer. It was fair to say that in comparison my second forced change of employer would be much more downtown Shropshire. Our new suitor wasn't even going to try and impress.

The introduction to Night Owls was to take place inside the familiar low-tech surroundings of the social club with hard copy handouts to support a six slide PowerPoint presentation. Six slides! Take a moment to think about it. I don't want to sound like a grumble-guts, but six slides didn't seem like a lot of presentation for a change in employer with multiple sets of terms and pensions to consider. Surely six slides at the very least would need a tiny font and a magnifying glass for every transferee. To make matters worse, I was experienced enough to anticipate the first slide would be 'Welcome' and the last would be entitled "Questions?"

As for the buffet my mind raced ahead, I expected an approach of similar calibre and therefore confidently predicted limp tuna and cucumber sandwiches still in their packing, an imposed ration of one cupcake per person, and resting by the door an Asda carrier bag to put the rubbish in. I anticipated our meeting would be accompanied at its end by a request from management that we 'leave the room as you find it.' It all felt demoralising, like we former civil servants were going back to an underfunded future. All those millions made from our labours in Tex4Tex, and we'd still been relegated from the Premier League to the Blue Square North Conference.

On the way to the presentation Tony and I had dawdled down the car park steps together in the time-honoured manner of office workers heading to a meeting they didn't want to arrive at – every stiff step was an effort and accompanied by either a groan or a sigh. Yet despite our lack of pace my chest was leaping like it had when Martin had been trying to sack me. Maybe it was a few coffees too many, maybe it was even my age, but there was a growing sweat across my forehead, and I felt uncomfortable and constricted.

Tension – I was beginning to recognise the symptoms.

I guess you might assume if I was being transferred for the second time then I should have been calmer than the first, but that wasn't the case. During the first transfer I had the fears of the unknown, they were shrouded in mystery, but by the second transfer I knew only too well. I even gave my fears names; Megson, Reivers and Night Owls. And of course, second time around, I was the most experienced member of staff facing transfer. I didn't like it, but I knew I couldn't sit at the back and leave others to fight my corner for me. I felt pressured to intervene, to take a lead, to act like the captain they said I was.

Idling by my side, Tony was indignant. I knew I could rely on him to say something. He angrily kicked loose gravel into the bushes every few steps. All the effort to energise his flagging career, to get promoted and in line for pay rises, and this was how Wiley rewarded him. The world was having a joke at Tony's expense. I sensed we were all going to feel his pain again, but rather than resign myself to it, today I hoped Tony would explode with righteous anger at the injustice and bring the transfer down like Samson and the Temple.

As for the forces of liberation, Paula had assembled a plan, just like Tony said she would. To my mind, it wasn't much of a plan though, 'we just have to split them up and then all pile in' was the best she came up with. If that was the best the union could offer, then we were probably doomed. As I said to you it wasn't much of a plan really, but I was too polite to say it to her directly. Talk of the devil she was stood on the steps impeding the access to the social club. I noticed she was wearing her fetching beanie with the panda ears; an unlikely outfit to wear to ferment dissent, not exactly Fidel in military fatigues. By her feet, a Tesco bag with leaflets and recruitment forms she was ready to hand out like bad news was manna from heaven for a struggling workplace union. And of course, it was and always has been.

She smiled when we reached her, bashing her mittens together and hopping excitedly from one foot to the other, keeping moving in the spring morning chill.

"Remember. I need you two reprobates to show some leadership for once," she chided. As she said it, she slipped a pair of encouraging arms around us to create a three-person cuddle. "The old ones must set the tone for the youngsters." She broke away two Mississippis later and pointed her mittens towards Jenny, Farah, and Louise gliding smoothly across the car park towards us. "You have to do it for them. We probably only have one shot. If we light a bonfire the union must come."

I put my hand in my jacket pocket and produced a box of matches to show I was prepared. Then I moved past her and once inside I positioned myself at the end of the second and final row of two lines of ten green plastic chairs at an access point for the buffet. If there was going to be a rush, then I was going to make sure I got there first, or at least before Toby Mullett began his human dustbin truck routine.

The managers were already here of course, and they stood chatting at the sides of a long rectangular table which was to provide the border of their territory when the meeting started. What is it about men and gadgets? They were taking turns, fiddling unconsciously with the projector which for the next hour would be their property – constantly touching and rubbing the poor thing like it was Aladdin's lamp, or something altogether more inappropriate. Weirdness aside, it was all amiable enough, the two sets of feuding alphas were joshing and jawing pleasantly together as they took it in turns to fondle the projector. All the time the ones denied access compensated by nervously playing with handouts and laptops checking everything was in hand. Yes, Les Reivers, and Jake Megson were chummily greeting Martin Monk and Cliff Wiley as though they didn't see each other every day in the office. Gloria was there too, but she stood aside from the others while compulsively scrolling down her phone. HR weren't yet quite a part of the macho world of transfer management, the men wouldn't require them until the formalities were complete and the cattle needed to be prodded onto the trucks.

The whole scene was curiously genteel, and polite, and therefore unnatural – out of keeping with the usual chaos the managers engineered. I had to pinch myself to remember the only reason the meeting had been scheduled for the social club was because it was nominally off-site and therefore neutral territory. Gloria had passed this information on to the transferees at a previous briefing, a Tex4Tex briefing, where we were allowed an early insight on the current employer's true feelings about losing the work. You see it was to be 'their' meeting, a Night Owls meeting, and Tex4Tex would refuse to allow 'them' access to 'our' staff at 'our' desks. Given the rationale for the transfer was a 'further enhancement of the harmonious employer ecosystem' supporting the department this publicly declared pettiness and mistrust between eco-partners seemed a strange, if long overdue, turn of events.

There again the whole trip had been strange. Tex4Tex had done nothing but accommodate Night Owls for the last twelve months. The bad publicity and political interference seemed to have cowed the company, it had become unusually passive and inactive. And weakness invites aggression, isn't that what they say? Yes, losing the work may have been unfair on the workers but it served justice on our employer. Previously Gloria had accepted Reivers's complaints about our staff at face value, and of course, thanks to Wiley stifling the harassment claims Jake had been given freedom inside the contract to manipulate the levers of power. And yet now, after all this time, at the bitter end, when their profits were affected and they were losing work, Tex4Tex had finally come to their senses and decided to recognise Night Owls as a manipulative rival and competitor and treat it accordingly. Hallelujah!

Things started making some sense to me now, as Paula said we had to split up the managers and show this transfer for the sham politics it was. It would probably be our only chance to do…to do whatever it was we were going to do. You see I hadn't thought that bit through. I wanted to protest, I didn't want to transfer, but frankly I didn't want to stay with Tex4Tex either. Yes I didn't really have a preferred outcome unless it was the one involving Dr Who and the Tardis, and a return to the civil service.

I took my seat.

Now timeliness is a virtue of I.T. workers, even for dreaded meetings we arrived on time. I sat there like a man waiting for the firing squad to position themselves hoping a last-minute reprieve would arrive. But it didn't. After vital minutes of physical stimulation, the projector tripped into brightness and Les Reivers tapped his pen on the table to bring the meeting together. We sat down with the customary clatter of chair legs across the floor. Reivers was symbolically in charge of the meeting, it was after all 'their' meeting as Gloria had put it, and he started off saying how much he was looking forward to working with us. He was incredibly pleased Jake was back to continue building on his good work with the team. Jake responded with a grin, and a wink towards the audience. Yes, it was extremely exciting – a breakthrough for Night Owls in its relationship with the department, "and Tex4Tex as well" Les added as an afterthought. He said Night Owls had been working to this end for at least eighteen months.

"That's about when the leaks to the press started then," Tony chipped in from the audience. Gloria smiled and nodded, but Les wasn't to be distracted from his speech.

"And thanks go to Cliff and Gloria for agreeing to consider Martin Monk's special request and cross our fingers we're pleased to announce that all the paperwork will soon be completed, and Martin will be with us to continue his work with you, except inside Night Owls from day one."

I don't know if he expected applause at the formal announcement of Night Owls' victory, but there was only a toe-curling moment of silence.

"I hope I'm not breaking any confidences," Les laughed, nervously looking around.

Yes, it was absolutely frigging hilarious. Good grief. Leaving Martin behind was one of the few benefits of the transfer. Next to me, Tony again vented automatically,

"Is this a fuckin' wind-up? Is this April Fool's Day already?"

There was a low murmur of support from the attendees.

Wiley patted his open arms to the table to try and quieten the room down whilst asserting himself as the centre of attention. He was trying to help whilst simultaneously usurping the authority of Reivers. Despite Wiley's intervention Tony refused to quieten down, I looked at my pocket watch and nudged Paula. Kicking off inside a minute was a new record for Tony, and it felt like he was going to complete nil-sixty mph in ten seconds.

"All this rubbish about Tex4tex Values and Ethics and you're sending us to that bunch of gangsters." Tony was commendably brave, pointing towards his future employers. He paused for breath.

"You can't transfer us, it's against your own policies."

"And why can't we transfer you? What policies are these?" Wiley replied calmly cutting across Reivers again, and temporarily staring Tony into silence. Tony sat back and began muttering something sweary before he turned to the table behind and angrily ripped the plastic cover off a platter of crisps. After taking a handful he passed the tray across the row and began chomping noisily whilst staring at the managers.

As soon as Reivers restarted on the Welcome slide, Paula was on her feet. She ignored the men and directly addressed Gloria, who was after all the HR representative, the keepers of the Value Codes, and Paula reminded the audience Tony was right, Night Owls were not a fit employer, the harassment claims were unresolved, and 'we' were seeking to send the women to their harasser. She pointed to Jake, who offered another contented grin and a shrug at his notoriety.

Alongside him Wiley merely shook his head, but across their row Gloria initially looked aghast at the accusation she was facilitating harassment and turned heatedly to engage with Paula. Gloria's body language implied she knew nothing of the complaints, which was surely a barefaced lie, unless of course Wiley had failed to report them. Directly in front of me the young women leaned forward taking a keener interest as Gloria continued her act of silence.

"There were no complaints," Wiley continued. "Well, nothing ever became formal. Or at least worthy of formal investigation," he turned and assured Gloria. "As you well know Paula, it was just hearsay and gossip." He smiled at his own slipperiness.

"You lying pikey bastard."

It was Tony who said it. Farah was on her feet. The others joined her.

'You're a liar!"

Farah pulled her phone out. She began scrolling through her messages from Jake before reading a selection out to the audience; "in a month's time you'll be my toy"; "I want to see you working under me."

And then Louise took over,

"Here's another one from Jake,' she said, "it says 'don't worry I'll look after you', 'If you do good for me, I'll make sure you're rewarded. Xxxxx."

The women stayed on their feet. They weren't going to sit until they received a reply.

We were still on PowerPoint slide one, and the meeting was capsizing. It was going under. At the table our chairman Reivers momentarily appeared to be losing interest. He petulantly threw down his script, and leaned back in his chair, his head as close to resting against the drop-down screen with its "Welcome to Night Owls" invitation. He ran his fingers through his non-existent hairline and was eying his potential new recruits with contempt. Was two hundred million pounds enough to take on this set of losers? The management team was breaking into small groups in front of our eyes. Les had taken his phone out and was inspecting it, Gloria was trying to engage with Paula, Wiley and Tony were jabbing fingers at each other, Jake was laughing, and the women were shouting at him.

While chaos reigned, only Martin was unmoved, as he sat there taking notes. It was the only thing making sense, after all he'd volunteered to join this madhouse.

I felt like it was now my turn to throw myself against their defences.

As you can imagine this chaos had calmed me down. I had overcome my nerves and was anxious to contribute to this free-for-all, add my thoughts to the shambles, and do my bit for the union movement. I rose slowly and carefully removed my watch from its waistcoat pocket hideaway to create a bit of theatre before clearing my throat. By my side Paula shushed the young women to create some quiet for me and urged them to sit. "Old man alert," she said as she patted the chair seats. I savoured the silence for a moment. It had taken my entire adult life, but I was starting to believe I could get to enjoy this 'taking part' lark.

"Modern management," I began. I shook my head and smiled, hoping for a look where I appeared to be admonishing a young puppy. Turning to face the young women in front of me, and those colleagues sat alongside me in the second row of hideous plastic chairs, the words started rolling.

"You know I joined the union on my first day as a civil servant because that's what we did back then. It seems now like a different age, like something out of a history book. You see being a civil servant was a dull job, but a safe job. It was as everyone knew, a job for life. That was the deal, we weren't well paid, but our jobs were secure, and we were looked after. I was guaranteed entry to a final salary pension scheme; I had guaranteed pay rises and overtime. I always thought things would inevitably keep getting better for everyone, nothing spectacular though, each year paid a little more, each year a little better treatment, but life has proved me wrong. For the new starters things are only getting worse. You young workers," I looked directly at Calum here, "you'll probably never have the terms I started out with on day one even if you stay here until you're sixty, or seventy, or however long they make you work."

I shook my head sadly. "You see New Labour has finished the work Thatcher started. I doubt our class will ever forgive them."

I sensed management's impatience with my social history lesson, to them my insight was irrelevant, Reivers was tapping Wiley's elbow, but Wiley just turned and grinned, as though he was saying 'yours to deal with pal. Welcome to my world.'

"I'm sorry we know you're in the union, we get that, but who are you?" I didn't answer Reivers, I just carried on regardless leaving him exasperated turning to remonstrate with Wiley again.

"You know, a few months ago, I sat next to Luke when Gloria and Martin dismissed him and the other male apprentices. The dismissal was supported by complaints made by you, Les Reivers...by Night Owls."

I saw him shake his head. Alongside me, Paula shouted and pointed, "Yes, you did."

"You conspired with Jake and Martin to sack a teenager in his first job." I faced my audience to ask them a question, "What kind of man does that? What's more, what kind of man does that, and doesn't even remember? How can this be allowed to happen in the twenty-first century?" I felt my audience approve of the message. I was the only one speaking, all eyes were on me.

"It seems to me that in Britain today the only justification you need is whether you can get away with it."

Les Reivers was still shaking his head, angrily now, but I continued regardless, I'd gone too far to back down now.

"And Les, you also made complaints, absolute fabrications against me as well. I bet you didn't give a thought to any consequence except to your own self-interest. You've had a hand in destabilising my team and my employer, and my best guess is that you and your colleagues are the ones leaking to the papers, because I don't know who else benefits." I opened my body up to my colleagues.

"Since Night Owls arrived, things have only got worse."

Alongside me heads nodded in agreement, even Gloria was taking notes. I looked up and heard the top table creaking as managers shifted in the plastic seats, perhaps considering their individual responses to my accusation.

"I think my friend Tony is right. We are breaking our so-called Tex4Tex values because to be honest if we weren't then our values are worthless." I heard a ripple of applause, but I struggled to end my contribution as I was momentarily dumbstruck by the ludicrous irony that Captain Pinkbeard could use Tex4Tex's corporate values for his own purpose. I was about to laugh, I was about to flounder, but then the words came.

"Privatisation was a good adventure to begin with, but it seems to me we've been sailing too close to the edge of the world for a while now." I raised my right arm with its tell-tale Punks Not Dead tattoo showing defiantly, and I pointed it towards the managers before finishing slowly and deliberately.

"And here… there… be… Dragons!"

My comrades and colleagues cheered whilst the managers sat stony faced staring out at their current or future staff. Wiley tried to gain control of the meeting again, asking people to calm down. If only there had been a microphone, he and Reivers would have been rolling on the floor fighting over it, but Reivers brushed him aside this time and shouted at me directly.

"I'm sorry, I'll repeat my question for you as you're clearly hard of thinking. Who are you?"

He smiled at his own clever wordplay.

The years of frustration, all those evasive smart-arse managers knocking me back and taking the piss, the familiar feeling of victimhood and powerlessness, those years welled upside me now, and sure enough the dormant volcano blew its top.

"I'm Captain Pinkbeard," I roared back instinctively. "You tried to sack me! I thought I had a stalker when you made so many complaints. And yet you don't remember me. You don't know who I am! Was the attempt to dismiss me just a joke to you? Was it a funny story for the jolly boys at the golf club?"

I broke away, to savour the silence again, enjoying the moment as everyone focussed on me. I was in full flow now. This speech had been years in the making without me even knowing.

"You want to know who I am. Well, I've worked here for twenty years. That's who I am. A press-ganged public servant in the private sector. That's who I am. This town is where I live, and always have. That's who I am. This place is where I work, and always have. That's who I am. This place, yes, this place is where I belong whoever my latest transient employer might be. You see the question is not who am I but who are you? All of you. And what is your game?"

I rested back in my seat and savoured the din of chairs scraping across the floor as others rose to replace me. At the front, the managers once again tried to calm us down and restore order, but the stand-off continued as half a dozen people were on their feet shouting at the top table.

I can't explain my actions here, although one day I surely must account for them. It just felt right is the best explanation I have. I casually leaned back in my chair and reached around for the cupcakes. I unwrapped the base, and then bit into the chocolate. I wanted to relax, and be seen to relax, amongst this broken meeting, but my plan didn't work, there was so much happening. I was too excited. As soon as I started trying to wind down, I realised I wanted to be back on my feet again with my comrades. It was instinctive I swear, but I realised I couldn't simultaneously mutiny and delight in a choccy treat, so for want of a better idea I gently lobbed the half-eaten cupcake towards the managers' table. You'd have thought it had exploded like a hand-grenade the way they stood and moved their chairs away.

More of the buffet was thrown as the managers took fright and looked to escape.

Tony was on his feet and ran to the door as fast as his creaking bones could carry him. He pulled the door open, and the distant rumble of traffic entered.

"Ten seconds. Ten fucking seconds!" Tony yelled to the non-committed to leave the room. And then, after they had bundled disorganised out of the room, Calum with some help from myself and Tony unplugged the vending machine and slid it across the door that provided access to the Tex4Tex car park.

And then we waited.

Silence.

And then we laughed at the relief of finally having done the right thing, at just having done something, and finally snapped back.

Unsurprisingly, it was Tony who broke the silence.

"Paula, just to let you know. If one of those PowerPoint slides says they're going to pay me a million pounds on transfer to Night Owls, I'm going to tear your fucking head off."

March 2009 (day 2)

I'm sure you know me by now and you've guessed who I am. Yes, it was that photograph which made me famous wasn't it? Well, when I say famous, of course I was never proper Hollywood world famous, but I was world famous in Shropshire certainly, at least for a while. And you know, all these weeks later, when the dust has settled and the world has turned, complete strangers still recognise me, and sometimes if I'm quietly minding my own business in the queue at the bus station or the chip shop, they will approach asking me questions about that turbulent week. They feel like they know me, but if they had truly known me, then they would have known not to bother me.

For it was nothing I did really, as you know I like to be left in peace, I don't seek attention. No, I hadn't sought fame, I wasn't one of those narcissist reality TV wankers. It was just the picture. Iconic is the word they use. You see there was a photographer kneeling on the bonnet of his Rover in the visitors car park, and he took the snapshot capturing our occupation. There I was performing look-out duties from the flat roof of the social club staring at the weird man balancing precariously on his car when I guess the shutter clicked, and he captured me forever. And fair play, he captured me well, my pipe was in my right hand, a bottle of Manns (circa1982) we'd found behind the bar in the other, a pocket watch chain dangling out of waistcoat. My dark trousers had ridden up above my Docs, plastic cutlass across my hips, and all of it wrapped inside an open black threequarter length coat. Behind my beard dark eyes stared with intensity directly into the camera. And on my head, in pride of place, a brown derby freshly decorated in union badges which failed to keep out the drizzle.

Captured by the artist, I was a modern curiosity, Canute the Great railing against the inevitable tide of history. Yes, at the heart of this dullest of the dull story inside the twilight zone of outsourced government services was an imposter from another time. You could say I was the key which opened the door. I imagine the right-wing journalists loved their own interpretation of our story. In their eyes we were noble savages from small town England raging against the high-handed New Labour metropolitan elite. By accident I'd become an unlikely godsend for the patronising London press with a story to file in a quiet news week.

"Union rebels challenge department over transfer" was one headline accompanying my picture on the Tuesday morning. "Telford says no to Whitehall" was another. But my favourite must always be the *Daily Mail's* article on our dispute. It is the only copy of that wretched newspaper I ever bought, and it hangs framed in glass on our landing wall.

"Union Pirate kidnaps women."

Paula didn't appear to mind me stealing her glory. She applauded the irony of a dispute involving young women where the media craved a picture of the old white man. Besides, the picture took her dispute from local to national press. She'd hit the motherlode. We were the biggest news story in Shropshire since T'Pau stormed to the *Top of the Pops*. Paula laughed. She said I'd given the dispute sex appeal.

"You just sit there looking pretty darling, but don't let the bad men take advantage of you," she joked as she edited another press release, "the *Loaded* cover shoot will have to wait."

It was all so unreal, for a brief period, only a matter of hours maybe, everyone wanted to know our story.

And yet only twenty-four hours before we had been dutifully following instructions to attend the social club for an update on our involuntary transfer. No one had wanted to know our story then, even our closest colleagues shrugged our cause as hopeless. What we thought about the transfer wasn't important, our feelings were irrelevant. Maybe it won't be too bad, stop moaning and get on with it, was the mantra we heard. Nothing was expected of us, except our acquiescence.

Yes, we'd surprised everyone even ourselves. The occupation hadn't been planned it was spontaneous. Organic. It just happened.

In a brief pause following the departure of the managers and the non-committed Paula called us together. Already the enormity of what we'd done had begun to sink in and I guess she must have sensed the anxiety. I looked around; it was myself, Paula, Tony, Calum, Farah, Louise, and Jenny in our corner, and Tex4Tex, Night Owls and the British state in the other. If I were a betting man I'd say the odds were against us, but as Paula talked, we all took heart from her streetwise home truths, and laughed; it would look ridiculous if we just opened the doors and backed down now. If we did, we'd probably get sacked for nothing, after all our impromptu strike was probably illegal anyway. No, we'd made our protest and taken our stand, and we had to see it through. And besides the best outcome of backing down could only mean surrender and transferring voluntarily to Night Owls as well as letting Wiley and Tex4Tex off the hook for the way they had treated us.

So yes, it was complicated, and we were in a tight spot, but we weren't the only ones. The way Paula explained the situation, our employers' prosperity was built on the myth they were infallible and always one step ahead. Industrial disputes were for the dim-witted public sector not the go-getting pelvic thrusters of private enterprise like Tex4Tex. Our protest was a humiliation for them, we were publicly rejecting them and all their profit margins and mission goals. Furthermore, Paula added, given time we'd highlight an unspoken truth, despite all their statements of partnership, our employers weren't just in dispute with us, they were permanently in dispute with each other. We laughed out loud and stamped our feet in approval when Paula asked us to visualise the finger pointing, blame gaming and shoulder sloping taking place in rival boardrooms.

Paula summarised, "We're the mouse that terrified the elephant." Our position wasn't as weak as it appeared. By making our protest it had substantially improved. Yes, we were in limbo, but we could take comfort, it was better than being inside Night Owls. Unlike the employers we could wait on events, we didn't need to pretend to be in control, and whilst waiting and standing together, we had to have faith we would gain a moment to shape our own futures. And of course, Paula said, we could count ourselves lucky our doomed transition meeting had broken down at the social club. The club had toilets, hot and cold running water, showers assigned for use by the cyclists and lunchtime runners, and behind the bar literally weeks of peanuts, crisps, and chocolate bars as well as bottled beers the social club had officially stopped serving years before. Theoretically we could survive on this diet for weeks. We had nothing to fear but fear itself.

Well almost. Nothing to fear but fear, and type Two diabetes.

The first rat-a-tat-tat knocking on the door startled us and came from the internal car park side shortly after our transfer meeting collapsed. Initially we didn't open for fear we were going to be physically forced out, but after taking in a deep breath, Paula leant out of the window, and then after Calum and a wheezing Tony had hauled the vending machine away, we opened the door.

As agreed with Paula, Matt, the security guard, mounted the steps and stood in the doorway. He said he needed to confirm how many of us there were, we were all safe and we were all there voluntarily. And then mission accomplished, he smiled and wished us luck, before he turned and retreated twenty yards. Once there he held his position while reporting into his walkie-talkie.

By my side I saw Paula clench her fist. For those initial hours it felt like every minute passing made us more credible and strengthened her hand. What we would come to accept as normality began. We would spend hours sitting on the chairs and sofas making our plans, refusing to acknowledge the boredom, focussing on what we wanted and what we feared. We all wanted to stop the transfer to Night Owls, but how could we go back to working for Martin or Cliff Wiley as if nothing had happened? It was a puzzle we were struggling to resolve.

On Monday afternoon I picked up my chair, hat, coat, and cutlass and took up my guard duties on the roof to ensure we weren't surprised by visitors again. I wanted both to play my part and keep my solitude. While others fretted over victory, I was just content to belong. I had been standing on the sidelines for twenty years passing comments on the efforts of others, and now finally I was a part of something that had made me proud. We had done this, we were busting the tank tracks of management, why would I want to reset the dial? I wanted to see things through to the end however it may end.

My lookout duties were three hundred and sixty degrees. I had two car parks to cover, and the next significant event happened early on Tuesday morning on the inward side. By now the first wave of union press releases had hit the media and either been picked up or ignored. I stamped my feet on the roof as I saw Roger approaching past our one-man security guard cordon. He was waving a white hankie in his right hand and had a smile on his face. As my eyes followed him, I imagined I could hear Tony bemoaning his luck at having to move the vending machine again.

A minute later, after calling me down from the roof, Paula agreed to let Roger in to address the mutineers. Despite the tense situation, Roger appeared as relaxed and low key as ever. I guessed Gloria and Texas Rose had chosen him as an intermediary to help with the corporate clean-up operation, and in doing so had wisely decided to keep our direct managers away. It was a good decision, he was our Tex4Tex Red Adair, firefighting was what he was good at.

He pulled up a chair and calmly took out his glossy Tex4Tex executive notebook with its personalised gold lettering from his shoulder bag. He said there was an official statement the lawyers had instructed him to read to us.

"It's got bullet points," he said with a smile, "with real bullets. Texan bullets dipped in chilli."

He cleared his throat.

"Tex4Tex needs to remind you that however you feel about your transfer to Night Owls, you are still our employees. As good faith we will keep your electricity and water running until this illegal dispute is resolved. You are not in dispute with Tex4Tex, it is not our decision to transfer you. It is the department that is handing the work to Night Owls, there is nothing we can do about that. You may be in dispute with the department, you may be in dispute with Night Owls, but we repeat you are not in dispute with Tex4Tex. You are causing uncertainty and damaging your colleagues' morale. We ask you to end this dispute immediately and then, and only then, will we jointly consider the next appropriate steps."

There was silence when he finished. Disappointment.

What Roger had read was nonsense, of course Tex4Tex could intervene, they didn't have to cooperate. They were a multi-national and had plenty of weight to throw around. Even if they didn't care for us, they should have been as angry at losing the work as we were at being transferred. We expected better from Roger, and initially at least it was hard to separate the messenger from the message. Twenty-four hours without contact, and all we got was a statement of corporate self-pity. Yes, the Texans hadn't given me a pay increase for years, and now they had the cheek to ask me to consider their feelings and capitulate to the inevitable transfer.

Perhaps Roger sensed our mood, perhaps he knew how the message would land, he was intuitive like that. So, he did the HR thing. He put his official Tex4Tex executive notepad back in his shoulder bag, before casually reaching for a different, battered conventional unlined notepad.

"Right then, so, what's your story? What are you doing here?"

The women spoke at once in a tsunami of emotion, firing accusations at Jake, Martin and Cliff Wiley, reading aloud the texts they'd received, and stating what Wiley and Monk had not done on their behalf, and how Wiley in particular had suppressed their complaints. After 15 minutes of unrelenting aggression and accusation Farah spoke.

"Paula is the only one in Tex4Tex who ever listened to us and believed us, despite all the evidence in our favour. We're not liars like they say we are." And then she cried in frustration as the others gathered around to support her.

"Wow!" was all Roger said initially; the women had left him in no doubt what they saw the dispute was about. And then instinctively the manager within must have kicked in. "Thank you. That's useful for me to know. And Calum you've been quiet, why are you here?

"Jake is only interested in shagging the women. He ignores me and he always has done. I can't get a look in. I used to like working for Tex4Tex, but Martin and Jake have ruined it. I think I'm only on the list for Night Owls because I asked Wiley for a transfer and in giving my reason, I demonstrated I knew about his cover-up of the harassment. I requested a transfer, and he transferred me to Night Owls. It's the kind of outcome he'd see as funny."

Roger looked frustrated with him. "Why didn't you talk to me? Just because I'm not your leader, I still could've helped."

Calum shrugged. "It's just all bad. No offence, but they got rid of you too."

Roger couldn't help himself; he gave a rueful smile and a nod in agreement.

"And what about you two sat there quietly? What's this I hear about the leaks?" Roger looked towards me, but as ever Tony needed no invitation and jumped in. He was going to make sure he grabbed whatever glory was going.

"It's just something we think should be checked. The leaks about failures. Jake was hired to fix those failures. The leaks about offshoring. Jake's boys offshored under his authority. The leaks from the Experience sub-committee. Jake was on the Experience sub-committee. We think the reason the company never caught the culprits was because they were looking inside Tex4Tex, and Jake's not solely on our network. The chances are that somewhere he'll have a personal email account he transfers data to, and from there he passes confidential material out. Night Owls, and maybe with the department's help, were leaking to destabilise the contract so they can sweep up the offcuts."

Then there was quiet again. Roger looked at Tony. He seemed impressed, possibly with himself. It was a look saying, I did the company a good turn the day I promoted Tony.

"And what about you, Jack? I understand Captain Pinkbeard found his voice in the meeting." He was smiling. "I wish I'd been there to hear it."

I was embarrassed. I gave a modest response.

"It's like everyone said. The transfer is a farce, Martin, Jake, and Reivers tried to get me sacked before. I expect they'll finish the job if I transfer."

Roger paused.

"Okay, but, and think properly here, did anything else happen after you spoke? They said people were throwing things at them."

"Just a cupcake," I laughed, incredulous at the stupid question and turned to a horrified looking Paula. She'd guessed something I'd missed.

March 2009 (day 3)

By Wednesday it was apparent we had unlikely allies in unexpected places. In faraway Dallas, HQ search engines were churning, and mentions of sexual harassment, contract mismanagement, trade unions and Tex4Tex in the same article sounded the alarm bells. And that photo of a bearded pirate, a Tex4Texer no less, drinking and smoking, waving a cutlass at the camera followed the company around. Yes, for twenty-four hours if you put Tex4Tex into Google up popped my picture. The horror! It was shocking. The barbarians were inside the gates and on the payroll. I imagined with satisfaction that the team of Amish Ultras I presumed wrote our corporate codes of behaviour policies were thrashing their backs with twigs in horror at the thought I may share with their employer.

So, gather round shipmates for these my friends are the vagaries of capitalism. A corrupt incompetent boardroom and the Stock Market held its nerve, a failing high profile contract and the share price kept steady, redundancies and a pay freeze were both met stoically. Our investors would ride out the global collapse of the finance system, but that photograph of a striking employee, the slightest whiff of a fightback, and suddenly the skies over Wall Street darkened with money men chucking themselves out of windows to escape the ignominy.

Against my best intentions I had become a catalyst. I didn't witness it for myself for I was engaged on my sentry duty, but now I know our contract managers came under pressure from above to intervene and end this dispute. Tex4Tex needed distance to preserve its reputation. The company now sought to present itself as a mediator honestly trying to resolve a problem caused by the failings of the department and Night Owls. And of course, there was an element of truth in their story.

Roger had become an hourly traveller to the club during day two, 'just touching base' acting as an arbitrator between officers and mutineers. He was a sympathetic face. He allowed us lap-tops so we could follow the news we were creating, and he was an honest touchstone we could use to keep up to date with the gossip inside Tex4Tex where we were led to believe calmer pragmatic heads were in a battle with Tex4Tex hardliners who wanted to cut our electricity. Our conversations with Roger led to a broad statement of aims we needed to resolve the dispute covering the immediate abandonment of the transfer to Night Owls; a commitment from Tex4Tex to tackle bullying; no victimisation of strikers; an end to sexual harassment and properly funded pay reviews.

Deciding what we wanted was the easy part. The tactical hard bit would be getting the seniors to realise their middle managers had run amok and weren't following policies. It seemed unlikely, but we needed a Tex4Tex big hitter to adopt our cause, bash heads together, and then cut their own managers adrift.

And then late evening on Wednesday, Day Three we had our breakthrough. At about nine p.m., after most of the day workers had departed Texas Rose arrived with Roger. Let us not forget, Rose was head of HR, she was the keeper of the policies we claimed the company had ignored. Roger must have prepped her, she'd dressed down for the occasion and dropped her intimidating padded shoulder power-dressing style for a casual sweatshirt and kegs, and when she spoke, she did so without the shrill hectoring style I was familiar with but with a warm friendly Texan drawl that could have been designed to surround us and place us at ease. She addressed the women largely ignoring the men, and she stated as a matter of fact she had spent her life fighting against men's judgments. Even after twenty years of continued achievement inside Tex4Tex, she felt she was still fighting them now. She wanted the women to know they could trust her, after all she was a fellow traveller.

Where I was wary, and even Tony kept his thoughts to himself, the women opened readily. This was what they'd been waiting to hear. Although I was familiar with their tales, I sat captivated while they spoke about the frustration of being a young woman in a corporate world. They couldn't dress how they wanted, they had to think about who they smiled at, or who they agreed with in meetings, every time they instigated a conversation, they had to be mind-readers, every interaction with some of their male colleagues was a swift toboggan ride downhill to the same question: 'Are you up for it?'

Our discussion followed the path to the conundrum we were all struggling with, the women didn't want to work for Jake, and they didn't want to stay and work for Wiley either. Rather than help with an answer Rose appeared to deliberately change the subject.

"Roger tells me, you said in the meeting, you had text messages?" She was getting to her purpose. "And Tex4Tex requires you to carry these same phones for work?"

Louise and Jenny nodded before responding and then both read some texts out as examples. Rose shook her head and frowned.

"I've never heard anything like it."

I'd like to believe she was telling the truth. And then as the meeting wound down Calum brought up something we'd overlooked. It was the Ranking List of Top Females issued on company email, during company hours, floating on the department's servers with a list of recipients who should have known better.

Calum carried his laptop over to show Rose.

The HR Director scanned down, shaking her head furiously, as she read the comments that discussed and ranked the women in a mocking tribute to the company's own performance management system. She remained quiet, but her lips were moving for us to interpret as she angrily read the thread, and its recipients. "Megson, Monk, Wiley, Reivers" she mouthed at the last, loud enough for us to hear. If she had arrived innocently at the social club with an intention of writing the whole experience off as lessons learned, then those hopes were eviscerated now.

She gently brought the laptop lid down and politely thanked Calum and the women. She took out her mobile phone and in full hearing of the women her urgent 'I want this done yesterday' management voice returned.

"Gloria, sweetie. Call me back now."

It was 9.35 p.m. and yet her phone buzzed instantly in reply.

"Hi Gloria, I'm sorry to disturb your precious family time but I'm afraid I need your assistance. I want Cliff Wiley in my room at nine a.m. tomorrow and I need you to fast track Martin Monk's resignation overnight. Can you do that for me, sweetie?"

"No, I don't care what his diary says he's got on tomorrow." She looked up and smiled at the women. "No… No… Gloria I tell you what, if he can't make nine a.m. tell him seven thirty. That way he won't need a nine a.m."

Finally, as she prepared to leave, she switched back into her warm American accent.

"Calum, isn't it?" she breathed. "Would you mind sending that email thread to me. Thank you so much." The older woman touched the blushing teenager's arm as he gathered his laptop. "You're so kind."

Ha! God Bless America. I never thought I'd think that.

March 2009 (day 4)

When Farah's friends tapped on the windows and delivered boxes of samosas sweating in their packets, I felt I could stay in dispute forever. This was no hardship at all. If our employer had ever hoped our support would dissipate after a few hours, and we'd be starved into submission, then their plan wasn't working. On the contrary, in the seventy-two hours since the mutiny began our union, other unions, families and ordinary people delivered trays of sausage rolls, packets of biscuits and dial-a-pizza delivery meals to the social club as fast as Tony and Calum, the bloody gannets, could demolish them. At one point a burger van appeared on the Tuesday afternoon in the visitors car park serving onlookers idling by to see if they could witness the moment when the West Mercia police would storm in Waco style.

Oblivious to distraction, inside our occupation we passed the hours calmly.

"It would be impolite to refuse," Tony would half-heartedly protest as another slice of pizza was folded before it disappeared down his gullet with a gulp. Or occasionally if the donations didn't meet his approval his response would be, "Vegetarian! I'm doing this for Telford! I need red meat!"

Yes, if our opinions carried as much weight as Tony's hips then we were home and hosed.

It amused me our occupation resembled an old man's fantasy. We were fighting for the working man whilst holding out in an unlicensed bar, surrounded by young women, with hot food being delivered to our door. On the face of it, it was the kind of industrial dispute James Bond would get involved in. Make no bones about it if needs must we blokes were in for the long haul. No surrender till the last salted peanut was swallowed.

Unfortunately, there are two sides to every story, and with due respect to Tony's colon others were making a greater emotional sacrifice. Each reminder of this fact came when Farah's or Paula's excitable toddlers were lifted shoulder high by Daddy and presented to an open window for Mummy to kiss. I realised it was only natural if others were getting itchy feet to settle and go back to what passed as a normal life. Yes, the parents in our gang were under a peer pressure I couldn't hope to appreciate.

Consequently, it didn't surprise me that after Texas Rose's visit the mutineers' conversations had turned optimistic, anxious even, focussing on the shock and anger on Texas Rose's face when she listened to our tales, and anticipating what retribution she may or may not take that would break the deadlock to enable a return to work, and home. Paula had promised the women we would get a moment of influence, surely this was it.

Yes, the women had made a friend in Texas Rose. They'd impressed a woman who believed in company values, believed they should be applied to all, and most importantly, had the power to make a difference when she put her kicking boots on. Paula's brief period of influence was passing. The company was moving, and the ground was shaking as a senior manager took control, made decisions, apportioned blame, and identified scapegoats. Confirmation of Rose's action came throughout on Thursday morning as colleagues approached in dribs and drabs to the social club windows passing on and picking up gossip, joining the dots on what we knew and what they knew.

The story ran that after her early morning ambushing of Wiley, Texas Rose had marched down to the unit with Roger, Gloria, and the security guards in tow to strip an astonished Jake of his site pass, suspend Toby Mullett, and hand Martin his notice of an immediate period of gardening leave prior to publicly confirming his resignation had been accepted and processed.

And while the guards took possession of Jake's courtesy laptop for investigation, Rose called the staff together. The unit was to be disbanded, all staff were invited to speak to HR about their dysfunctional management, and the investigation into the leaks to the papers would be renewed. And yes, everyone was to undergo Values Training again – every silver lining has a cloud. Meanwhile Roger would return to fill the void, keep Martin's team ticking over while a permanent solution was found. As far as I could gather at no point had she mentioned the union, or the social club, or the occupation. It was like she wanted staff to believe she'd just woken up with a bee in her bonnet and a hunch about the unit and Night Owls. The company was going to hard sell the whitewash.

To the surprise, and the disappointment of some, Rose didn't return to update us, and even Roger didn't return until the Thursday afternoon to colour in the shapes. We took our seats tense but hopeful management had caved in, but then we groaned as he took out an official statement.

"There's good news and bad news," he said, as he unbuttoned his collar to allow his neck to breathe.

"Tex4Tex have this morning written to the department and Night Owls. We have advised that we have put the transfer of our staff to Night Owls on hold pending investigation. We have requested the department permanently cancel the transfer. Following preliminary investigative interviews this morning we have suspended several staff in response to your allegations into discrimination and the circulation of a Ranking List grading women staff, Martin Monk's resignation has been accepted, and every Night Owls contractor has had their passes blocked. An initial investigation of outgoing emails indicates contact between Night Owls staff and outside organisations. We have advised the department to perform their own investigation into leaks. We expect you all to back at work on Monday."

By my side Paula let a brief satisfied smile pass her lips. Although Rose had now assumed control it was Paula who had organised the giant killing; they couldn't take that away from her.

As others welcomed the outcome, I followed Paula's lead and kept calm. I noticed Roger's tired drawn expression and stayed impassive. I can't say I knew what was coming, but I'd seen enough to know there had to be payback. Even though Paula and the mutineers had in effect orchestrated a campaign identifying rotten managers and contractors, and keeping a fifty million pound per annum contract inside Tex4Tex, it wasn't about finance, it was about credibility, a struggling union couldn't be seen to win otherwise others may rush to join.

"You said there was bad news as well?" I ventured to Roger.

"Well, I'm returning to the unit to replace Martin. That's bad news," he laughed, but then he wiped his hand across his face, and when it passed his smile had gone. "Yes, but seriously Jack I'm afraid there is bad news. I'm really sorry about this, I was hoping to grab a few words with you privately." He held my gaze and took a deep breath.

No!

No, I trusted Roger, but I wasn't going to play the game.

"Surely all of us should know if there's a price for returning to work?" There was that familiar tetchy edge in her Paula's voice.

"Mmm, okay then." Roger took a deep breath, and then deliberately pulled out his notes to indicate he was returning to the script, and these weren't his words. "All disciplinary charges against the so-called Telford mutineers will be dropped pending co-operation with the investigations into bullying, corruption, and harassment. All except one charge that is – the breach of company values, the disruption of a customer meeting, and the throwing of objects, inciting younger staff to throw objects, at both managers and customers alike." He folded his notes again. "In effect management believe Jack should be prepared to answer a charge of gross misconduct. They see him as the provocateur inciting bad behaviour and bad publicity."

There was a pause. We were ninety five per cent there, but they'd put a sting in the tail and a price on our agreement. It was so typically corporate, taking petty retribution to ensure the union was seen to be defeated even though management had been the ones backtracking. Their contrived positioning set a moral equivalence between months of harassment, dysfunction and lies, and gently lobbing half a cup-cake. It was bloody typical, it was a joke, I wanted to laugh, except it wasn't funny.

There I was edging my way to the wrong exit door again. I knew I should respond, but I couldn't trust myself. I was lost for words. Ha! If only I had a cake to hand. I was pleased when Paula piped up, after all she was probably a better advocate for me than I was.

"Jack's as big a victim of lousy management as anyone else here," Paula protested. "They're always picking on Jack, how many more times?" And then, she gathered her thoughts and returned to union mode. "So, what you're saying is that unless we agree Jack should be disciplined, we remain in dispute?"

"No, we believe there is a case to answer, they have not predetermined the outcome."

There were more groans as he prevaricated. Roger was trapped in decent managers no-man's land referring to Tex4Tex as 'we' and 'they' as though he didn't know which side to take. He redoubled his efforts.

"Yes, the company believe they have made a fair attempt to resolve the dispute. Your dispute has been illegal. The hawks wanted to cut your electric and move against you on day one. Take your victory, the transfer to Night Owls will not happen. If you reject this offer in its entirety you remain in dispute and management intermediaries like me will be sidelined and the Tex4Tex hawks will take over."

More bloody power games.

There it was, that groan again, but stifled this time. I sensed others were frustrated, but I also guessed they were too polite to say what they thought and were waiting for me to respond. Perhaps my comrades also saw how Roger was struggling, a decent man in a bad place. If Paula had let him speak to me alone, they wouldn't be getting guilt tripped this way. For my own part I'm sure they didn't want to abandon me, but at the same time it was a good offer for the others, I knew it was, and this was our moment. It was the right time for the union to settle before the wheel turned. I felt conflicted. I continued to keep my head down studying the hands locked across my lap as the silence dragged on.

I heard Roger, call "Jack," like he was calling me to attention, but I didn't respond, and I kept my pose. By my side, I heard Tony shift in his seat. I felt uplifted, I needed my friend to fill the void as he had done so many times before.

"For fuck's sake!"

It wasn't Shakespeare I grant you, but it broke the silence. I knew Tony well enough to know there was more to follow.

"But if you're in temporary charge, Roger, won't you be the one to discipline him? He's worked for you for years. How can you do this?"

"Yes, I suppose I will be. And yes, there are mitigating circumstances and I'm sure Paula will make sure I don't overlook them." He smiled, but he was gulping for the words. I half expected him to make a run for the door.

Bizarrely, I was embarrassed for Roger. I'd always liked and respected him, and I instinctively understood Rose had set him this loyalty test to see whose side he was on. All the dishonesty we witnessed daily, and now having used Roger's credibility to resolve the dispute, taking advantage of the fact he was both union and management, they had decided to bring him to heel and prevent him getting ideas above his station. As an ex-civil servant, he would never be an insider; he needed to be taught the lesson.

Management is a pit of vipers. Isn't that what Roger had said all those years before?

However, Tony wasn't finished. Whereas I was tongue-tied he still had more to say.

"But you can't sack us all," he said, "what if I said I threw the cupcake?" Tony grinned.

"Yes, I threw it." He looked around for support, he was onto something. All over Shropshire the National Grid was spontaneously firing up. "I threw it. I'm Spartacakes." He released his childish giggle, laughing at his own silly joke, and then he paused, calmed himself, and stood and spoke slowly, loud and proud.

"I'm Spartacakes. All of us, we're all Spartacakes."

And then Calum, I heard his chair move, and I guessed he was on his feet behind me.

"I'm Spartacakes, too," he laughed. By my side Tony gestured to the others.

And then they all rose, Jenny, Ruby, Farah, Louise, Jenny even Paula. There were all Spartacakes. This protest was getting silly but quite affecting none-the-less.

I looked over at Roger, he was smiling at our solidarity as we kept repeating that we were Spartacakes.

Finally, after thirty seconds of giggling and chanting, Roger broke the silence.

"I admire you all," he said, "I'll take the message back and see what we can do."

As the meeting ended Paula followed Roger to the door for a chat. I knew it would be about me. Paula would no doubt be doing what she did, picking her way through the minefield trying to get us all intact to the other side. And I hoped, no I knew in fact Roger would be assisting her. I didn't want to stand there earwigging so I picked up my green seat and took up residence on the roof of the social club.

I sat on the roof alone with my thoughts, hoping a solution would miraculously present itself when the dust had settled, and we'd all had a night's sleep. Spartacakes! The daft sods. Mind you in the film he was tapping Jean Simmons so bar the unnecessary crucifixions it wasn't all bad.

Paula and Tony popped up in the late afternoon to share the gossip with a few bottles accompanied by outdated packets of crisps. Her news only added to the absurdity. The complaint against me came from Martin. He hadn't known at the time, but he had unknowingly spent his last hours in work writing it. Paula as ever had a plan. "They daren't sack you, they won't sack you," she assured me, "but you must trust me. And you should trust Roger is working to find a way out for you. We can still win our dispute and save your job. They're just hoping we'll crack under the pressure of being so close. Trust me by the weekend they're going to be begging you to settle with them."

And with a mischievous smile she shared a copy of an embargoed press release she was going to send to management to goad them into dialogue.

"Tex4Tex striker faces sack for throwing cup cake." And alongside the text was that picture of me the company feared so much.

"They're gonna hate this," she laughed. "You see, we're going to drip-feed stories to the press, one a day until they cave in. We're going to tell the world what it's really like here." She was still laughing at her crackpot scheme. "The beauty is that we know it doesn't need national attention to get picked up by the Dallas search engines and put our managers under pressure."

"Telford 1, Texas 0" Tony laughed along. We all did. How had it come to this?

Tony rebooted after a taking a swig at his bottle.

"Me and you are like them hobbits on an adventure in *Lord of the Rings*." My eyes widened at the unlikely comparison before Tony corrected himself. "Not Frodo and Sam fighting Sauron you realise, but those other two irritating hairy-footed twats that hung around with them."

Tony's jokes made it harder to care about my future and I gave up worrying about next week. You can beat the bosses once, maybe even twice, but they will always come back at you. That was the nature of things, for the workers life is a fight from cradle to grave.

This was my lesson in the neverending class struggle.

So, the three of us sat there amiably chewing the fat over the changing times as we watched the mist close in over Telford. So much and yet so little had changed over the years, it was just the details had got sharper. We still all wanted to leave but had refused to transfer. We wouldn't consider resigning from an employer we had never accepted, and we'd fight like mad to save our jobs until the same employer gave way and paid us off. It was an issue of principle. Was everywhere in Britain like this? Abandoned working class people drifting aimlessly in deep waters desperately hoping to get marooned by chance on a retirement island paradise.

Soon those walking by were little more than dark blurs on their way to start their engines for the drive home, and the only detail which remained was each other, the three long-standing workmates, the fabric that holds us all together.

The bottles of beer were empty. Before Paula left, I thanked her and told her that whatever happened next, she'd organised the best and most rewarding week of my working life.

"D'oh! Your working life so far," she corrected me. And with that she hugged me close and whispered one more time. "Trust me, they wouldn't dare."

The next morning, the Telford mutineers woke to find the door open.

After twenty years I'd taken brief control of my destiny and celebrated it by taking a leap in the dark. I trusted Paula. By going home for breakfast I'd brought the dispute to an end.